BEAGLEMANIA

A PET RESCUE MYSTERY

BEAGLEMANIA

LINDA O. JOHNSTON

WHEELER
CHIVERS

This Large Print edition is published by Wheeler Publishing, Waterville, Maine, USA and by AudioGO Ltd, Bath, England.
Wheeler Publishing, a part of Gale, Cengage Learning.
A Pet Rescue Mystery.

The text of this Large Print edition is unabridged.
Other aspects of the book may vary from the original edition.
Set in 16 pt. Plantin.

LIBRARY OF CONGRESS CATALOGING-IN-PUBLICATION DATA

Johnston, Linda O.
  Beaglemania / by Linda O. Johnston. — Large print ed.
    p. cm. — (Wheeler Publishing large print cozy mystery)
  "A Pet Rescue Mystery."
  ISBN-13: 978-1-4104-3944-4 (pbk)
  ISBN-10: 1-4104-3944-5 (pbk)
  1. Dog breeders—Fiction. 2. Animal rescue—Fiction. 3. Animal shelters—California—Los Angeles—Fiction. 4. Large type books. I. Title.
PS3610.O387B43 2011
813'.6—dc23   2011021448

BRITISH LIBRARY CATALOGUING-IN-PUBLICATION DATA AVAILABLE

Published in 2011 in the U.S. by arrangement with The Berkley Publishing Group, a member of Penguin Group (USA) Inc.
Published in 2012 in the U.K. by arrangement with the author.

U.K. Hardcover: 978 1 445 86544 7 (Chivers Large Print)
U.K. Softcover: 978 1 445 86545 4 (Camden Large Print)

Printed and bound in Great Britain by the MPG Books Group
1 2 3 4 5 6 7 15 14 13 12 11

ACKNOWLEDGMENTS

Conducting research for *Beaglemania* and future Pet Rescue Mysteries has been fun and rewarding, as well as eye-opening and, sometimes, sad.

There are a lot of wonderful people who gave unstinting time to answer my questions, show me around their facilities, and be generally supportive of my plan to turn Lauren Vancouver into one determined pet rescuer.

I admit to using poetic license in my writing, so any inaccuracies are mine, definitely not theirs.

I want to thank them all, including:

Detective Susan Brumagin of the LAPD, who is the head of the Los Angeles Animal Cruelty Task Force, as well as the many devoted members of her team.

Kathleen Davis, general manager of the Los Angeles Board of Animal Services Commissioners, who helped to put me in contact with others to interview.

Captain Karen Knipscheer-Cox, commanding officer of SmART, D.A.R.T., and Animal Emergency Preparedness, who showed me around an amazing, yet unopen, Los Angeles Animal Services care center, and didn't flinch when I told her I might use her position — but not her — in my story. Also, special thanks to all the members of the Small Animal Rescue Team (SmART) who let me observe their training sessions and answered a lot of questions — especially Team Leader Armando Navarette (Nav).

Los Angeles Animal Services Officers Daniel Gonzalez and Eric Gardner, who, individually, graciously provided answers when I ran into them and started asking a lot of questions.

Thanks, too, to some amazingly dedicated, friendly, and helpful animal shelter administrators and others:

Arlene Ober, Office Coordinator, and more, of Pet Orphans of Southern California, as well as all the wonderful staff members and volunteers.

Tina Ito, Director of Administration of the Glendale Humane Society.

Ricky Whitman, Vice President of Community Resources of the Pasadena Humane Society and SPCA.

Thanks also to my excellent editor, Michelle Vega, and my incredible agent, Paige Wheeler.

This book is dedicated to animals everywhere, especially those pets who are awaiting new forever homes. I wish I could help all of you!

It's also dedicated to those . . . well, *dedicated* animal rescuers who work hard to take care of those animals, and to help them find the right forever homes.

And, as always, to my husband, Fred, who helps keep me sane. I think. Most of the time.

CHAPTER 1

I am not a killer.

At least not a killer of animals. I save their lives whenever humanly possible, especially pets. Their sole purpose on this earth is to love and be loved, like perpetual children.

People are something else.

Right now, I'd have gladly used my own hands — nice, strong ones for someone in her forties, since I do a lot of enclosure cleaning, lugging and opening of animal food containers, and other physical labor — to strangle Efram Kiley, the man who stood in front of me. His expression was the picture of innocence even as he squared his thin yet sturdy body, as if attempting to hide the filled floor-to-ceiling cages in this torture chamber of a mega shed from my view.

Impossible, considering how many there were.

He couldn't hide the smell, either. It was

awful. The caged puppies and their parents obviously had no choice but to eliminate their wastes in the same place they lived and ate and suffered. The only surface beneath them was wire mesh that undoubtedly hurt their feet. No comfy rugs or mats for them.

And the sounds. Their cries. Their barks.

The outraged comments and shouts of the three Los Angeles Animal Cruelty Task Force members who'd leaped in like superheroes to reinforce regular animal control officers, all intent on saving these poor creatures.

Efram must have read the fury in my expression. Or maybe he'd learned enough about me, in the past few months, to know what I was thinking.

He quickly turned, and before I could say anything, he'd plucked an adorable beagle puppy from one of those appalling crates and gently placed her into my arms.

What could I do but nestle the squirmy little body close to my face, stench and all? "You poor little thing," I whispered against one of her long ears as I used my free hand to extract a small towel from the tote bag over my shoulder and wrap her in it.

"She'll be all right now, Lauren," Efram assured me. As if he had anything to do with this rescue. Instead, the opposite was true. He was a party to the horror of this puppy mill. Even so, he said, "Isn't this just a terrible place?" He shook his head slowly, as if he was as upset as I about the condition of this hell house and the innocent beings who lived here.

"Yeah," I agreed. "Terrible. So why do you work here?"

"I don't."

"Then are you one of the owners?" I demanded.

"You know better than that, Lauren."

What I knew was that he was involved. I didn't need to know exactly how, although I doubted he owned the place. But I'd have bet he profited from it somehow.

I glared into Efram's doleful brown eyes as I shifted the puppy in my arms. Towel or not, that smell was getting to me. But I wasn't about to release her till I saw she would be taken care of.

She was just one of dozens of puppies here that the ACTF and animal control officers were handling with great care and angelic concern. And I would, eventually, have to hand her over to them.

Efram was in his twenties, with dark, messy hair that hung over his forehead. He worked out a lot and favored T-shirts with torn-off sleeves to show off his muscular biceps. His jeans were worn, his sneakers new.

He did a lot of work for me at HotRescues these days — the no-kill animal shelter I had helped to open a few years ago and now ran.

Oh, yeah. Efram was an animal care apprentice tending to creatures in need. He even had a choice about it: either learn how not to abuse pets and help care for them while they waited to be adopted, or forgo the substantial amount of money that was part of the legal settlement we'd entered into a while back.

Guess which he'd chosen.

Last year, Efram had threatened to sue HotRescues and me for rehoming his dog, Killer, without attempting to find the lost pup's real owner. I, in turn, had been furious about the condition of that poor dog, now called Quincy, who had been brought to HotRescues as an apparent rescue from a public shelter, or so I'd chosen to believe. The settlement of our dispute had been fair. It resulted in Efram's being paid to learn how to really care for animals. I'd even thought that, after all we'd taught him, he had become genuinely contrite for having abused Quincy. He certainly had seemed to throw himself energetically into his quasi-volunteer work with HotRescues.

I wondered now if every bit of it had been an act.

"You're Lauren Vancouver, aren't you?" One of the uniformed animal control officers I'd glimpsed outside approached me. She was tall, her ginger hair pulled starkly back from her round face.

Efram looked relieved, as if this official, who could arrest him, was easier to deal with than me. Maybe she was.

I expected J. Gibbons — the ID on her nametag — to demand that I leave. Now. Civilians weren't particularly welcome here, in the middle of an official investigation. I knew that.

But this wasn't the first animal rescue that I'd crashed. Nor would it be my last.

"Yes, I am." I mentally prepared my argument to stay here.

"Ralph told me to come get you."

That would be Officer Ralph Alazar, who'd gotten to know me on some of my forays to the East Valley Animal Care Center. I'd seen him outside, too. He was a good guy, didn't usually give me a hard time.

Even so, I hesitated. Should I go find out what he wanted or remain here and see how

13

I could help more with the pup in my arms and the others?

Officer Gibbons' next words quickly convinced me that I should head outside. "The SmART team just arrived. Ralph thought you'd want to be there."

I absolutely would. SmART was the Small Animal Rescue Team of Los Angeles Animal Services. All animal control officers were trained to conduct some rescues, but SmART was called in for situations beyond normal, where special expertise and equipment were needed.

Like puppies trapped in storm drains.

I threw an accusatory glance at Efram as I gave the baby in my arms one more hug, then handed her to one of the rescuers.

Efram wasn't looking at me. Instead, he was helping the uniformed ACTF members remove puppies and older dogs from the cages, check to make sure they were alive, then place them gently in cleaner crates, stacked on wheeled dollies, before taking them outside to change their lives forever. As if he'd come here, like me, to help out.

I knew better, but I'd have to let the ACTF, including its Animal Services members and LAPD cops, do their job. I was aware from the tip I'd gotten that at least some of them suspected Efram's complicity in this situation.

Following Officer Gibbons, I hurried out of the well-insulated backyard shed that had appeared so inconsequential from the outside — a moderate-sized steel structure that looked like a rural barn's younger brother, complete with red sides resembling painted wood. It was at the rear of a nondescript two-story commercial building that could have held anything from a bakery to an accounting firm. I suspected it contained only the office of the puppy mill owners. Could be they even lived there. The place was large enough.

It was a wonder that the nearby neighbors, even in this commercial area, hadn't complained to authorities before about the sounds and smells emanating from here. Maybe they had. Or maybe they'd indirectly collaborated in silence because they, too, were hiding things.

At least one of them — finally — had been horrified enough to report this place. Or maybe it was a visitor. Or a curious passerby. Someone complained and that was why rescuers had converged here at last.

I hurried over the concrete-paved driveway, skirting an animal control officer confronting two people — an obviously angry man, who was gesticulating and shouting, and a crying woman. Were they the puppy mill owners? I'd heard that a married couple was at least partly to blame. Efram wasn't in this all by himself.

I exited through the open gate in the tall picket fence that was in dire need of painting. I'd used the gate along the main avenue to enter, but this one opened onto a narrower side street, now an ER triage of activity, especially in the area of the gaping slash of a hole along the curb that led to the storm drain. Despite all the conversations, the sound of crying puppies wafted from somewhere below street level.

Poor little creatures.

They'd been down there when I'd arrived. I'd heard some Animal Services people trading shouts about it as they headed that way. At the time, I'd been single-mindedly intent on confronting Efram. But now, I wanted to know what was happening.

I excused my way through the crowd of onlookers being herded out of the way by animal control officers. On the sidewalk was a stenciled, stylized picture of a leaping dolphin, labeled, "No dumping. Drains to ocean." But someone apparently had started dumping puppies there, hoping the current below would drain away some of the evidence of what was going on in the nearby shed. I felt my teeth clench at the very idea. Had it been Efram? The emotional couple in the driveway? Once again, my urge to do something in response surfaced. Fortunately, I've always had a lot of self-control. Even in situations like this.

Even more important, I'd achieved what I'd set out to do initially — confirm Efram's inexcusable presence here. Now, I wanted to do all I could to help in this rescue.

At least whoever had done this hadn't gotten very far before Animal Services arrived. Otherwise, there wouldn't have been so many small canines still shoehorned into that faux barn.

Muffled puppy cries continued to rend the air. They were alive, and, somewhat luckily, the sounds emanated from a storm drain and not a sewer. If the animals were trapped in a sewer, I understood that the SmART team members would have to wait for appropriate Department of Water and Power personnel to help deal with any gases and other dangers.

At a van parked nearby, three people — two men and a woman — dressed in brown T-shirts with white letters and the round logo of Los Angeles Animal Services, Small Animal Rescue Team, pulled equipment out. The shirt worn by one of the men indicated that his name was Renz, and he was the team leader. They all wore red caps. Another man, dressed in a more standard Animal Services uniform, observed them, issuing orders.

They seemed ready to roll quite fast, as if experience and sympathy drove them. Approaching where I stood in the crowd, the two men unfastened the grate around the storm drain while the woman, the slimmest of the three, strapped on a harness and a red hard hat. Using equipment they'd carried here, they lowered her into the drain.

"I see them!" she called. "Four. There's a small ledge down here and they're all on it, out of the water. Were there any more?"

"Unsure," shouted the man in charge. He looked around, his gaze alighting on the team leader.

"That's the number Animal Services was told," Renz replied.

In only a few minutes, small beagle puppies, much like the one I'd snuggled so briefly inside, were lifted one by one, in a collapsible and flexible cage attached to a cord, out of the drain and into the arms of waiting Animal Services people.

I couldn't resist. I'd had a taste of hugging one subject of this imperative rescue and wanted to savor it — and these little ones would probably be even needier. When the third was extracted, I slipped over to where the action was.

Officer Ralph Alazar was one of the animal control officers helping the SmART team. He looked at me, bared sparkling white teeth as he grinned beneath his fuzzy black mustache, and interpreted my pleading expression correctly. He handed me the puppy he held. He then slid over to take possession of the last one brought to the surface.

I pulled another towel from the tote bag over my shoulder and wrapped it around the pup. Even so, the poor, small creature shivered in my arms. It was another little female, with long brown ears and soulful eyes. If she'd been in the water she'd had time, while waiting, to dry off somewhat, but she was still damp. I hugged her even closer than I had the other one, murmuring reassurances.

"Who are you?" demanded an angry voice. I looked up to see the guy apparently in charge of the SmART team glaring at me. He was over six feet tall, so he wouldn't have fit easily into the storm drain. On the other hand, his knit shirt seemed to hug substantial muscles, so I could imagine him rappelling down a mountainside to help save an animal that had tumbled into a ravine. The ID tag clipped to his shirt identified him as Captain Kingston. A captain? From what I knew of the hierarchy of Animal Services, he was definitely the go-to guy here.

"I'm Lauren Vancouver, Captain. I run HotRescues, a local private animal shelter. I came here to help." Never mind that I was told of what was going on, unofficially, by one of my employees who happened also to volunteer at a city shelter. He didn't need to know that. Nor did he need to know that I'd had an additional agenda: checking out Efram's presence.

His glare didn't waver. I could feel him assessing me, even as I still held a puppy bundled in my arms like animal control officers did with the others nearby. I knew exactly what he saw — not that I could interpret what he thought about it. He appeared around my age, maybe a little younger, so he should respect his elders. Besides, I look okay for my age. I keep my dark hair clipped short so it doesn't get in my way. My high cheekbones made me think I had model potential when I was younger and cared about such things. My green eyes glared into his brown ones.

Yeah, I assessed him right back. And

found the guy good-looking. As the officer in charge, he had every right to give me a hard time for interfering in this rescue. But I wouldn't admit that to him.

The puppy in my arms squirmed some more, nuzzling against my chest as if seeking to be fed, like a human infant. I looked away from the scowling captain and down at the baby beagle. I smiled and hugged her tighter. "We'll find your mama for you soon, sweetheart." I looked back at the man, glanced at his name badge again, and said, "Right, Captain Kingston?"

Guess he must have had a heart that melted for animals, too, since his look softened. "I'm Matt. And, yes, we'll find this pup's mother as soon as we can."

Eventually, I had to yield the puppy to official care, but not before her companions from the storm drain had also been stowed away for transporting to a city shelter.

"Be good now," I whispered to her as I slowly handed her to J. Gibbons — Janeen. She'd told me her name. "Stay out of trouble. No more swimming, got it?"

The animal control officer grinned as she took possession. "We'll make sure she behaves." I watched the morose little beagle eyes until Janeen turned her back.

21

I observed for a while as other animal control officers loaded the crates filled with dogs and puppies from inside the shed into a van. Regular cops had arrived and kept onlookers back. ACTF members appeared to be interviewing people — neighbors, maybe. Helicopters hovered overhead, and I wished I could tell them to go away. Their noise must be disturbing the rescued animals.

It was certainly disturbing me. Especially since I'd been involved before in situations where choppers arrived, and not only those from the LAPD. I doubted any today were from D.A.R.T. The other Animal Services rescue group — Department Air Rescue Team — came in when large animals like horses needed help, not abused puppies. Had the media gotten wind of this operation?

Probably. News traveled fast. Hadn't I heard about it myself in an unauthorized manner?

I saw Ralph Alazar come through the gate, accompanying Efram. I knew better, but I approached them.

"Thanks for letting me know when the SmART folks arrived, Ralph," I said, not looking at Efram. "The rescue was amazing. And successful, thank heavens — assuming there weren't more puppies down there than the four brought to the surface. There weren't any more that washed away before help arrived, were there?"

That last was snapped directly at Efram. I watched his face. He gave a small shake of his head before he apparently caught himself, and I compressed my mouth into an ironic grin. I had my answer.

"So what's the official theory?" I addressed my question to Ralph. "I suspect it was my buddy Efram, here, who tossed those puppies into the drain. I know word got out before you arrived that you guys were coming. Was he planning to protect his butt, intending to toss every one of those poor animals down there, so they'd drown?"

I turned my gaze back onto the man I'd once thought had come around fairly well in his treatment of animals. His mouth was open, his expression startled, as if I'd read his mind.

He didn't say anything, though. I continued, "I'll assume you're admitting it, Efram, since you're not denying it." And I'd seen his reaction. "Your effort at getting the animals out of their cages while I stood there was pitiful. Did you really think you'd convince me you gave a damn? I'm not sure whether you'll be prosecuted as an animal abuser, but I know the truth and so do you. You can bet I'll tell Dante, make sure you don't get another dime of settlement money, at least until you're proven innocent. Which you won't be."

Dante DeFrancisco was the wealthy benefactor of HotRescues. Efram had threatened him with the rehoming lawsuit, too. Dante had helped to work out the settlement by funding our attempt to rehabilitate this abusive S.O.B.

"That's not the way the legal system works, bitch," Efram growled.

"It's the way *I* work. And I'm the one with Dante's attention. Maybe we'll even sue to get back the money you didn't earn. You certainly didn't learn how not to harm animals."

"You'd better keep that ugly mouth of yours closed," Efram demanded. He suddenly feinted one way, causing Ralph to grab at air instead of Efram's arm, which he'd aimed for. Instead, Efram grabbed my arms and started shaking me. Hard.

Painfully.

"Hey!" Ralph again tried to take control of Efram, who planted himself behind me, still holding on.

I'd had enough. I was sorry I wore soft-soled, comfortable shoes along with the jeans and the HotRescues T-shirt I'd put on in anticipation of working at my sanctuary later that day. Shoes with more substance — too bad I owned no stiletto heels — would have been more effective. Even so, I prepared to kick backward, hoping to collide with his groin. Of course, I'd be satisfied with bruising his shins if I did it hard enough.

Instead, he was suddenly lying facedown on the ground, being handcuffed by Captain Matt Kingston, with Officer Ralph Alazar's help. My arms were free.

So were my legs, but I resisted kicking him.

"Thanks," I said to the animal control officers. To Efram, I said, "Don't bother coming back to HotRescues. Ever. Even if you somehow manage to avoid getting prosecuted for animal abuse — I'll make sure you're arrested for assault. Next time you see me, I'll be testifying against you in court."

CHAPTER 2

A short while later, I drove my car — a dark gray Toyota Venza crossover equipped with a bunch of pet-friendly accessories — into the HotRescues parking lot, off Rinaldi Street in Granada Hills. I pulled into my reserved space.

This wasn't quite the northernmost part of the vast city of Los Angeles, but it came close. It definitely wasn't far from Pacoima, where Efram lived, and also where the puppy mill was located. And where my mind remained, at least for now.

How could Efram? How could *anyone?*

I entered the main building through the side door, right into the back of the cheerful room where we greeted visitors. Bright lemon yellow walls displayed photos of happy pets with their new adoptive humans. In fact, most of HotRescues was designed with happiness in mind — for the sweet animals waiting for their perfect forever homes, and even more for potential adopters, to put them in the right frame of mind for picturing themselves bringing home a new addition to their families.

The most eye-catching piece of furniture in the welcoming room was a waist-high reception counter of leopard print veneer — a new addition, after Dante sent a friend, CEO of a renowned furniture company, here to adopt a dog. This was how he'd shown his appreciation, including a full redecoration of this room.

Nina Guzman, in charge that morning in my absence, sat at a table behind the counter, answering phones and working on a laptop computer. Walking in from the side entrance, I saw that Nina was online, scanning a Web site that described local animals available for adoption at a high-kill facility run by a neighboring city. One of our favorite sites . . . not. But we visited that shelter often, bringing back as many dogs and cats as we could to ensure their continued longevity. And, hopefully, quick adoption.

I was glad Nina staffed the welcome room that morning. She was one of the few people I wanted to talk to just then.

"Trawling for new residents?" I asked before she noticed me.

"Lauren!" She stood immediately and rushed to where I stood near the door. "Tell me what happened. Was it really a puppy mill? Was Efram there?"

"Yes to both, as if you didn't know."

Nina was taller than me, a bit more curvy, and over a decade younger. I could have been jealous of even one of those features, and all three, blended together, might have made a less tolerant person in charge want to fire her perfect butt right out of there.

Not me. I really liked Nina. She was conscientious and energetic, and one of the most pet-oriented people I'd ever met. On top of everything else she did, she helped to coordinate our volunteers. Plus, our divorces gave us something in common. But as much as I now despised my ex, he was only a fraction as appalling as Nina's. She'd been divorced now for about eighteen months — and had a restraining order against the jerk who'd abused her before she'd finally gotten the nerve to walk out.

"Okay, I want to hear all about it." Nina headed back to the table, where she pulled out another chair in invitation for me to join her.

I complied and sat, but still asked, "Anything I need to know about or work on first?" I doubted it. If something had come in that required an executive decision, Nina, my assistant administrator, would have gotten it started, and if whatever it was demanded my immediate input, she'd have contacted me.

"I took a call from a woman who said she was bringing her dog in later. She lost her job and can't take care of it anymore." Nina, seated again behind the computer, grew silent. We stared at each other. Nina's brown hair was shoulder length, and bangs framed her waiflike, large eyes. Her skin was taut and pale, with worry lines creasing her forehead — hinting of the angst she had once faced every day of her life.

"Did she seem for real?" I finally asked.

"Who knows?"

As a private facility, HotRescues was not permitted by its LA Department of Animal Services permit to take in stray pets off the street. If anyone brought in an animal they'd found, we had to turn it over to LA Animal Services, at least temporarily. Of course, our turnovers always came with a strongly worded request — demand, really — that if no one adopted the pet within a reasonable period of time, they were to let us know. We'd take it back.

Assuming custody of endangered pets from high-kill shelters was another story.

That was how a large percentage of our wards came under our protection. We always attempted to take in animals that were suitable for adoption, and avoided those with aggressive tendencies unless we were certain we could resolve them with training.

We were also permitted to take in owner relinquishments — animals whose owners couldn't keep them any longer, for whatever reason.

And when the reason was combined with sorrow — which wasn't always the case — those situations became difficult not only for the person bringing in his or her baby for placement in another home, but also for us. Especially when we had to turn animals away for lack of room.

Fortunately, HotRescues wasn't just any shelter. It had been founded by Dante De-Francisco, the same guy who'd paid for the settlement with Efram. Dante was a wealthy business mogul who'd gotten rich selling pet supplies at the huge HotPets network of stores. He still provided most of the funds for HotRescues, a nonprofit corporation, and remained on the board of directors. Where situations could be resolved by throwing money at them, he could usually be counted on to help.

I already had to let Dante know about

Efram. If the woman brought in her pet, I'd mention that to Dante, too.

Of course she could just be one of the numerous, unfathomable people who shed crocodile tears about how sad they were to give up their pets but were utterly relieved to get rid of them.

"We'll see how that goes." I proceeded to tell Nina about the rescue of the dogs from that hell-inspired puppy mill. "How could *anyone* throw those adorable, tiny beaglets down a storm drain?" I spat. "Let alone Efram. After all we taught him here."

"You're sure it was him?"

"No, but he didn't exactly deny it."

"What a horrible excuse for a human being."

"Absolutely. But . . . he'll pay." My ire had risen enough to make it hard for me to talk. Nina obviously noticed, since she went into the small kitchen near the entry and brought me a cup from the coffeemaker we kept in there. I took a sip of the hot, strong brew as visions swirled through my mind all over again of those poor, frightened, abused dogs.

"I'll check on the rescued doggies later," she assured me. "I'm scheduled to volunteer this evening at the East Valley Care Center. They'll probably be taken there. If not, I'll find out where they are. Did all the parents look like they'd be okay?"

Typically, in puppy mills, adult male and female purebred or designer dogs were bred over and over again, procreating as fast as nature allowed, until they could no longer reproduce, and then they were adopted out, too.

Or kicked out on the street.

Or, much too often, they were in such bad shape that they had to be euthanized if taken to a vet or a shelter.

"As far as I could tell," I said. "I didn't see them all. I was distracted by Efram and the little beagle he handed me while I was inside, so I'm not even sure what other breeds were there. All relatively small ones, though. I saw Yorkies and cockapoos and maybe some Boston terriers, but there could have been others, too."

"I'll find out." Nina's connections had told her about the rescue in the first place. She spent even more time than I did, if that was possible, helping to care for animals. I was affiliated with only HotRescues, but she also devoted her off hours to volunteering at city shelters. She made a lot of helpful associations that way. And she'd made it known that anyone who heard of a situation where animals were being rescued, and might ultimately need someplace to go if not adopted quickly, was to tell her. She, in turn, told me.

"I know you will," I responded with a laugh.

"So . . . I'm a little jealous," Nina said. "You got to see SmART in action. I haven't been able to do that yet."

"Even with all the people you know?" I was surprised.

"Well . . . it's partly my own fault. It's bad enough to understand what they're up to — SmART, D.A.R.T., and the Animal Cruelty Task Force. But bringing myself to go see the endangered animals before they've been rescued . . ."

I got it. As kindhearted as she was, Nina had gone through her own version of hell and didn't need to see other creatures, human or not, in that kind of peril.

I decided to nudge the subject a bit. "You know, the whole time I was there I didn't even think to ask who the puppy mill owners were, though I think I saw them. I was just so upset that Efram was aiding and abetting . . . Did you happen to hear more about them?"

I wouldn't really have a hard time finding out. By the time I'd left, media vans besieged the area, with their little satellite dishes reaching way up into the ether to send whatever sensational pseudo-news stories they could to their media home planets. Between them and the vultures in the helicopters, they would either know whose property it was, or they'd find out.

"I think their name is Shaheen," Nina said. "Patsy and Bradley, or something like that."

I wondered how Efram knew them. Not that it mattered. He was there that day. The place was a puppy mill. He hadn't ratted on them but instead had seemed to know the place.

I might have jumped to conclusions — but his believed affiliation was one of the things that had been conveyed to Nina by whatever Animal Services contact had mentioned the then-pending raid on the puppy mill.

I'd watched Efram officially taken into custody by a member of the Animal Cruelty Task Force after my last little altercation with him.

Only then had I felt I could leave.

I left Nina in charge again as I headed from the offices and through the gate. It was time for my first walk of the day through the important part of the shelter.

I visited our residents often. The sensation was always bittersweet. Mostly sweet — for me.

Our habitats were, of course, well built and maintained, and as cozy as Dante's generous monetary contributions and pet supply connections could make them. Not to mention my own insistence on making each enclosure as homey as possible.

But no matter how nice every residence was, how spacious and filled with toys and comfy bedding, ample water, and regularly served food, it was still a cage — the easier to keep it clean and safe.

Dogs, except the smallest, were housed in enclosures that were partly inside long, low, temperature-controlled buildings, and partly open-air. Toy dogs had fully inside accommodations. Each dog had its own kennel, unless they were mothers with pups, known littermates, or otherwise had lived together previously without issues. Despite our attentive staff, we couldn't watch each pup every moment of the day to ensure that two together weren't fighting.

Cats tended to be more tolerant, so they were usually housed in groups — after we made certain each new addition got along well with the rest. As we brought each one in, though, we kept them in separate enclosures during their normal quarantine period and sometimes beyond, depending on their friendliness.

We also took in other pets, like birds, guinea pigs, and more — a veritable Noah's ark of rescue, providing the most suitable habitat possible. At the moment, we had a few rabbits and hamsters in residence.

But as safe, secure, and well cared for as our animals were, they were all, in fact, homeless. Waiting for someone to adopt them, who would love them even more than our great employees and volunteers could.

Fortunately, we had a lot of success in placing our wards.

As I entered the fenced, primarily canine area, I met up with Ricki, one of our volunteers. She had been coming here for over a year, loved it, and was just about to begin training as a veterinary technician — starting out as I had done years ago, smart kid.

Wearing a yellow knit shirt with the HotRescues logo displaying a happy cartoon dog and cat on the pocket, she was prepping Elmer, a black Lab mix, for a walk outside. Our volunteers often exercised dogs behind our facility on a relatively quiet street that had sidewalks.

A fresh-faced African American girl, with long, loose hair the shade of rich cocoa,

Ricki tossed a happy smile at me even as she gave a small tug to show Elmer who was the alpha of the two of them. "Hi, Lauren," she greeted me effusively. And then she frowned. "Was it really a puppy mill?"

Word had gotten out.

"Sure was," I said grimly.

"How awful. Oops!" She almost lost her balance as Elmer gave a tug on his leash. "Heel!" she ordered and pulled the eager Lab back into place at her side.

"Have fun," I called as they hurried along the path between cages, their presence triggering a roar of barking from jealous inhabitants. Or maybe they were just being watchdogs. Or both.

I approached the nearest enclosure. Sharp yaps emanated from it — or, rather, from the little white Westie mix — part West Highland white terrier, and part who knew what.

I waited until she was quiet, not reinforcing behavior that might make her less adoptable. "Hi, Honey," I said to her. That was her name. It was printed, as with all our residents, on a page slipped into a plastic folder mounted near the top of her enclosure, along with her age, breed, health condition — which was updated as needed — and date she'd been brought in. Honey had been saved from a high-kill shelter not very long ago, one of our rescues that I was especially proud of.

My BlackBerry rang then. At least it vibrated. I could barely hear it, thanks to all the canine noise in the area, but it tickled my leg beneath my jeans. I pulled it from my pocket and glanced at the display. Tracy was calling.

My twenty-year-old daughter attended Stanford University. She was in her sophomore year. It was now April, and I hadn't seen her since Christmastime.

I hustled away from the doggy bedlam toward the gate to the quiet — well, quieter — offices.

I stopped near the feline-decorated greeting counter. "Hi, Trace. How are you?" I felt a smile draw curves up my face, hoped she heard it in my voice.

"Hi, Mom. Or should I say, 'Hi, YouTube star'?"

I was comfortable using the Internet for HotRescues' purposes — like checking out animals that needed rescuing, which were posted online by high-kill shelters.

I didn't get into any of the social networking sites, although Nina did — also to scout for useful information for our shelter.

And YouTube? I occasionally saw a link to

something that looked cute, like a clip about dogs that danced or cats that sang. But I had no idea what Tracy was talking about.

I told her so.

"You don't know? Oh, Mom, that's so uncool. You should at least be aware of it when someone posts something about you or HotRescues. I'll e-mail you the link."

"HotRescues is on YouTube?"

Nina walked out from behind the desk and looked at me quizzically, obviously eavesdropping.

"No, you are. Somebody shot video on the rescue of dogs from that puppy mill, and you're in the middle. You were holding a poor little pup in a towel, and whoever took the pictures said in the narration that it had just been pulled out of a sewer."

"Storm drain," I corrected absently.

"Whatever."

"Did they mention HotRescues?"

"Nope."

My mind started tearing in several directions. Was it a good thing for HotRescues that I got a moment of fame from this? Not likely. If I'd known I'd been filmed, I'd have chattered about being affiliated with this epitome of a private shelter and about the joys of adopting a rescued pet.

"That guy with you — the one in the

animal rescue shirt? He's really a hottie."

Ralph? No — he wore a regular animal control officer uniform. It had been Captain Matt Kingston who'd been closest to me as I held the rescued pup. Sure, he was a hottie, but I cringed about my young adult daughter telling me so.

"I didn't notice," I lied. "But I want to see the clip. Please send me the link as soon as you can. And thanks for letting me know. Everything okay?"

"Everything's fine, Mom." Of course she'd have said that even if her grades were iffy and she had a cold. But we were close enough that I believed she'd tell me if there was anything I really needed to know.

At least I'd succeeded in changing the subject. "Take care, sweetheart. I love you."

I had hardly hung up before the phone rang again. This time, outside the doggy area, I actually heard its musical peal.

It was Kevin, my son. He was a student at Claremont McKenna College, approaching the end of his freshman year. I could guess what he was calling about but decided not to let him know that Tracy had stolen his thunder.

Sure enough, he'd seen the YouTube clip with me on it, thanks to a tip from his sister.

Didn't these kids do anything but surf the

Net? I certainly was paying a lot of tuition for them to keep their noses to the grindstone — or at least in their textbooks.

But they both got good grades, so I couldn't complain.

"You rock, Mom," he told me, sounding gleeful. "I'm showing all my friends how you stick up for animal rights and all that."

Despite my momentary irritation, I grinned. I was proud of both my kids, and it felt even better than eating chocolate to think they might be proud of me, too.

I chatted with Kevin a few more minutes, glad for the opportunity to touch base with him, make sure he was still handling his first time away from home well — even though his college was in Claremont, just east of LA. Unlike with Tracy, I actually saw him on weekends now and then.

I soon hung up.

"Hey, Lauren. Come over here." Nina was back at the table behind the computer. I saw that she had brought up the YouTube clip. She turned on the sound, but only for a few seconds before my BlackBerry rang again.

The caller ID said Dante DeFrancisco was on the other end. "Hi, Dante." In case this conversation needed to be kept private, I walked down the hall toward my office.

41

"Hi, yourself," he said. "I've got you on my speaker phone. Kendra's here, too."

Kendra Ballantyne was Dante's lady friend, a lawyer who'd helped with the Efram situation when he'd threatened to sue us. She was also a pet-sitter and pet lover, an ideal combination to help work out the solution with Efram.

Did Dante already know what I intended to tell him about Efram and his relationship to the puppy mill? The guy did seem to know just about everything. Scary, sometimes.

I closed the door, then sat on the chair behind my desk, braced for whatever. "Hi, Kendra."

"Hi, Lauren," Kendra replied. "The whole puppy mill thing — I heard about it from a few sources and told Dante. That clip on YouTube — it's going viral."

My mind sprinted with possible results. I was identified, at least, so I still might be able to use it for publicizing HotRescues and how we save endangered pets. It also showed the concern and dedication of the LA Animal Services folks, particularly special teams like SmART, as well as Los Angeles police on the ACTF. And, it might emphasize the plight of dogs bred in puppy mills.

On the whole, I liked the possibilities. But what if Dante didn't? Even though I was the HotRescues director of administration, he was the personification of the golden rule: he who has the gold makes the rules. At least around here.

"I haven't watched the entire thing," I said cautiously.

"Well, I think it's great," Dante said, and I felt the breath I'd been holding slide out in relief. "I'll talk to some of my PR folks at HotPets and see how we can use it to promote HotRescues and the good work you're doing."

"Great idea," I said, glad we were on the same page.

"It's really cool," Kendra added. "I'll be sending links to all my animal-law and pet-sitting clients."

"Wonderful!"

But it was time for me to toss a monkey wrench into this celebration of puppy liberty. I told them about my confrontation with Efram.

"We'll deal with it." I heard the grimness in Dante's voice. As I'd told Efram, his settlement payments were toast, and that nearly made me cheer.

After I hung up, I headed back to the welcoming area. "Run that clip again, please," I said to Nina. "When we're done, please send the link to your Animal Services contacts, including anyone at SmART."

"Already done," she responded proudly, and I grinned at her. I should have figured.

Hopefully, Captain Matt Kingston would see it, too, if he hadn't already. His SmART team deserved the Internet pat on the back a lot more than I did.

And the little film, distributed so far, should help in the prosecution of the puppy mill owners — and Efram Kiley.

CHAPTER 3

I sat in my office at HotRescues, watching
the YouTube clip yet again on the clunky
desktop computer that had been my secretary and more for at least five years. There
were lots of extra bells and whistles on
newer PCs, but I was much happier directing our funding toward more important
things, like caring for our residents. Yes,
Dante would have paid for something better. No, I didn't want it, at least not now.

Three days had passed since I'd first
watched myself on YouTube. I'd even for-
warded the link to my good friend, Dr. Carlie Stellan, but hadn't heard back from her
yet. No surprise. In addition to her busy
veterinary practice, which included being
head of the HotRescues medical facility of
choice, Carlie hosted *Pet Fitness,* a TV show
devoted to pet health. It aired on the
Longevity Vision Channel, a cable TV station that had the theme of exploring life

paths for all species, including humans. Carlie was somewhere in the eastern United States now, filming a segment, and sometimes didn't check her e-mail for days.

My parents, who live in Phoenix, had also seen the YouTube entry, thanks to the kids' contacting them. They'd called to tell me, and to let me know they were showing me off to their friends. Their excitement made me smile. Of course they'd told my brother, Alex, who lived near them with his family. He'd also called.

Each time I peeked at the clip, I segued from basking in quiet pride for having been at the puppy mill rescue to reliving the joy of holding those little beagles to recalling what it felt like to watch puppies being liberated from the storm drain . . . to restoking my outrage at the puppy mill owners, whom I'd heard confirmed in newscasts as Patsy and Bradley Shaheen.

Their pictures showed up often on the news. I was surprised they looked vaguely familiar, though I hadn't gotten close enough to see them well at the puppy mill. They did, indeed, live upstairs from the ghastly holding cells. Their apartment must somehow have been noise proofed — and smell proofed.

Their hearts had to be compassion proof.

46

I also thought a lot about Efram Kiley. Our failure with him. He clearly hadn't learned not to abuse animals. But I didn't blame myself. I'd known what sort of low-life he was originally. Was he capable of rehabilitation?

Apparently not.

I finally had enough of admiring myself on YouTube, at least for the moment. Although I did look pretty good there, for an aging broad. Not that anyone but family would be watching me. All eyes would be on that sweet puppy in my arms.

I took a quick peek at a Web site of the unofficial network of pet rescue administrators that I belong to, Southern California Rescuers. On a discussion group linked to it, we all share news of upcoming events, animals that need quick rescue — especially if we can't get there fast enough or haven't the room to bring them in — and other information that we thought our counterparts might find interesting.

I wasn't enamored of the methods used by some of the other shelters in the network to care for or rehome their wards, but I kept my opinions to myself, in the interest of sharing useful information. So far, none who'd joined seemed to be abusing any of their residents, or my stance could change.

Nothing of interest there. No one had mentioned the puppy mill rescue, nor should they. No private shelter was officially involved.

I clicked back to my computer desktop and pushed away, observing the stack of files I needed to review. They sat on the right side of my antique-style wooden desk. I'd found the ornate, L-shaped desk used around the time I'd helped Dante to open HotRescues. He'd been willing to buy me a new one or a real antique. But I hadn't thought either necessary. I had engaged my multitalented, strong hands to refinish this one and liked it a lot. It was large, with ring-like, drooping drawer handles that looked like aged pewter.

The desk occupied one side of my fairly large office — which had been designed and mostly furnished by Dante, not me, as the administrator's hangout. The other side was basically a conversation area that I used for private meetings. It contained a really at-tractive sofa with brown, leathery uphol-stery, beige pillows, and curved wood legs. A little pretentious, but I liked it. I appreci-ated even more the wooden bookshelf that also had a role as a file cabinet. And I especially liked the window view of part of the shelter area, although right now the

48

shades were drawn.

The files on my desk were labeled with names of our most recent adoptees. HotRescues was savvy enough to keep computerized track of all residents, but being medium tech instead of high, I also kept paper files for information not scanned or typed directly onto the computer. We maintained as many details as we could on each animal, including everything placed on the data sheet posted near their enclosures and more. The files I stored in my office were devoted to our residents waiting for someone to take them home — paperwork I kept readily available to make copies for potential adopters.

Right now, I had to go through folders on animals we'd placed recently. I'd soon organize their files in a storage room, but I always liked to chuck out unnecessary papers first. We always maintained some things, though, like special notes from volunteers who took pets for walks or played with them. And data about their spaying or neutering, since no animal left here unfixed, if they weren't already, unless they were too young — and in those cases, we insisted that they be brought back so we could make sure it was done. That way, they'd never have offspring who could become similarly homeless.

We also kept data on who turned noses up at a meal, or expressed rage by attacking another dog, or had any other behavior or health issue. And . . . well, I actually didn't recycle much.

I hadn't a lot of time to sort through files now anyway. A pet owner was supposed to come in to talk to us about relinquishing her dog. Maybe. It was the same woman who'd called a few days ago. She hadn't kept an appointment yet.

Which might be a good sign. Perhaps she wouldn't abandon her dog here after all.

I glanced at the clock — a modern digital gadget that didn't go with my desk's antique look. It was nine thirty A.M. The woman had said she would show up at ten o'clock. I decided to take the opportunity to walk through the shelter area again.

"Be back in a few," I told Nina as I passed through the entry. She was once again staffing the welcome area. The volunteer who had promised to sit there this morning had phoned in sick.

"Say hi to everyone for me," she called.

Outside, dogs started barking the minute I appeared, as always — even though I discouraged it. I began to stroll down the path with habitats on both sides. At each enclosure, I stopped to say hi to its resident, smiling and putting my hand through for a pet as long as that pup wasn't barking. "How are you, Elmer?" I crooned to the Lab. "You're looking adorable today, Honey," I told the Westie mix.

I passed the middle building, on my right, which housed our toy dogs, most rescued cats, and other smaller animals.

As I reached the turn toward the next row of kennels, I saw Si Rogan and Angie Shayde come through the back entrance, near the end of the storage building. "Hi," I greeted them both.

"Hi, back, Internet star." Si grinned as I rolled my eyes.

"That's so three days ago," I countered.

Si was an animal behaviorist who helped to retrain our most energetic or belligerent residents to make them easier to adopt. Around my age, and cute in an aging boyish kind of way, he was a nice guy who'd worked here part-time since we'd opened HotRescues. I'd gleaned by his attentiveness now and then that he wanted to get to know me better, but I'd gently discouraged him.

"But it's still so adorable." Angie was also smiling. A new veterinary technician who had only recently started working here, she had a classic oval face that looked almost cherubic, and short, curly hair. I was certain that she put all the animals she treated at ease with her warm attitude, too.

"Would have been cuter if the circumstances had been different," I reminded her.

Her expression clouded. "That's for sure."

They both headed for the center building as I continued my stroll. I glanced at my watch. Time to return to my office to see if the woman who'd talked about leaving her dog here showed up around when she'd said she would.

I soon sat at my desk again and made myself begin plowing through files but kept checking the clock. When 10:10 showed, I heard a noise in the outer area. Looked like, this time, she had decided to keep her appointment. I sighed for her dog and turned my expression into a smile of dispirited compassion before rising to join them.

"What are you doing here?" I heard Nina's voice raised from beyond my half-closed door.

"I'm back again to help out." Or at least that's what I thought I heard. The voice was muffled, yet unpleasantly familiar. No more ghost of a smile on my face, only anger. I burst out of my office.

Efram Kiley stood there, leaning over the

reception counter with a grin that appeared menacing in its innocence. He wore jeans and a HotRescues T-shirt that looked similar to my outfit that day — not prison garb. But he'd just been arrested three days ago. What was he doing out of jail?

What was he doing *here?*

He turned to look at me. Something unsettling passed across his face — rage? Hatred?

Or maybe nothing at all. It could have been my imagination, since it wasn't there when he aimed his unwelcome grin at me. "Hi, Lauren. I hope we can get past that misunderstanding the other day. Honestly, I was at that puppy mill to help."

"Help the puppy mill owners?" I goaded. "I didn't have any sense that you were helping the dogs."

His eyes turned sorrowful and pained, as if I'd unexpectedly grown cat claws and drawn them across his face. Real emotion? I doubted it. Especially not after the way he had grabbed me during the rescue. Attacked me, until Matt Kingston took him into custody.

"Like I said, it was a misunderstanding. But now I have to prove it in court. They arrested me." He sounded genuinely baffled, but I knew how skilled an actor the guy was.

"I'm out on bail. Had to hire another lawyer, can you believe it?"

"Yes, I can. And I think you'd better go talk to your lawyer. Or at least get out of here. You're not welcome any longer." I moved closer, intending to force him to back off. I didn't want him here. His presence reminded me of those poor, suffering puppies and dogs in those horrible, cramped conditions. Not to mention the pups rescued from the storm drain.

When he didn't move, I glanced at Nina, who sat behind the desk, pale and clearly upset. "Please go call 911," I told her.

"But I don't want to leave you . . ." She glanced at Efram.

I didn't especially crave being alone with him, either, but I wanted her away from this volatile man. "Go," I insisted. Nina darted past us into my office.

I was concerned, sure, but at least Efram and I faced off in a relatively public place. The woman wanting to leave her dog was due any minute. Volunteers and employees of HotRescues always signed in here, in the main reception area. I had nothing to worry about. Besides, he abused vulnerable animals that were smaller than him and couldn't fight back. His grabbing me before didn't really mean he'd hurt people.

I hoped.

As we stood there, Dr. Mona Harvey walked in. Short, professionally clad in a shirtwaist, she was our esteemed staff psychologist and part-time adoption counselor. "Hi, Lauren. Efram." She glanced at the latter shrewdly and inquisitively but didn't ask why he was there. Instead, she signed the sheet on the desk and continued through, obviously reluctant to interrupt.

I nearly asked her to stay, but what good would that do? Besides, the cops would be here soon, if Nina had called as I'd requested. And I was sure she had.

Efram didn't leave, but the steam of his anger appeared to be cooling. "Lauren, can we talk?" His voice held no menace now. He actually looked exhausted, and worried. Was this change of attitude for real?

I didn't believe it. "No," I said. "Please leave."

Instead, he turned and planted himself on a chair at the side of the elongated table for visitors, where people interested in pet adoption were interviewed and filled out forms. It was located under the window that opened to the street. "Please, Lauren. Sit down."

I ignored his request, sharpening the intensity of my glare.

He leaned forward and clasped his large hands between his knees. "I want things the way they were before. I was learning how to really take care of pets, you know that. I love animals. I wouldn't do anything to hurt them, especially now."

"I'm not the judge of that," I responded evenly. I could act a role, too, if I needed to. And right now, displaying any of the anger that seethed inside me wouldn't boot him out of here. "I'm not the one who arrested you. But I did see you there at that puppy mill. And someone threw those poor little beagles down the storm drain."

"Not me!" he shot back, half standing. I tried to keep my expression indifferent, but he scared me.

I could admit that to myself, but no way would I admit it to him.

Matt Kingston wasn't here to pull Efram away if he attacked. Neither was anyone else. Even if Mona had stayed, I doubted she'd be able to do more than attempt, in her shrink's way — most likely unsuccessfully — to get this obviously upset man to chill out.

"Maybe not." I kept my voice neutral as I glanced at my watch. "I'm expecting someone any moment who's supposed to bring in a dog. Really, Efram, leave. Now."

His face became a mask of annoyance that he bit back as fast as a Jack Russell terrier chases a ball. "Soon," he said. "Right now, I want to visit the animals." He rose suddenly and darted past me.

By the time I caught up, he'd opened the gate into our shelter area. Albert, a gray miniature poodle mix in the first enclosure on the right, saw us and started barking, which turned the entire locale into a cacophony of dogginess. Despite how I usually discouraged that kind of noise, I wanted to thank Albert for starting the ruckus this time. Instead, I said to Efram, "You've seen the animals. Now, get out of here, Efram."

Auspiciously, Pete Engersol came out of our center building just then with a leash in his hands. An energetic senior citizen, he was one of the all-around assistants who cleaned enclosures, fed animals, and did whatever not-too-physical labor was required. "Hi, Lauren and Efram," he called over the remaining barks. I waved, glad to see someone else around but wishing it was some big, burly, younger guy acting as my Superman. Or anyone with handcuffs and authority to arrest Efram for trespassing.

Too bad Matt Kingston wasn't around. I'd have to invite him for a visit here one day soon.

As Pete headed for the rear of the shelter area, Efram stood there without answering me, his arms crossed, clearly intending to hang out here longer no matter what I said.

"Can I walk a few of the dogs today?" he asked. "Like I said, I want things to go back to normal."

"That's impossible." Keeping my voice calm was becoming more of an effort. "You're not welcome even to be here, let alone to get any closer to the animals. Get out, Efram." This was getting damned repetitious, for all the good it did. I felt ineffectual, like a Chihuahua yapping at a hungry coyote, and I hated the feeling. Even worse, my fear, rational or not, was elevating as if I was one of those small dogs facing a skulking predator.

"I told you I didn't do anything wrong." Efram's voice was suddenly raised as if to combat the now nearly nonexistent ruckus from the nearby dogs. His anger seemed barely in check, and I glanced around, glad to see a couple of pit bull mixes nearby that, if necessary, I could let loose. These two were sweethearts, but with the breed's reputation of violence, they might scare Efram into backing off.

Or not, since he seemed to be gearing up to start his own reputation of violence.

"That may be," I said, forcing my voice to sound more angry than afraid — even though the two emotions vied for priority. "But I couldn't help watching the news over the past few days. The neighbor who claims to have called in the complaint to Animal Services about the puppy mill in the first place has said in interviews that she knows the owners, the Shaheens, and that she saw someone else throwing the puppies into the storm drain. Someone in shadows, whose description could be yours. The Shaheens have been interviewed, too. They're not saying much, but they seem pretty upset that someone — not them, though they haven't identified the culprit to the media — dared to throw pups into the drain, like they were trash, not beloved animals."

Strange, that the Shaheens seemed to give a damn about the mistreated offspring they'd bred into the world — even if it might only be because they saw dollar signs floating in the storm drain instead of puppies.

"Not me. I want the money you and Dante promised me, Lauren, and I'm willing to work for it."

Ah. This had to be the crux of his demands, his real reason for coming here. "I'll talk to Dante about it again," I responded civilly, although I already knew the answer — the same one I'd gladly hurl into Efram's face now if he weren't so menacing. Including a demand that he pay back all the money he hadn't really earned. But that could come later, when I wasn't alone with this vile man. "I really think you'd better leave now, though, till all this is resolved."

I turned and started walking back toward the entrance gate, my hand outstretched in invitation to Efram to go through it — permanently.

He grabbed my arm and twisted it. "No way, bitch. I want my money."

Ignoring the pain that speared through my arm, I wrested it away. "That's enough, Efram. Get the hell out of here, immediately." I still couldn't force him to do anything, but I'd shouted so loudly that the dogs all started barking again — and my voice was even more voluble than theirs.

I was relieved when Si and Angie emerged hastily from the center building. Both had assisted in our attempt to reeducate Efram, so they knew him.

They approached us, which hurled my emotions into further turmoil. I didn't want them endangered, but maybe there was safety in numbers.

Or maybe not.

"What are you doing here, Efram?" Angie demanded. "People who work at puppy mills aren't welcome. Those poor animals!"

"Like she said." Si looked at me, as if trying to confirm my opinion.

I nodded. "Efram was just leaving." I didn't look at him.

"Yeah, okay, I get it," he growled. "I'm leaving for now. But you can be sure I'll be back. And if you think I may have abused animals before, just wait till you see how nasty I can get. And not just to the damned dogs and cats you keep here." He paused, and only then did I glance at him. His face was a feral mask of rage. "Everyone here had just better watch their backs," he said in a voice so low it was hard to hear. "All of you — especially you, Vancouver." He shot an extra-menacing glare at me, and then he strode toward the rear exit — even as I finally heard a siren from down the street.

CHAPTER 4

Unsurprisingly, Efram vanished before the police arrived. I told the officer who interviewed me — a young African American guy who clearly loved animals — what had happened. I gathered that, despite Efram's ugly threat, he would probably not be arrested for his intrusion into HotRescues that day.

I had Nina take the cop for a walk around the shelter, ostensibly to make sure Efram wasn't hiding in some remote alcove, but also because I had the sense that the officer was interested in seeing our residents, and I wanted to encourage that. His partner, an older, no-nonsense female cop, pretended disinterest, but she accompanied them.

I returned to the welcome area. It was long past the time when the woman who'd called so often said she was bringing in her dog. Maybe she had at long last made the final decision to keep her pup at home.

But that wasn't the case. A thin thirty-something lady was standing there when I arrived. She wore tight jeans and a loose shirt in a colorful print pattern.

Sitting on the floor at her feet, his leash slack since he wasn't moving, was a golden retriever mix. He looked toward me with anxious eyes as I joined them.

I believe that pets understand a lot more than most people give them credit for. Often, they recognize words. Even more, they read moods, especially of the people they love.

This dog clearly sensed something terrible was afoot.

"Hi," I said, immediately taking charge. Approaching the woman with my hand outstretched, I continued, "I'm Lauren Vancouver, director of administration of HotRescues."

"I'm Brooke Pernall, and this is Cheyenne." Brooke didn't shake my hand or meet my eyes. Her face was narrow and gaunt, her mousy brown hair a sparse, unstyled frame around it.

If I wasn't mistaken, she was ill. Which made this situation potentially even more heartbreaking.

"Hi, Cheyenne." I knelt beside the dog, whose tail gave a halfhearted wag. I couldn't help it. I hugged him.

63

"I have to leave him here, with you. He needs a good home." As Brooke spoke, her voice grew louder, as if she gained strength from expressing her decision.

"Yes, he does," I agreed. "Please have a seat." I motioned toward the chairs at the table near the window. I nearly shuddered, since the last time I'd seen anyone occupy one, it had been Efram. But helping to resolve this situation might cleanse the area of its bad karma — I hoped.

Brooke took the seat I indicated, and Cheyenne sat on the tile floor beside her, looking more alert, as if sensing an ally in me. If so, he was one smart dog.

"So," I said, "I get it that you want a good home for Cheyenne. What I don't get is why your home doesn't qualify."

What little color there was beneath Brooke's papery skin drained away as if sucked quickly inside by an invisible vacuum. Her light amber eyes flooded with tears, making mine grow moist in empathy. I waited.

"I love Cheyenne," she said hoarsely. "I wish I could keep him, but . . . my home is being foreclosed on. I'm not sure where I'm going to live, or *if* . . ." Her voice tapered off, and I realized that the emphasis on her last word was a statement.

She believed she was dying.

"Tell me about it," I said gently, not sure how I could bear hearing her, but I felt certain she needed to talk.

Her story was probably not unique these days, after the economic crises over the last few years. She had a heart condition, was on medication that helped but the stuff was expensive. Interestingly, she'd worked for a major private investigation firm as an operative — until she became too ill to go out in the field. They'd given her an inside desk job for a while, but as the economy slowed, so had their business. They had recently let her go. When she'd lost her job, she'd also lost her medical insurance, and the combination meant she would additionally lose her home.

Now she was about to lose her beloved dog, too. But, unselfishly, she wanted to give Cheyenne the best possible chance at survival and happiness, no matter what happened to her.

"Where are you living now?" I asked her.

"I'm still in the house for the time being, but the bank has said they won't extend that beyond another month or so. That's why I need to make sure Cheyenne is taken care of right away."

"Got any family who could help?" I had

to ask, but anticipated the reply.

"Not really."

Cheyenne stood and put his head on Brooke's knee. She bent over and hugged him.

I wanted to hug them both. Fix things for them.

Well, I couldn't cure Brooke. But I had an idea about how to make things better for them, at least over the short term.

"Okay," I said briskly, standing. "Here's what we'll do. You take Cheyenne home with you for now. As Nina and I told you over the phone, we can help by supplying dog food. The moment the bank says that's it, that you have to leave, you can bring Cheyenne back. If necessary, we'll work out a good adoption for him, one where you'll be able to visit if you want to. But before we get to that point, we'll see if we can make things better."

Brooke looked up skeptically. "How?"

"Can't tell you now," I replied. "And there are no guarantees. But let me do some checking, see if I can come up with anything so Cheyenne and you can stay together while you're dealing with your illness. Is it a kind that could be . . ." I stopped. Her prognosis was really not my business.

"Fatal?" she finished. "Potentially, although there are new medications and other options I could try. I'd have a better chance if my insurance company hadn't dumped me, though."

"Got it," I said cheerfully. "We'll see what we can do. Are you okay to drive Cheyenne and you home?"

"Well, yes," she said, sitting up fully in her chair. Cheyenne backed away slightly, and for the first time he started really wagging his tail. "But —"

"But you'd braced yourself for going back alone. I get it. Cheyenne doesn't, though. Are you willing to take a chance on being able to keep him now?"

"Well, yes," she repeated. "But I don't see how —"

"Even if I can't help, you'll at least have had more time with Cheyenne. Isn't it worth it to try?"

"Oh, yes!" Brooke bent again to hug her best friend — and then came over to hug me.

I only hoped I wasn't just blowing smoke around both — all three — of us.

But the HotRescues benefactor — who also contributed to other worthy causes — was out of town. His secretary said she'd give Dante my message but suspected I wouldn't hear from him until the next day. He'd decided to confront a problem at a HotPets warehouse in the Midwest himself.

That meant it would be handled quickly, efficiently, and well. It also meant I couldn't follow through on my idea to help Brooke Pernall right away — and I hated delays, even if I couldn't control them. *Especially* then.

My idea? Throw money at her. Dante's money, not mine, since I hadn't much to spare. But maybe he would lend me his clout to lean on Brooke's former insurance company. Or —

Hey, a lawyer could do that. I could talk to his lady friend, Kendra Ballantyne. She might have some ideas, too.

I lifted the phone in my office again, but the door from our reception area burst into the room, followed by Nina.

"Lauren, everyone here knows about Efram, and how he acted. They're worried. Could we talk to them?"

My second in command looked worried, too. Justifiably. Brooke Pernall's woes had distracted me from my own. HotRescues' own.

The bank hadn't kicked Brooke out yet. I didn't have to fix things for her this instant, if I could at all. But addressing the menace around here couldn't wait.

"Absolutely," I told Nina. "Let's get everyone who's here together in the meeting room upstairs in twenty minutes."

"I'm on it." Nina looked relieved as she left again, pulling the door closed after her.

If only some inspiration would leap into my fragmented thoughts so I could convey genuine optimism to my gang — some way to permanently banish Efram and his threats from HotRescues.

The main HotRescues building was a solid, attractive two-story structure that Dante had designed to his specifications when he created the shelter.

The upstairs was planned around a conference room. Doors opening onto it led to offices used by staff members like Nina and Mona to meet with potential adopters and decide if they were worthy. And, in Mona's case, counsel them. There was even a shrink's couch in her room. I preferred to have my office downstairs in the mainstream of what was going on.

When time for our impromptu meeting arrived, I stayed in our welcome area as the others headed up the stairway near the exit to the shelter grounds. I didn't count heads, but after a few minutes I followed — not before locking the outer door. Any visitors could ring the doorbell.

By the time I arrived at our meeting, nearly everyone else had, too, massing around the conference table. They'd thoughtfully left a chair at one end for me — a good idea, since I had every intention of presiding over this gathering.

Like our reception room, this one's walls were decorated with photos of our successes — pets and their new owners. I know I'm prone to anthropomorphism, but yes, even the animals seemed to smile. Why not? They'd each found a new home.

I planted myself on the empty seat — wood that matched the table, blue upholstery, and wheels for ease of movement.

"What's going on, Lauren?" Mona frowned beneath her narrow glasses. She held a notepad and pen, clearly prepared to take notes. No surprise that she spoke first. As a psychologist, she liked to know what everyone was thinking — human and not. "Does this have something to do with Efram?"

"It sure does," said Angie. "The S.O.B. threatened us, and the animals, too. He has some nerve, hurting those poor pups, then coming here." A veterinary technician — clad, as usual, in a turquoise lab jacket —

she always seemed highly empathetic with animals.

Of course, everyone in this group gave a damn, or they wouldn't be here. I'd make sure of it.

"I don't understand the guy." Si Rogan shook his head. "I worked with him a lot. Really thought he was coming around, doing a good job learning how to care for animals." He looked at me as if for confirmation, and I nodded.

"Too bad you couldn't train him as well as you train animals," Pete Engersol said to Si, drumming his aging fingers on the table. Our all-around caretaker had spent a lot of time with Efram, too, but I didn't bring that up.

Our young volunteers, Ricki and Sally, looked from one speaker to the next, both wide-eyed.

"What kind of threat did he make?" Sally ventured. She was a short brunette with lovely Hispanic features, dressed, like Ricki, in a yellow HotRescues knit shirt. The actual employees — me included — wore similar shirts in blue.

"Nothing specific," I replied, "but the fact he'd threaten HotRescues at all is why I called this meeting. You're all on notice to be careful. If you see Efram, stay away and come get me. Better yet, if you feel even a little nervous, call 911 first, then warn the rest of us."

"I don't get it." Nina had taken a seat beside me. "I hated what the guy did with Quincy. But he always seemed so nice around here — took orders, even showed initiative in doing things for our residents."

I'd hated his abuse of Quincy, too — enough to work out a way to make sure we'd gotten the dog from a shelter, since our permit doesn't allow us to take in strays. Efram had claimed we were wrong about the abuse. He'd also claimed we hadn't looked at all for Killer's owner. I had . . . but not very hard.

"Because he was paid to," Mona reminded Nina. Efram's threat of a lawsuit, and the settlement we'd entered into, were no secret, though the actual amounts Dante was paying were.

"Anyway," I said, "I'm through, unless anyone else has anything to discuss. Just be careful. Don't trust Efram. We'll do what we have to, to ensure he gets what he deserves and leaves us alone."

"Amen," said Mona, and the gang all started to dissipate.

As I began to follow, Si joined me on the narrow stairway. "I really hate that Efram threatened you, Lauren." He peered down from the step above me. His hair was dark with gray strands, with a similar pattern in his five o'clock shadow. His narrow-lipped scowl turned his high forehead into a contrail of parallel wrinkles.

"I hate that he threatened everyone around here," I replied. "As well as our animals. We'll all have to be cautious."

"Let me know later when you're ready to head home. I'd be glad to make sure you get there safely."

We'd reached the bottom of the steps, and I smiled at Si. "Didn't I hear that you were teaching a new beginner's dog training class starting tonight?"

"Well, yes, but it's not until seven o'clock."

"I'll be fine, Si. Besides, the rumor I heard said you've been hired to give a class at a major pet store chain that doesn't belong to our chief benefactor. If that's true, you'd better just slip away late this afternoon without any fanfare."

"Really?" He looked horrified.

I was joking. Si did a great job of retraining some of our most challenging dogs to help squelch objectionable traits that could hinder the possibility of finding them homes. But he was free to work for whomever he chose when he wasn't busy here.

"Just kidding. I know it's not your first gig for that outfit, which shall remain nameless around here."

He smiled back. For an instant, I had the impression he was going to bend down and try to kiss me.

I pivoted and edged away. "You're one great dog trainer, Si." I hoped he heard my silent message — again: I gave homage to his training skills, but, personally, I had no interest.

Maybe one day I'd have to say it out loud, openly hurt his feelings. I liked the guy . . . as a friend and employee. And I'd hate to have to start looking for a new trainer.

But men and I . . . Well, my beloved first husband, Kerry, had been the absolute best, but he'd died years ago from a rare and untreatable form of cancer. Thinking the kids needed another father — and I needed company — I'd remarried. That second marriage had been an utter mistake. Now, I liked my life. My independence. My non-reliance on any man.

So even if Si was the most outstanding guy in the universe — I simply wasn't interested.

"Let me know how your new class goes tonight," I finished, and headed for my office.

■ ■ ■ ■

My BlackBerry rang as I closed my door. I pulled it from my jeans pocket. It was Dante.

"Hey, thanks for calling back," I said, settling into my chair.

I glanced toward the window, which opened onto the shelter area. Ricki and Pete were checking on our doggy residents, and I saw Sally enter the central building's back door. Everything looked fine. No sign that we were under pressure from that miserable Efram. But I hoped that enough had been said to put everyone on guard.

I intended to tell Dante first about my discussion with Brooke Pernall and Cheyenne so I could ask how charitable he felt that day. Before I could start, though, he said, "In case you're wondering, I've stopped all payments to Efram Kiley, as of today. Didn't get around to it earlier this week. I'd arranged for automatic deposits into his bank account, subject to his keeping his promises, but he's reneged on them big time. Of course Kendra reminds me that the guy's innocent under the law till proven guilty. But she's the lawyer, not me. If he's found innocent, I'll make up any amounts he should have been paid."

"Good move." I wished I'd known about Dante's actions before our meeting, though, since Efram was even more likely to turn his threats into frightening reality once he learned his money source had terminated. At least nearly everyone had been warned. I told Dante about the threats, and he was clearly angry and concerned. "You be careful, too," I warned him, "in case Efram includes you in his vengeance."

Next, I told Dante about Brooke Pernall and Cheyenne. "So . . . what do you think? Can we help her?" I finished.

"You mean, can *I* help her?" He at least sounded cheerful again. "Get me more info about her and her predicament, like confirm what her medical condition is and how money might help cure her, that kind of thing. Then we'll see."

"Thanks." I smiled as I hung up. I had a feeling that some assistance would soon be dancing Brooke and Cheyenne's way.

Another good thing about having a shelter funded by someone as rich as Dante was that we could afford good security. Consequently, we had an alarm system we turned on at night, security cameras placed in strategic locations, and a security company

— EverySecurity, also used by Dante at his HotPets stores — that sent a patrol around HotRescues several times between dusk and dawn.

I wondered now, though, as I had in the past, if we should hire someone to stay overnight. But some other private shelters made do with even less, and this system had worked fine since HotRescues opened.

We'd never been threatened before, though, and now not even all that security was enough to ease my concerns about Efram.

I decided to call Captain Matt Kingston to update him and ask obliquely whether Animal Services could do anything else to rein in Efram.

Matt had called me the day after the puppy mill rescue to keep me in the loop about the conditions of the dogs who'd been saved — and he had better firsthand knowledge than Nina's sources. All were expected to survive, even the parents, who were in the worst health. Matt promised to let me know if any of their lives became at risk due to overcrowding in public shelters.

He'd given me his cell phone number so, still sitting in my office with the door closed, I called it.

He answered right away. "Hi, Lauren. No,

we're not giving up any of the dogs for you to rehome yet."

I laughed. "You've got me pegged. But as long as you find them great new families I'm fine with it. I'm calling about something else." I filled him in on Efram's threats. "Everyone here is on alert, so I'm sure we'll be fine . . . but if there's anything you can do to expedite his trial or whatever —"

"Damn!" he exclaimed. "I'll contact the LAPD and make sure there'll be extra patrols in your neighborhood. But be careful, Lauren. That guy's a danger, even when he doesn't make threats."

"Thanks," I said.

"You up for dinner one of these days? To discuss the puppy mill operation and Efram and the other suspects, I mean."

Grinning slightly, I told him I'd love to talk business with him, someday soon.

Only Nina was still around late that evening, and she was heading home. We stood in the reception area.

"I called EverySecurity to let them know we need additional patrols," she said, brushing her long hair away from the shoulder strap of her pocketbook.

"Good idea," I said. "I did, too."

It was already dark outside. "Let's both

leave together," she said. "We can watch each other's backs as we get into our cars."

"I'll watch yours, but . . . well, I'm staying here tonight. Sleeping upstairs." I'd done it before, when we had an ill animal that needed nursing or I had some unavoidable paperwork that kept me busy till long into the night.

"Bad idea." Her normally pale face flushed, so I knew she was upset.

"Maybe, but I'll feel better if I'm here." Thank heavens my kids were at school and I had no pets at home. That gave me leeway to do what I needed to . . . and I wouldn't worry that Efram could harm them, too. "Our security guys will call me if there's anything suspicious outside or if the silent alarm goes off, or whatever. Plus, Captain Kingston of Animal Services promised he'd alert the LAPD. And I'll call for help right away if I hear anything. I'll be fine."

We argued a little longer, but Nina finally caved. She's worked with me long enough to know that, when my mind's made up, that's that. And so, she left.

I hung out downstairs awhile longer, going outside to check yet another time on our dogs, and inside the central building to look in on the smaller animals.

All seemed normal — as normal as could

be with an environment filled with sadly homeless creatures. But I was uneasy enough to check other doors, like one into our large storage building at the rear of the fenced property that also contained our laundry facilities. Everything there seemed fine, too.

I eventually went upstairs in the main building and sat on the couch in Mona's office. I'd slept there before — although that night I didn't anticipate getting any real sleep. I slipped on the black hoodie I kept at HotRescues in case it got chilly, since I didn't intend to put the furnace on. It was late April and unlikely to get very cold.

I actually must have conked out, since I was startled awake when the dogs outside began to bark. Sounded like all of them. Upset and loud.

I reached for my cell phone, but didn't call the security company . . . yet. One dog might have thought he'd heard something, started barking, and spurred the others to join in.

Maybe.

But I'd be careful.

I pulled my shoes back on and tied the laces. I didn't even turn on all the lights as I went downstairs. They could disturb the animals even more or alert an intruder —

Efram? — to my presence and endanger me further. I'd been prepared enough to bring a flashlight.

I tried not to hurry, since I didn't want to fall down the steps. I wished I could call out to the dogs. Calm them. Tell them I was on my way.

At the bottom, I turned toward the door to the shelter area. And then I opened it.

The barking was louder outside without the building's insulation to muffle it. My nerves were even more frayed, making my trembling hands cause the light beams to scintillate. The hell with it. I flicked the switch to turn on the lights.

As I looked around, I hesitated. What was that? A pile of something lay on the pavement way down toward the far end of the closest row of enclosures. It hadn't been there before.

It looked like clothes. Only . . .

I swallowed hard. Something — someone — was in those clothes.

Who else was here? Was he — she — hurt?

Had Efram somehow made good on his threats after I'd headed upstairs?

Holding my BlackBerry in my hand, fully on alert and ready to call for help the instant I needed it, I inched toward whoever lay on the ground. I wore athletic shoes — not that

I'd have made much sound on the concrete walkway anyhow. Especially with the dogs still barking, telling me about the intrusion — or something else.

As I reached the lump of clothes, I recognized it. I also saw a large puddle of red seeping onto the ground.

Efram. Bleeding.

"Efram!" I shouted. Was this a trick? If I knelt to see if he was okay, would he lunge at me?

But he wasn't moving. I didn't even see him breathing. I took a few more steps and stooped, carefully reaching out to touch his neck.

"Freeze!" shouted someone behind me. Startled, I stood and pivoted at the same time.

Three cops stood there, aiming guns at me.

CHAPTER 5

I immediately put my hands in the air, trembling as the cops edged closer. "I'm Lauren Vancouver, officers." I wished the usual note of decisive authority could interject its way into my voice now. "I'm director of administration of HotRescues. I just found Efram here, and — is he going to be okay?"

The female officer knelt on the ground as I'd started to do, feeling Efram's neck. "Let's get the EMTs here," she said, which gave me hope that he was alive despite my initial assessment. No matter how miserable a human being he was, at that moment I didn't wish anything too bad for him — except that, as soon as he was well, he'd spend a nice long sentence in prison after being convicted of animal abuse. "But I think this is one for the coroner."

My optimism blew away with my audible sigh. I hadn't even realized I'd been holding my breath.

"Come over here, ma'am." One of the male cops gestured for me to follow. At least they'd lowered their guns, but I had no illusions. I wasn't sure why they'd arrived at that critical moment, but they'd seen me with Efram. And Efram had apparently been killed.

I'd spotted, on the ground, under the bright, artificial lights of the shelter, what might have been the weapon used to stab him. It was one of the overgrown knives we kept in the storage building to rip open large bags of dog and cat food. I wasn't the only one, but I did, sometimes, feed our charges. My fingerprints could be on that knife.

And I'd been arguing with Efram. These cops didn't know that . . . yet. They'd probably find out.

But I hadn't hurt him. I hadn't even known he was here. Not that I was entirely shocked by his presence.

Only his condition.

I stood alongside the cop who seemed to have taken charge of me. His name badge said he was Andrews. He appeared young and gruff, or maybe that was his way of dealing with crime. I didn't remember walking as far as the main building, but now we stood outside it. I became aware then that the dogs were still barking. Under ordinary circumstances, I'd have been fully mindful of it at all times. Would have tried to calm them. But now, with my nerves this edgy, I could easily have joined them, shouting and venting any way I could. Maybe even bawling.

Efram clearly couldn't hurt me now. But I was terrified of the situation. Not that I'd show it.

"What happens now, Officer Andrews?" I asked as calmly as I could.

He reiterated, as his female cohort had said, that the EMTs and coroner would arrive soon. So would a team from the SID, which he explained was the Scientific Investigation Division — the LAPD's version of CSI.

"And one of our Robbery Homicide Division detectives will want to talk to you, ma'am."

There wasn't much I'd be able to tell them, though. I'd try to help, but I wasn't stupid. Efram had been stabbed. I was here. No one else seemed to be around but the cops . . . now.

Therefore, I would be a suspect.

The dogs quieted down a bit. Or maybe I was tuning them out. I hoped not. They were upset for a good reason.

I badly wanted to take another quick walk through the shelter area, make sure all the animals were okay in their enclosures despite their restlessness.

Whatever Efram had been doing here, I believed he had intended to carry through on his threats, which encompassed our residents, too.

Only . . . what person had gotten to him first?

I wasn't sure how much time had passed, but daylight was starting to transform the black sky to light, hazy blue. Officer Andrews had allowed me to go into our main building, and I now sat on a chair at the table near the window.

Soon, people who belonged here would start arriving. What would they think? Would they assume, as these cops probably did, that I'd killed Efram?

My subordinates knew, even better than the cops did so far, the ill will I'd felt toward the man who clearly had no problem with abusing animals.

But despising him was a huge chasm away from killing him.

Officer Andrews hadn't sat down. He seemed to be studying every inch of our reception area, as if it would provide a clue about what had happened to Efram. The place, even with its cat-print counter and happy pictures of animal adoptions, no longer seemed so welcoming, even to me.

The door opened, and a man wearing the deep green uniform of our security company walked in. I recognized him. His name was Ed Bransom, and he was a manager. He visited now and then to check out the system, make sure it was working optimally. If he hadn't, I'd have been on the phone making a lot more demands of the company.

"Hi, Lauren," he said now. "No alarm went off at our offices, but one of your cameras suddenly lost its picture. Per our agreed-on procedure for HotRescues, we tried fixing it remotely, then dispatched someone and called 911. By the time our guy arrived the cops were already here."

Somewhere along the line, they were supposed to call my BlackBerry, too. Maybe they'd thought that was to happen only after they'd checked things out. I'd have to review our agreement with them.

"Is everything under control?" Bransom continued. He glanced toward Officer Andrews, who just watched silently.

"Not really."

"Then tell me —"

"Please step outside, sir," the cop said.

87

"Someone will talk with you shortly."

Ed met my eye, then looked at the officer. "A crime was committed, then?"

"It appears that way, sir."

"We'll talk later, Lauren," Ed said.

He had barely left when the door opened again. The man who walked in wasn't wearing a uniform. Or maybe he was — a suit, dark, with a blue-striped tie. And a frown.

He yanked a badge from his pocket and waved it toward Officer Andrews, who nodded, rose, and slipped out the door.

I felt like following. But I had a pretty good suspicion that this man was here to talk to me. Maybe not only me — I hoped. But I didn't really want anyone else at HotRescues to go through this experience, either. And it was getting close to time that the gang would start arriving.

"Hello." The man stood next to me, effectively blocking me from rising. Assuming control. I had to tolerate it, but I didn't have to embrace it. "I'm Detective Garciana of the Los Angeles Police Department." He held his badge out in case I wanted to study it. I didn't.

"Hello," I said, then cleared my throat, hoping to erase my uneasy huskiness. "I'm Lauren Vancouver, director of administration of HotRescues."

The dogs outside, previously quiet for a minute, now rent the air with a volley of barking. I wondered what was happening but suspected I wasn't welcome to go out and see.

"I'm here to help figure out what happened tonight," the detective continued. "Mind if I ask you a few questions?"

I did mind but said nothing. The more I pondered the situation, the more concerned I got. Any attempts on my part to help the cops could ricochet back and slam me in the gut. Efram was at least badly injured, probably dead. I'd been found with him. And I'd had a damned good motive to harm him: his threats and his animal abuse.

What could I say to get me out of this mess?

The best I could do — maybe — was tell the truth. Some of it.

"Go right ahead," I finally said, trying to sound as if I meant it.

He sat in the chair the police officer had just vacated. I leaned on my arms on the table as I waited for him to start, trying to hold back my body's quivering. So what if I had nothing to hide? I was as nervous as if I'd stabbed Efram. Which I hadn't.

Detective Garciana had straight, dark eyebrows knit nearly together as he watched

89

me, giving his deep brown eyes an air of sincerity that I didn't trust. His complexion was dusky, his black hair long enough to show its waviness. I wondered if he liked animals.

"You were here when the first officers arrived, correct?" After laying a recorder on the table, he extracted a small notebook from an inside pocket and poised a pen over it.

"That's right." I considered giving him a blow-by-blow of all that had occurred, but I watched enough TV cop shows to know better. I'd just wait for his questions.

And tell the truth. Carefully. I wondered if I should ask for a lawyer, but that might make me look like I had something to hide. I wasn't in custody, and cop shows indicated that an imminent arrest was what triggered Miranda rights and lawyering up.

But, damn, I was churning inside like a smoothie machine. I leaned back, in a futile attempt to calm down a little.

"Do you know the victim's identity, Ms. Vancouver?" he asked.

"His name is Efram Kiley."

"How do you know him?"

I explained only that he volunteered sometimes at HotRescues. No need to mention that his work here had started as the result of settling a dispute.

"He was arrested earlier this week because of his alleged affiliation with a puppy mill," said Detective Garciana.

That wasn't a question, but I still nodded. "That's my understanding."

"And according to news reports, you were also at the rescue of those puppies."

"Yes."

He eyed me with what could have been amusement — or irritation. Was he used to those he questioned blurting out their entire life histories?

If it helped to get him to believe in my innocence, I'd do that. But who knew what he was really thinking?

"So . . . Mr. Kiley helped out here. Was he usually around late at night?"

"No," I answered.

"Are you?"

"When I believe it's in the best interests of our residents."

"Did you arrange to have Mr. Kiley volunteer to help out tonight?"

"No." The vehemence in my tone got a surprised blink out of the detective.

Maybe it wasn't wise, but I decided I'd had enough of Twenty Questions — or A Hundred Questions, the way this was going.

"Here's how it is, Detective Garciana. I was definitely unhappy with Efram and his apparent work with that puppy mill. He and I had a disagreement about it, and he threatened me, my staff, and our residents here at HotRescues. I decided to sleep here because I was concerned about those threats. I didn't actually expect Efram to show up tonight, but I'm not surprised he came. I'd even asked our security company to keep close watch on us."

The detective seemed to relax, as if my outburst put him at ease. Did he believe he would get my confession any minute? My assumption was bolstered by his next words. "So, you heard him here, maybe saw him, and feared for your life?"

"If you're asking if I stabbed him in self-defense, the answer is no."

Those dark brows raised in obvious interest, and I realized what he might assume from what I'd said.

"And don't think I'm confessing to stabbing him *not* in self-defense, either," I asserted, feeling my hands ball into fists in my lap. "I didn't stab him at all. I heard the dogs barking, worried about what was going on, and came downstairs to find out — and found him lying there." I closed my eyes as I felt tears rush into them. Mistake. The image of Efram, bloody and still, popped into my head, and I again opened my eyes to find the detective still watching me keenly.

"So . . . you were staying here all night. Did you lock all the doors and gates?"

The way he looked at me I guessed that was a loaded question. I mentally started going through all entries. I'd certainly checked the ones in front, and into the parking lot. There was a fence around the perimeter of the entire site, with a couple of gates here and there, including one leading to an alley from which we brought in the heaviest bags of food since it was closest to the storage shed. It was always kept locked, and I'd checked it. Had Efram nevertheless sneaked in through there? Did he have a key made for that or any of the other locks while he was volunteering here?

He'd obviously gotten in somehow and turned off the alarm. And whoever killed him must have accompanied him.

But his being on the premises at all was another strike against me, most likely, in this detective's eyes.

Worry coursed through me in an ever-increasing stream. Would he arrest me?

What was the evidence against me? Possible fingerprints on the knife on the ground beside Efram. My animosity toward the guy. He was here, and he shouldn't have been. I was here because of him. And he had threatened me.

But —

As I've said before, I'm not a killer . . . of animals.

And even though he'd been a terrible man, I hadn't hurt Efram for any reason, self-defense or otherwise.

Somehow, I had to convince this skeptical detective of that.

CHAPTER 6

I'd been surviving on adrenaline for what seemed like hours. Probably *was* hours. But fatigue eventually trumped all other sensations.

The detective hadn't eased up. Wasn't he tired, too? Hard to tell. His questions were sounding familiar, so maybe he was. More likely, he was hoping I'd begin spouting inconsistent responses to prove his assumption that I was lying.

Which I wasn't.

My leaning on the table once more was no longer intended to resemble eagerness, but to hold me up. I couldn't tell much of what was going on outside. How long did a crime scene investigation take?

How were my poor charges out there doing?

"So, Ms. Vancouver," Detective Garciana was saying, "please tell me about the last time Mr. Kiley volunteered here at HotRescues."

I'd only responded to that three times before. Instead of answering now, I posed a question to him — not for the first time, either. "Detective, please. When can I go outside and check on the animals?"

"Soon. Now —"

"Sorry, but that's not good enough," I snapped, earning a glare. "I gather you're not much of a pet lover, but a lot of animals out there need to be fed and given water. Maybe have their enclosures cleaned. My staff will arrive soon. If you won't let me out there, will you at least promise to —"

My BlackBerry rang. Not asking for permission to answer, I yanked it from my pocket. Nina's number appeared on the display.

"Hi," I said. "Are you on your way? I need to tell you —"

"What happened, Lauren? I just woke up and . . . Thank God you're okay. You are okay, aren't you? HotRescues is all over the news. They say someone was hurt, and I was so afraid —"

"I'm fine," I assured her. I glanced toward the detective. He glowered but didn't insist that I hang up. Not that I'd pay attention if he tried. "The thing is — well, I can't go into detail now, but Efram showed up here. He's the one who was . . . hurt. And now the place is a crime scene and I'm not being allowed to go into the shelter area to take care of the animals."

I was whining, damn it. And to someone who might empathize but wouldn't be able to do anything about it without permission.

I moved the phone away from my mouth as I said to Detective Garciana, "Will you please let some of my employees check on our residents?"

"It's a crime scene," he growled, as if tired of telling me so. Well, gee, it wasn't as if the guy didn't like to repeat things.

"Would you be this way if the crime scene was a hospital? Or a nursery filled with hungry kids?"

"I'd have taken you to the station to question you if I wasn't aware that you were needed here," the detective responded as icily as if his saliva was freezing in his mouth.

"Who are you talking to, Lauren?" Nina's voice sounded distant, and I realized I still held the phone off to the side.

"A detective who's been questioning me." I looked back at him. "Like I said, some of my staff will arrive soon. Can they take care of the animals? Please?" Lord, it hurt to act polite, let alone beg.

Before he answered, one of the uniformed cops came into the room. "Excuse me, Detective," he said.

Garciana rose and joined him near our reception desk, while I spoke softly into the phone. "I think Efram's dead, Nina. I found him that way."

"Where?" she demanded. "How?"

I didn't have to choose whether or not to give her any of those details since the detective was already back in my face. "Later," I told her. I again looked at Garciana. "I'm talking to one of my assistants. She'll be here in a little while . . . okay?" Like, when was he finally going to give permission for me to do, or arrange for, what was necessary around here?

"I want a list of all your employees," Garciana said. "They're apparently starting to arrive."

Big surprise.

He glanced over his shoulder toward the cop who remained near the door.

"Fine. And then, will you —"

"We'll work out a way for someone to take care of the animals," he confirmed.

For the first time in what had seemed like eons, I smiled a little. Then I told Nina it was okay to come here right away.

After I complied with the detective's request for a list of employees — to which I also added volunteers scheduled that day — he let me flee into the shelter area. Not alone, but accompanied by a uniformed cop, a lady this time — Officer Plummer.

When I first went through the gate and onto the walkway, I stopped, stunned. The place hummed with people, some in uniform and some not. I watched for a short while as they flowed around one another as if experience had choreographed them. Some took measurements, others crawled on hands and knees with tweezers, picking up dust and twigs that had blown onto the paving.

The scene didn't completely resemble the crime scene investigations portrayed on TV. On the other hand, I'd heard for a long time that those shows made good drama but were not based a whole lot on reality.

At least the dogs in the outside kennels seemed to be taking it all in stride now. I noticed a couple of crime scene folks talking through fencing to some of our residents, including Dodi, a sheltie mix, who wagged her tail eagerly, obviously delighted at the attention, and Junior, a Doberman, whose ears perked up as he listened to whatever was being said to him. I wanted to hug them both. But not yet.

I realized that some of the dogs had probably witnessed what happened. Might they bark more at the killer than anyone else? Not likely. But it was an interesting thought.

Pete Engersol stood with a woman in a suit almost as formal as Detective Garciana's, and he looked down at her with an earnest but puzzled expression. Was he being interrogated, too?

I had to assume that everyone would be questioned, employees and volunteers alike, as soon as they came in. Maybe they'd even be sought out at their homes or alternate places of business. Some, like Mona and Si, were only part-timers, after all.

With the evident media coverage, it was unlikely that potential adopters would visit today. If they did, I'd be wary of placing any of our residents with them anyway, since that kind of person would have to be nuts to run the media gauntlet, or might be just publicity seekers. Not likely, either way, to be good candidates as new animal parents.

With Officer Plummer at my side, I ventured through the crowd to the first enclosure. Elmer, the black Lab mix, lay dejectedly on a nice, fluffy dog bed from HotPets until he saw me, and then he dashed to the front of his cage, wagging his tail so hard it looked as if it could act as a helicopter rotor and lift him from the ground.

"Hi, sweetheart," I said, glancing inside. The surface of his habitat needed a good cleaning. His water bowl required a refill. And he was undoubtedly hungry.

My responsibility — and pleasure — now. Pete would want to help, and so might any volunteers who got through, but I couldn't wait to see if I'd have any backup. Physically, I'd have no trouble doing everything myself. But I hated to keep any of our residents waiting.

Unless . . . "Officer Plummer, do you happen to like animals?"

She was about my height and weight but only about half my age. Her previously blasé expression suggested that she wanted to appear as if this all wasn't fairly new to her. But now her feigned nonchalance disappeared into a broad grin. "I have a golden Lab at home, Ms. Vancouver. Her name is Trixie."

"Great. This is Elmer. Can you help me take care of him? I'll want to keep on the move, since he's just one of a whole lot of dogs and cats who need some care right away."

"Sure!" She demonstrated her sincerity by talking softly to Elmer as she took the pooper scooper from me and slipped inside the enclosure when I opened it. She picked stuff up and placed it into the biodegradable bag I handed her. I wondered if she'd get in trouble for suddenly assuming the role of a HotRescues volunteer.

I did the same in nearby enclosures, using only bags, not a scooper, for the initial cleaning. Hosing things down would undoubtedly have to wait until later. When I was able, I headed toward the back of the shelter area, skirting around where I'd seen Efram without looking down, as if he were still there. His crime scene outline might be. His blood . . .

I needed to get food for the animals from our shed.

Pete was still near there, talking with the probable lady detective. He looked up at me with concern adding new wrinkles to his already lined face. "Are you okay, Lauren?"

"As good as possible under the circumstances," I assured him.

"We're done, aren't we?" he pleadingly asked the woman. "I need to help take care of the animals."

"All right." But she didn't sound entirely convinced. Even so, she let Pete go.

Together, he and I took care of all our charges. A couple of cops besides Officer Plummer helped with the feeding, although no others assisted with cleaning.

I assumed that no one else who belonged here had been allowed through the police lines yet. They were probably being interrogated as they appeared.

Eventually, the cops apparently finished with all they needed to do. Detective Garciana again joined me. He asked if we'd covered a security camera for any reason, and gestured up toward one that had something tossed over it that appeared to be a dog blanket. Otherwise, it might have filmed what had happened here.

Shocked, I said, "I've no idea how that got there. Maybe Efram did it when he broke in. He'd have known how to angle himself to stay out of the camera's way until he covered it." It certainly explained why the picture had suddenly disappeared at the EverySecurity offices.

"Maybe." Garciana didn't sound convinced or enthused. Just skeptical. He didn't ask any more questions, thank heavens. He didn't assure me he'd never be in touch again, either. In fact, he gave me a business card, told me to call if I thought of anything he should know. I glanced at it, saw that his first name was Stefan. My assumption was that Detective Stefan Garciana and I would get to know each other a whole lot more than I'd ever want to do over the coming days and weeks, until whatever happened here became clear.

As the crime scene folks' presence receded, Nina and some volunteers rushed in, including Ricki and Sally.

I was quickly the center of their attention, including Pete. I assured them that I was fine, and so were all our residents. And I extracted from Pete that he, too, was doing okay.

Knowing the animals would need him, he'd come in through the back entrance near the shed — and, yes, the gate hadn't been locked. There'd been cops around, sure, but he'd somehow talked his way inside, bless him. He only wished he'd been able to start helping our residents faster.

When the group started asking me what had really happened to Efram, all I said was, "I wish I knew. But whatever you think, whatever you hear, you can believe that I didn't touch him."

While most of my crew nodded sympathetically, I have to admit, but only to myself, that the skepticism I thought I saw on a few of their faces hurt a lot.

CHAPTER 7

As the morning inched along, more control of the property was returned to me. I realized this was a concession not always given so fast at a crime scene, but the nature of our rescue facility made the difference. Maybe I should have felt grateful. Instead, I just wanted the whole official crew gone. They were still disturbing our residents.

Not to mention me.

But they weren't our only tormentors. I thought about letting Nina or the volunteers handle the endless phone calls from the media, but I'm no coward. And I had no doubt I'd dispose of them more easily than anyone else.

Capitulation wasn't in my vocabulary.

But irritation definitely was. As I sat at my desk, the blinds pulled so the crime scene people couldn't watch me, I had to stop myself more than once from shrieking, "Leave us alone," into the HotRescues phone. Fortunately, no one had gotten my BlackBerry number . . . yet.

I didn't give a damn whether I was raked over the coals on TV or in the press — except that it might anger Dante. There was no job in the world that I wanted more than this one. Plus, I thought I did a damned good job of taking care of our animals. Symbiosis. I didn't want the paparazzi to ruin it for any of us.

So, with each call, I went through a litany in my mind: *What's the best way of getting rid of this creep without giving HotRescues a poke in the eye?* Or, *What would Dante want me to say here?*

As it turned out, I was given the perfect opportunity to find out. Dante was one of the seemingly endless callers, but he was the only one who called my cell. I was calm and professional when I answered, and I agreed with pleasure to meet him for lunch and give him an update.

When I hung up, I sagged in my desk chair. How could I put as good a spin as possible on this deplorable situation?

I'd just tell the truth. Dante was no fool. He was fully aware of the hell occurring around here.

And the idea that I might be suspected of murdering Efram?

Well, he'd been a murder suspect, too, not long ago. At least that was what the media jackals had howled. No apologies to him after the real killer was found, of course.

Just as there wouldn't be to me now, by the cops. But I sure hoped the truth flashed to light soon.

The situation was hurting more than just me.

Dante's office for his HotPets pet-supply store chain was in Beverly Hills. HotRescues was located in Granada Hills, in the northern San Fernando Valley.

I was, in some ways, Dante's employee. He could easily have insisted that I meet him near his offices. But he was kind enough to suggest someplace in between, more or less.

We met at a restaurant in Encino.

It didn't surprise me that we weren't alone. His main squeeze, Kendra Ballantyne, joined us. I wasn't sure where she lived or pet-sat, but I'd heard that her law office was in Encino.

I didn't mind her presence. In fact, I was sort of relieved to have a lawyer to speak with, under the circumstances.

Not that Kendra represented me. If anyone, she represented Dante. And, maybe,

HotRescues. She'd once represented all of us, when Efram threatened to sue, but her loyalties now lay more with the others, not me.

I'd always appreciated Dante's lifestyle, as I saw it. He didn't insist that we meet at the most expensive brasserie in the area, although he could have. And since he was treating — as always — he could have selected anyplace at all.

He chose an eatery that was part of a family-style restaurant chain. His only concession to wealth was to slip some money to the hostess as we walked in, buying us a table in a corner, as private as possible under the circumstances. I couldn't tell how large the tip had been, but the hostess became really attentive, really fast.

Dante was a bit of an old-fashioned gentleman, holding chairs for both Kendra and me before seating himself. He was definitely a good-looking guy, with wavy, dark hair and intense, deep brown eyes. He was dressed somewhat formally in these days of business casual — a white button-down shirt — but at least he wore no tie or jacket. Here, at least. I suspected he had them available at his office, if not in his car.

"Let's order first," he said quietly. "Then we'll talk."

I nodded and picked up my menu.

"Unless you've got something you want to say right off," Kendra contradicted. Obviously she wasn't impressed, or cowed, by the authority granted by his wealth. Probably a good thing, considering their relationship.

He just shot her an indulgent glance, one that made me smile. I was glad to see Dante so happy.

Although I admitted, but only to myself, that I wondered why he'd settled his heart on this particular woman. Oh, it wasn't that Kendra was anything but lovely. Her face was youthful, her blue eyes sparkling and inquisitive, her light brown hair skimming narrow shoulders clad in a stylish gold blouse tucked into dressy brown slacks. I had the impression that she loved giving the right appearance, no matter what the occasion, but not in an obsessive or arrogant way.

But someone as rich as Dante could have his pick of women. Mostly, anyway. Although I admired the guy, he wasn't my type — assuming I even had a type anymore.

We all ordered as soon as the server came over — very quickly, probably cued in by the hostess. I opted for a grilled chicken sandwich with a side salad — and figured it would make a good dinner of leftovers, too. With everything that had happened over the last — was it only twelve hours? — I really hadn't much of an appetite.

The black coffee tasted good, though. Hopefully, the caffeine would keep me awake. Or maybe the company would be enough, since I'd have to remain focused on the conversation.

"So," Dante began. "Fill us in on what happened."

"You mean you haven't heard all about it on the news?" Sarcasm wasn't really called for, but I knew I could get away with it around him.

"Of course. And if I paid attention to it, I'd figure you lured that S.O.B. Efram to HotRescues in the middle of the night and skewered him with a knife. And set it up so you could claim you did it in self-defense because he threatened you, but that wasn't credible since he was stabbed in the back."

Yes, that was what the reports were claiming now. I hadn't seen the actual location of Efram's stab wounds, but if that was true, no one — me included — could believably claim self-defense. Not that I intended to.

"Did I leave anything out?" Dante's grin was full of ironic pleasure.

"Yeah," Kendra said. "How about, she's

not allowed to discuss it without her lawyer present. So . . . would you like me to refer you to a criminal lawyer, Lauren? It's not my area."

Interesting that she would say that. I'd intended to ask her for just such a referral.

I shouldn't need a lawyer, of course, since I hadn't done anything wrong. But the smattering I knew about the legal system was enough to tell me to mistrust it.

"Yes, I believe I'd like a referral. But let me tell you my side, and you advise me if it's necessary. Let me know if you think anything I'm saying would lead to any kind of self-incrimination, and I'll plead the Fifth Amendment right here and shut up."

Dante laughed as Kendra said, "I gather you like to watch crime shows on TV or the movies."

"Enough of them," I admitted. I'd already told Dante a little, so for Kendra's edification I described Efram's visit to HotRescues yesterday, ending with his threats. I let them both know that I'd decided to stay there last night . . . and all that had happened since.

"So you weren't aware when Efram came onto the HotRescues property?" Kendra asked.

"Only when the dogs started barking."

"And as far as you knew, you were the only one there — human, that is," said Dante.

"Right."

"Then what's your opinion about who killed Efram, and why? And how they got in." Kendra stopped and waved one manicured hand in the air. "Forget I asked. That's something you should probably only talk to your own counsel about."

"But do you have any ideas?" Dante asked.

I shrugged. "Not really . . . not yet, at least."

Our lunches arrived, and I found I had more of an appetite than I'd originally believed.

Our conversation turned to other things — like the puppy mill rescue, and our current batch of HotRescues residents and how we were seeking homes for them.

I mentioned the situation about Brooke Pernall and her dog, Cheyenne, too, but told them I hadn't yet started to get the information Dante wanted about her background or illness.

Inevitably, the topic returned to what had happened at the shelter and how it might affect our ability to rehome some of our inhabitants.

"Sometimes being in the news could be a

good thing," Kendra said. She looked at Dante, whose expression looked almost sour.

"Or not," he said. I had the impression that this was a subject they had discussed before. I already knew that the HotRescues benefactor, though well known as a wealthy mega-mogul of the pet industry, preferred to let others hype his stores, products, and generosity in the media. I gathered it was because there was something about his past that he wanted to downplay, and I'd never asked.

"Whatever," Kendra replied. "But, Lauren, as you may know, I . . . well, I feel a little responsible for what's happened to you."

"What?" I stared at her, even as Dante laughed aloud.

She mumbled something that I couldn't quite hear, then took a quick bite of her sandwich.

"Pardon?" I said.

"I'm a murder magnet," she said more loudly.

I gaped at her. Oh, sure, I'd heard that she'd once been considered a suspect in a murder or two. And I, of course, was well aware that Dante, too, had been the subject of a murder investigation. Then there were other rumors about her friends and acquaintances either becoming murder victims or suspects, but I'd always chalked that up to jealous gossip of other women who wanted her out of Dante's life.

But she had just admitted it — as bizarre as that was. And unbelievable.

"I appreciate what you're saying, Kendra," I said. "But I promise I don't blame you for my being a suspect in Efram's murder." That even sounded odd to say. But since her guy was my boss, and more, I needed to make my opinion clear.

"Well, thanks for that," she said. "Look, you may not know it, but I've had a number of friends who were investigated as potential murder suspects. I helped them all clear themselves. So . . . well, I'd be glad to look into Efram's murder, see if I can figure out what really happened to him."

I managed to smile at her. Then I looked Dante straight in the eye. "I can't tell you both how much I appreciate your confidence in me. I want to stress that, whatever happened to Efram, I didn't do it — not as a murder, and not even in self-defense. If it turns out that the cops really zero in on me as a suspect . . . well, Kendra, I really would appreciate your giving me a referral to a good criminal attorney. Otherwise, I'll keep your very kind offer in mind, but there's no sense in your wasting your time looking into this."

For years, I had relied only on myself to figure out solutions in my life, and in my kids'. And I genuinely hadn't done anything wrong.

Sure, I'd despised Efram and what he'd done to animals, especially being involved in that puppy mill situation.

But I hadn't killed him.

And if that Detective Garciana or other cops decided to try to pin a murder on me, I'd find a way out of the mess.

In other words, if I needed to figure this out, I'd do it myself.

CHAPTER 8

My mind darted from one topic to another as I drove back to HotRescues, like balls on an animated pool table in a computer game my son, Kevin, used to play. My responsibilities at HotRescues. That lady, Brooke, who needed help. The puppies who'd been saved, both from the storm drain and from terrible living conditions. Their parents. The wonderful Animal Services folks who rescued them. The likely puppy mill owners. Where had I seen them before?

Efram and his threats.

Efram's death.

My relief at Dante's ongoing support.

By the time I pulled my car into the HotRescues parking lot, it was only mid-afternoon but felt like late night. I was dragging. But my responsibilities here trumped my discomfort, or anything else. A bunch of wonderful dogs, cats, and some other small animals needed new homes.

Of course, when these guys were adopted out, they'd be replaced by other equally needy creatures. Who'd be replaced by others. Then others. Till I dropped — and even then, more people would take up the HotRescues gauntlet.

I couldn't stop people from failing to take proper care of their pets or get them all to spay and neuter to prevent so many unwanted animals from being born, but I could do my part.

So the fact that I was exhausted? Irrelevant.

Hearing voices as I opened the door from the parking lot, I slipped into our welcome area. Nina was there with a middle-aged couple, who sat at the window table apparently filling out forms. We required a lot of paperwork, including a contract adopters signed to make sure they knew what we expected of them.

Nina turned toward me. "Hi, Lauren. Remember the Tylers? Frannie and Morris. They were here last week looking at pets to adopt, and they really fell for Elmer."

"We'll probably change his name, though." Morris was a bit flabby, with more hair on his eyebrows than the top of his head. His broad grin looked almost sappy as he spoke about our resident, and I couldn't help smiling back. That kind of caring was what I really liked to see.

"If that's okay." Frannie, equally chubby, was dressed in a loose Pepperdine University T-shirt. She looked worriedly from Nina to me, as if we'd snatch Elmer back from their waiting arms out of anger that they might dare to name him something else.

I wouldn't, of course — not for that reason, anyway. But I needed to know more about them than the way they completed our adoption papers. "So . . . has Nina asked questions about your home, if you have any other pets, and where Elmer will sleep?"

"She sure did," Morris said.

"They have a house with a nice yard, no other pets — and Elmer will sleep in their bedroom," Nina added. All the things we wanted to hear, although other compatible pets were fine. If we didn't get these answers, or other suitable ones, we wouldn't allow our visitors here to adopt.

"And after you were here last week and met Elmer, how many other shelters did you visit?"

A flush crept up Frannie's cheeks. "A few. But we didn't meet any dogs we liked as well."

"Great." I still had another question,

though. I leaned back against our reception desk and folded my arms. "Did you come back today because you saw HotRescues on the news?"

Morris stood, frowning. "We almost didn't come back because of it. But we couldn't blame poor Elmer for what happened here."

"He needs a good home, away from all the excitement," his wife asserted, also confronting me. "I know the reporters are saying you're a 'person of interest,' or whatever, in the death of that man found here. The main thing is that we'd already decided to come back, see if we could adopt Elmer, so all that really made no difference to us."

I smiled. "Just the kind of people I look for as possible dog adopters!" I still had to officially okay them, of course, and my standards were high. But so far, approval seemed likely.

Both appeared to relax. Me, too.

"Okay, then." Relief erased some of the tension from Nina's face. "We still have formalities to go through, even after you fill out the paperwork. We'll want you to meet with Elmer in our visitors' park, away from the stress of his cage and having all the other dogs so close. We'll see then how you get along. For minor issues, our part-time animal trainer is here to help."

So Si had come in today. That was a good thing.

"We'll also want you to meet with our adoption counselor. She's due here in about an hour. Okay?"

"Whatever it takes," Frannie agreed. "We brought some pictures of our home, like we were asked to last time we were here, so you can see where our dog will live."

I watched with pleasure as Nina accompanied them into the shelter area. I suspected all would go well between them and Elmer — or whatever they later named that sweet black Lab.

I marveled at the fact that another thing, besides lunch with Dante and Kendra, appeared to be going right that day.

I was in my office later when someone knocked on the door.

Better that kind of interruption than all the phone calls I had been ignoring. I'd learned from my kids how to silence the ringer on my BlackBerry when I went to meetings or shows. They'd taught me about apps as well; some I used a lot and others I used less.

Today, I'd glanced at my gadget now and then to check the list of missed calls and return those of people I actually wanted to hear from.

I'd let one of the volunteers — Bev today, a senior citizen who came here at least once a week, usually more — answer my office phone when not outside walking dogs or performing other duties, and she let me know if it was someone I wanted to talk to.

But now, Si Rogan stood at my door.

"Hi," I said. "Have you met with the Tylers and Elmer yet?"

"I sure did." His broad smile told the story he was about to relate, but I could hardly wait to hear it anyway.

"Have a seat." I pointed to the two chairs facing my crowded desk.

He maneuvered his way into one so quickly that I hardly had time to blink. Not surprising. The guy was a dog trainer, skilled in teaching agility. That meant he was nimble, too.

Today, he wore one of his own company's T-shirts: Rogan's Dog Obedience Studio.

"So tell me all about it," I said. "How did the Tylers get along with Elmer?"

"Great! Elmer is a pretty enthusiastic guy, like most Labs, but he was willing to obey some pretty basic commands — come, sit, down, whatever. When he wasn't moving, you could tell from his eyes and the beat of his tail that what he really wanted was to leap up and shower them with attention. They loved it! I did give them pointers, like making sure to be disciplinarians right away so he'd consider them the alphas of his new pack. They can let up in the future, if they want."

"So they're still enthused about Elmer?"

"Looks that way. We'll see if Mona approves them later." Si's smile drooped. "I'd planned to come here today anyway, Lauren. What really happened here last night?"

"You mean you don't believe everything you hear in the news?" I didn't attempt to keep the irony from my voice.

"Not even when it's consistent stuff, but the reporters were all over the place in what they were saying. What really went down?"

I told Si my version of what went on here in the middle of the night. His expression grew more and more sympathetic. He even stood and leaned over my desk toward me, as if he wanted to give me a hug.

Under most circumstances, I wouldn't let that happen. But at that moment I wasn't averse to sympathy.

Even so, I broke away quickly and sat back down. "Thanks, Si. It's good to have so many friends in my corner, like you."

A tiny look of hurt passed across his face,

replaced by a sad smile. "You can always count on me, Lauren."

A little while later, volunteer Bev popped her head in to say that Dr. Mona Harvey had arrived. Bev had taken the Tylers upstairs to meet with our chief adoption counselor.

"How long ago did they start talking?" I asked.

Bev was short and thin, and had just a touch of a slouch that suggested osteoporosis. But she had as much energy as any of the volunteers a third of her age. She looked at the outsized watch on her skinny wrist and said, "Ten minutes or so."

"I'll go see how they're doing," I said.

Si walked out with me on his way to see what he could do to help. I left Bev staffing the welcome area and headed upstairs. Passing the conference table, I knocked on the door of Mona's office but didn't wait for her invitation before entering.

Mona looked relaxed behind the small wooden desk. The Tylers, too, did not seem overly stressed. I gathered I'd interrupted a mutually enjoyable conversation.

"So how's everything going?" I directed the comment to our part-time shrink.

She pulled her glasses off and rested them

on the desk, a gesture I'd learned was positive. If she was unhappy, she generally used her glasses to hide behind as she frowned.

"Did you know the Tylers have had Labs in the past? They know a lot about the breed and the dogs' temperaments."

Actually, I did know. Our application forms required that prospective adopters tell us about pets they've had before as well as current ones. But Mona's second sentence told me more.

"We lost our last one about a year ago," Frannie said sadly. "Morris wanted us to adopt again right away, but I thought we needed a mourning period."

"Frannie jumped in to start looking for a new dog as soon as she thought enough time had passed," Morris said, beaming.

"So we don't have to go through as hard a period as this again, we might even consider adopting another Lab, or a Lab mix," Frannie added. "Plus it would be great for Elmer, as you call him, to have a friend. Please keep us in mind if you get any others as wonderful as he is."

I aimed another quick glance at Mona, who nodded.

It looked as if Elmer was about to find a loving home, whatever his new name might be.

■ ■ ■ ■

Mona and I watched from the parking lot a little while later, while the Tylers drove off without Elmer.

No matter how good potential adopters seem, we almost never allow the placement to occur on the day they first make their decision about which pet they want. At adoption fairs — well, we allow it sometimes, as long as we really like the adopters and make it clear how intrusive we'll be in their lives until we feel comfortable a re-homing is working out.

Generally, though, we continue to review applications for a day or several, often visit homes, and give people the chance to change their minds.

But I felt fairly certain this one would work out, especially since the Tylers had come back so enthused after meeting Elmer before.

"I'd like to talk to you about what happened here last night," Mona said as we reached the door. She seemed to examine my face, as if she could read my emotions. Maybe she could. She was, after all, a shrink.

"If you've seen the news, you've gotten

the gist of it. I found Efram. He'd been stabbed, possibly in the back. The cops found me with him and assumed I'd been the one to stab him."

"But you didn't, of course."

"I didn't. I had a motive, though."

Mona nodded. "His threats. If the cops look at that as the motive, though, it would fit everyone here. The animals, too."

I returned her smile. "You going to tell them that?"

She sobered immediately. "Probably. I'm scheduled to talk to a detective. He's meeting me at my office, and I'm already running late. Oh, well." She didn't sound at all repentant.

"Is his name Garciana?"

She nodded.

"I take it you didn't sneak in here in the middle of the night and stab that miserable excuse for a human being, did you? If you admit it to Garciana, you'll get me off the hook."

"Even if I did it, I'd never admit it, Lauren. Not even to save you."

We were both joking. Darkest humor.

Even so, *someone* had done it. Right now, everyone I knew who was connected at all to Efram was a suspect, no matter who the cops leaned on.

■ ■ ■ ■

"Some detective has been calling you," Bev told me when I returned to my office.

"Garciana?"

"Yes," she confirmed.

I reached into the pocket of my jeans for a card I'd gotten from Kendra at lunch. It had information on the lawyer she had suggested I contact if I needed guidance in dealing with Efram's murder investigation. I glanced at it. The name was Esther Ickes.

"Thanks," I told Bev. At my desk, I called Esther right away. She was in her office and told me that Kendra had given her a heads-up that I might be in touch.

"I'd suggest that we meet, maybe . . . How's one o'clock Monday afternoon?" It was Saturday now.

"Fine, unless I have to speak before that with the detective who's been calling me. The one who asked me questions last night, when I found Efram's body, left me a message."

"Don't talk to him any more without my being with you," Esther cautioned. "Go ahead and return his call, but let him know you're now represented by counsel."

"So I've 'lawyered up'?"

Esther sounded both amused and kind. "That's right."

I'd have stayed at HotRescues that night if it had been in the best interests of our animals, no matter what had happened there with Efram.

But I'd been in touch with our security company. Though they'd done a crappy job last night, allowing Efram to get in — and his killer, too — and not staying in touch with me as they should have, they were still under contract with HotRescues. Without admitting any responsibility, they had checked out our on-site cameras and offered to send even more patrols to the area that night.

Plus, I figured the cops would still have a presence in the area.

Before I left, Pete Engersol and I went through the facility enclosure by enclosure, making sure everything was clean and secure, that every animal's records indicated they'd eaten when they were supposed to, and that they all had plenty of water. Then I'd walked through again and headed home.

My place was in Porter Ranch, not far from the Granada Hills location of HotRescues. It was a pleasant house in a gated community, a good place to have brought up my kids. I knew my neighbors, at least to wave to and to give treats to their pets as they went for walks in front of my house when I happened to be home during the day. That was now a rarity, especially since my kids were both away at college.

I'd had pets at home before, when the kids were younger — dogs, hamsters, cats. The last, a Boston terrier that Tracy had especially loved, had died six months ago. I'd been here alone then. Grieved deeply over poor Bosley. Hadn't wanted to grieve again that way, so although I'd considered adopting a pet from HotRescues, I'd not done so. I had definitely empathized with the people who'd adopted Elmer that day, though.

Tonight, alone here after all that had happened, was the first time I really regretted having no pets to greet me.

Now, I just wanted to head straight for bed. I'd picked up a salad at a fast-food restaurant's drive-through, though, so I decided to eat first.

I turned on the TV and sat through the beginning of a cop show, chewing on the irony of it along with my dinner. Then I pulled my BlackBerry out of my pocket and used its online function to view news about what had happened at HotRescues, and finally checked it for anyone whose call I should return.

My friend Carlie's number, my kids', parents', brother's, and Nina's, appeared with a bunch I didn't recognize. Some of the unknowns had called a few times.

I tried returning Carlie's call first. As far as I knew, she was still on her trip to the east to film a segment for her pet health TV show. It was three hours later there — after eleven o'clock — so she'd probably have her cell phone turned off, but I could leave a message.

To my surprise, she answered. "Can't talk now," she whispered. "In a meeting about what we're doing tomorrow. But" — I heard voices in the background, then Carlie said — "you've been a busy girl. In the news here. You okay?"

"Yes, but —"

"You kill him?"

"No!" I practically shouted.

"I figured. Talk to you soon." She hung up.

I stared at my BlackBerry for nearly a minute, willing Carlie to call back, but, of course, she didn't. Sighing, I next checked in with family, although I'd spoken with all of them earlier, too. I again assured them all I was doing fine. Then I returned Nina's call.

"Everything okay?" I asked. I knew she was doing her regular volunteer work at a city shelter that night.

"Fine. But Captain Matt Kingston got in touch with me. He said he's left you several phone messages, but you haven't called him back."

"I've only returned a few other calls besides to you," I told her. "And none was to him. Which one's his number?"

She told me, and I pushed it into my cell phone. It was fairly late, so I expected I'd just have to leave a message, too, but at least I now would recognize it when he called back.

But he answered right away. "It's about time, Lauren. Look, I don't want to talk to you over the phone. Meet me for a drink." He named a place not far from HotRescues. "There are some things you should know."

To hell with my exhaustion. I let curiosity and the need to be in human company — especially the company of Matt Kingston — outweigh common sense and agreed to meet him in half an hour.

132

CHAPTER 9

We met at the bar of a great Mexican restaurant where I'd eaten lunch occasionally. The place was crowded — it was a Saturday night — but we still found a table for two along a wall.

I was tired enough that I considered ordering something nonalcoholic, but not long or seriously. I deserved one drink, as long as it wasn't too strong. A strawberry margarita whet my appetite and it would soon wet my lips. Matt chose a Dos Equis beer.

I'd taken time to shower fast and change out of the HotRescues outfit I'd worn for nearly two days, sometimes with the hoodie for warmth and sometimes not. Now, I wore a yellow long-sleeved shirt tucked into khaki pants. I'd decided to throw on something that would make me appear cheerful. I was afraid that what Matt wanted to see me about had something to do with the disposi-

tion of the animals from the puppy mill —
in a manner I'd hate.

That would only add insult to the injury
of being a suspect in killing a wretched
member of the human race who'd hurt
them in the first place.

Last time I'd seen Matt, he'd worn an
Animal Services uniform. Now, he had a
sport jacket on over a shirt and slacks. Trying to impress me?

More likely, he'd been to some kind of
meeting before.

When our orders were taken, we chatted
amiably for a while, loud enough to hear
one another over the endless thunder of
conversations in the bar. I knew we were
here on business — the very important business of saving animals. Even so, we edged
into some personal small talk about our
favorite things about LA, our jobs and
mutual acquaintances. I hadn't dated for a
while, but this felt a bit like what I remembered.

Then Matt leaned over and asked quietly,
"Are you okay, Lauren? I tried some official
channels to learn all I could about that guy
Kiley's death and heard that some of the
garbage in the media may have been true."

"What, that I killed him?"

"Only if you've literally backstabbed him."

His eyes, a much deeper brown than the drink the server now set in front of him, bored into mine, apparently trying to read my mind.

"Not guilty." I kept my tone light as I took my first sip of the cold, fruity cocktail I'd ordered. It tasted great, though its alcohol content needed boosting.

"What about killing him in self-defense? I'm playing devil's advocate here — maybe he turned around fast."

I stood and glared down at Matt. "So you do believe the crap those damn reporters are spewing to improve their ratings? I had nothing to do with what happened to Efram Kiley. He made threats against me, my employees, and my animals. I made him leave, told him never to come back. I hung out at HotRescues to protect everyone that night. Then I found him there, in the middle of our shelter area. I didn't even wish him dead, just incarcerated forever. I'd rather he'd have had lots of time to think and suffer over what he did to those animals. Now, unless there really is a hell, he's free."

"Whoa." Matt waved me back to my seat. I ignored him. I'd come for information about those poor dogs. If he wanted to insult or even tease me, he could drink alone. "Sorry. I figured Kiley was enough of a jerk to threaten you. That was the part of the news stories I bought. As to the rest, I wouldn't have blamed you even if you had rammed a knife into him and twisted — especially in self-defense. But I believe it when you say you had nothing to do with it."

"I had nothing to do with it." I said each word slowly and with feeling, but I did sit down again. I took another sip of margarita as my blood pressure slowed just a little.

"Got it. So . . . any idea who did kill him?"

"Not really." Not yet, at least. I had a feeling I'd be considering the possibilities even more, though, unless the cops started acting like the knowledgeable pros they were supposed to be — and stopped treating me as the most likely suspect. Sure, I happened to be with Efram when they showed up, but that wasn't proof I hurt him, for *any* reason. "The only thing I can figure is that maybe someone was following him and caught up with him at HotRescues. Maybe those people who ran the puppy mill." A thought struck me. "Is that possible? Your folks arrested Efram but he was out on bail. Were they released, too?"

Matt nodded. "Unfortunately, yes."

As I sipped my margarita, I pondered the inequity. Humans were much more likely to

136

harm other beings than most pets were, and they got away with it too often — no matter whether those beings were other people or defenseless animals.

I considered Nina and the abuse she'd suffered at the hands of her ex. Her restraining order was valuable only to the extent that particular jerk chose to heed it. Fortunately, he'd apparently moved to another city.

And I was relatively fortunate, too. My ex, the dishonorable Charles Earles, hadn't laid a hand on me. Only on my already slim bank accounts so he could have a grand time feting his sexy young paramours. The louse.

Why the hell was I even thinking about him now, while in the presence of one really hot guy? Not that I was into hot guys, or any other kind of guys, these days. Charles had weaned me of any interest.

But this particular hot guy could help me resolve my current dilemma. "So what's the talk around Animal Services? Does anyone think those puppy millers — the Shaheens — killed Efram? Or maybe another animal lover who hated what he'd helped to do to those pups? Or —"

"Right now, everyone's applauding you, Lauren. Under the assumption, of course, that he went there to attack you and the animals, and you defended yourself."

"Oh." So they, too, were taking the easy way out. Good thing they weren't investigating Efram's death.

"But I meant what I said. You told me you had nothing to do with it, and I believe you."

He caught my gaze and held on — till I looked away. Felt my face grow pink. The guy was flirting, even as he essentially accused me of killing someone. No matter how he denied it.

Time to change the subject. I first took another long swig of margarita, only to find I'd nearly emptied the pretty but shallow glass. I frowned as I set it back on the table.

"Another one?" Matt asked.

"Well . . . it looks like you'll take a while to finish your beer. So, yes, please." I wanted to blame it on him.

But I'd be careful. I still had to drive back home. And I certainly didn't want to be pulled over by the cops with everything that was going on.

Matt waved over a server and ordered my refill. Then I said, "I'd thought, when you asked me to meet you, that you wanted to talk about the rescued pups. How are they doing now? And their parents?"

His smile lit up the angles of his face as if

he were a proud parent. "Amazingly, they're all just fine. I've seen larger puppy mills, and ones that abused the animals even more. This one wasn't so bad, all things considered."

"*Not* all things considered," I reminded him. "Some of those guys were thrown into the storm drain."

"Yeah." His tone underscored his sudden anger.

"Did anyone admit to doing it?"

"No, although the neighbor who called in the complaint told us, and not just the media, that it appeared to be one person, probably male, who trotted out of the gate at least twice. The description she gave fit Efram a lot better than Bradley Shaheen, and both Shaheens swear it was Efram. But they also swear that they just love animals and that they took good care of them and made sure any pet stores they sold puppies to — at inflated prices, of course — promised only to resell them to people who would give them loving homes."

"But of course." I enjoyed Matt's grin at my obvious sarcasm. "Too bad you nasty folks at Animal Services impounded them. I assume you'll have to hang on to the whole lot as evidence in prosecuting the Shaheens, right?"

"For now. But I can assure you they're being well cared for."

"Can I come visit them?"

"They're all being housed for now at a shelter in the north Valley that hasn't had enough funding to open to the public. That way the pups can grow to adoption age in peace."

"So . . . can I come —"

"Visit them? Sure. We'll work out a time next week. I have an office there. But only on one condition."

"What's that?"

"I want a similar pass to visit HotRescues. I've heard great things about it, for a private shelter. I'm always looking for new ideas for the public shelters, so maybe we can exchange suggestions."

"Sounds like a plan." I smiled. "And you're right. HotRescues is a great private facility. Let's touch base early next week to see when we're both up for meeting?"

"Fine."

For the rest of our time together, we talked about animal rescues in general, trading war stories.

Later, Matt reminded me of our "date" sometime next week as he held my car door open for me.

"I'm looking forward to seeing HotRescues," he said.

Cynic that I am, I wondered if he was most eager for me to show him the spot where I'd found Efram Kiley's dead body.

CHAPTER 10

I arrived at HotRescues bright and early the next morning. I even beat Pete Engersol, usually the first there. He mostly arrived around seven A.M., even on Sunday, the better to check on the animals and start cleaning enclosures before mealtime.

My preferred hour to appear wasn't usually until eight thirty, but it was barely six thirty now. Despite my exhaustion thanks to all that had happened, I hadn't slept well — big surprise — and had even called the security company to make sure they were complying with their promise of extra patrols. And to ask if the cameras were all working, and whether they were monitoring them closely during hours we weren't open. And to ask if they saw anything unusual. They assured me that all was well.

Even so, I was still considering alternatives as the result of their prior failure. A replacement security company? A person hired to be here all night?

Would Dante buy into either?

It was obviously too late to save Efram from being killed here — and to save HotRescues from being the subject of a media frenzy for reasons other than its awesome dedication to saving animals. But I still didn't know who'd killed Efram or even how the killer and the victim had gotten onto the HotRescues property the night before last — although I gathered that it had been via the back entrance near the storage shed.

Worse, I didn't have a clue about the killer's motive. Did Efram die because of his ill treatment of animals? I could understand that. If it was something else, though, the animals we were caring for could be at risk.

As I parked, I considered walking into HotRescues without entering the security code. I'd test EverySecurity by letting the armed system send its silent alarm. But I wasn't sure how helpful that would be now.

Instead, I called them again as I entered. Turned out they were genuinely on the ball, since Ed Bransom, the company's main representative to HotRescues, got on the line fast. "Take a look at your parking lot, Lauren," he told me. Key in hand, I'd been about to open the side door to the main building. I turned to see an officially marked EverySecurity vehicle turning in, its driver waving.

They had, in fact, been watching . . . now. Even so, they still hadn't explained the presence of Efram and whoever killed him the night before last.

As far as I was concerned, they were still on probation.

I slipped inside and flicked on the lights, since dawn was just starting to rip nighttime's blackness from the sky, turning it gray instead. Not much light filtered into our welcome room, especially since I had been careful to close the narrow slats on the rust-colored window blinds when I left the night before.

Usually, I appreciated any solitude I could get in the HotRescues admin building. Not now. I kept thinking about the eeriness of staying there the other night. How startling the dogs' barking had jarred me in the wee hours of the morning.

How I'd shaken in fear when I'd discovered Efram — and been confronted by the cops.

Okay, so my nerves were still on edge. Too bad. I had animals to check on.

I headed for the shelter area — and

rehashed my drink with Matt Kingston last night. What would he think of HotRescues?

Unsurprisingly, the dogs began greeting me aloud from their enclosures, all of them in the outdoor portions to see what was going on. "Hi, Honey," I said to the adorable Westie mix who was now in the first pen on the left as soon as she grew quiet. She all but purred when I reached in to scratch behind her ears.

I stroked each dog in turn, including Elmer, as I headed toward the rearmost enclosure along this path . . . and kept maneuvering so my back faced the place on the ground where Efram had lain. Even so, I glimpsed his outline — but, fortunately, his blood had been cleaned up.

The camera facing that area was no longer covered. I waved at it. I turned the corner at the back of the shelter, heading along the storage building toward our next doggy row. When I reached it, its inhabitants, too, barked in acknowledgment of my presence. I laughed aloud. Nothing like an enthusiastic welcoming committee.

Not that I'd directly encourage their barking. It could make them less adoptable.

As I knelt to say good morning to the now-silent Babydoll, a shepherd mix whose coat coloration suggested that she wore a skirt, something grabbed my shoulder. I gasped, stood, and pivoted.

Pete stood behind me, his features startled and his face ashen. "Are you okay, Lauren?" he asked.

I glared. "I was till you grabbed me."

"Sorry. I called out but guess you didn't hear me with the dogs barking. I didn't expect to see you here so early. Is . . . is something else wrong?"

I all but hugged him. His aging face seemed braced to handle anything I might tell him. "Just my worry," I said. "After yesterday, I needed to get here early to re-assure myself everything was okay now."

"Same goes." He looked a lot more at ease now. "Do all our residents seem okay?"

"I've only checked the first row of dogs," I said. "I'll help you look in on the rest."

"Great. Don't suppose you'd want to give me a hand cleaning kennels, too, would you?" His lopsided grin told me he was kidding.

"Nope. Good try, though."

But as I continued down the next row of dog enclosures, I couldn't help wondering if there was another reason for Pete to show up here half an hour early.

Okay, I was getting paranoid. Reading things into signs that didn't even exist.

Pete was a sweetheart. He'd been here helping out from the very first, when HotRescues had opened. He had no reason to harm anyone — not Efram or the animals or me.

Even so, I temporarily locked the center building's door after going inside to check on the animals housed there. I took my time, enjoying my visit. A couple of volunteers always showed up a little while after Pete did. I'd feel more at ease when there were a bunch of us here today, keeping close watch on each other.

But the rest of the day was uneventful. It was Sunday, after all. We didn't have many visitors, although those who came were great! With the diligence of my staff looking into the Tylers, their home, and the other information they'd supplied, we approved their adoption of Elmer, and they returned for him almost as soon as I'd hung up the phone. As they left, I felt like waving a sad goodbye, although my usual personal heartache at losing a resident to adoption was always countered by sublime happiness for the animal I might never see again — if I sent someone else to do the follow-up at the new home.

Two cats and another dog had visitors who fell in love and applied to adopt them that day. We'd see if they worked out, but I felt optimistic.

With all that had happened, I'd been neglectful in the situation with ailing Brooke Pernall and her golden mix, Cheyenne, but I finally remembered to call her from my office and obtain the information Dante had requested about her health condition and lender.

"I've been working to get someone's attention at the bank to try to negotiate something, but no one will talk with me." Her defeated tone suggested resignation to the inevitable.

I wished I could reassure her, but I couldn't . . . yet. I had seen how Dante's strengths often included achieving the impossible in his business and charitable endeavors, but I couldn't guarantee his success this time.

"It won't hurt to try," I told her. "Give Cheyenne a hug for me." When we hung up, I realized that her sense of futility had somehow traveled over the phone connections to perch on my shoulders, and I shrugged it off.

I called Dante's cell and relayed the information to him. "Anything you can do would be great," I told him.

"We'll see."

I kept busy at HotRescues for the rest of the day, refusing to dwell on that sad interlude. Later, though, when I left for home, it vaulted back into my mind, once more sharing space with the Efram situation, which had never left. That night, I talked to my kids before calling my friend Carlie, who was still out of town. I'd have liked Carlie anyway, just because she was a veterinarian, TV star, animal lover, and genuine all-around nice person. But since she had given the first forever home to an adoptee when we opened HotRescues six years ago — a Cocker mix named Max — I especially cherished her friendship. She answered right away, sounding harried but cheerful. At least reaching all of them helped to uplift my mood.

It rose even more after I talked to the guy on duty at EverySecurity before I went to bed. No signs of problems there, he promised. I even slept a little that night.

Paranoia could become my watchword, I thought the next day. I dashed to HotRescues early once more to check on everything — and fortunately spotted no problems.

A little later, I called ahead to check with Esther Ickes, making sure we still had an appointment scheduled for one o'clock that afternoon. The criminal lawyer confirmed it, so I eventually headed in a timely manner for her office in Westwood.

It was an appropriate place for her. I'd Googled her — sure, I trusted Kendra's referral, but being armed with information could only help. Esther had gotten her law degree at UCLA quite a few years back, and the university was located in Westwood, too. I hadn't thought to ask Kendra about Esther's age. Not that it mattered. The more experience, the better.

Her office was in a building on Wilshire Boulevard. Esther came out to greet me in the reception area.

Yes, she apparently had a near lifetime of experience. I guessed she was seventy or older. She looked somewhat frail, definitely a senior citizen.

Could she really do a good job representing me if I was actually arrested for harming Efram?

That paranoia swelled like a tidal wave when she ushered me into her office, with its files and law books scattered everywhere. Was she of an age that she felt more comfortable with the old-fashioned stuff like physical volumes than research done on the Internet? Even I knew there were a lot more resources available online these days. Keeping as current as the opposition was surely as necessary as experience.

Esther wore a peach linen suit. Her hair was nicely styled, but definitely gray. Her face looked grandmotherly.

I took the seat she motioned toward with her aging hands, wondering if I should instead excuse myself graciously and scurry out.

"So here's the thing, Lauren," she said as we faced each other. "I talked to Detective Garciana. He wants you to come in for another interrogation, and he doesn't sound happy that you're now represented by counsel. Tough shit, right? Anyway, it'll be tomorrow. Right now, I want to go over everything from day one with you. When you were born. Where. When you first met the victim. Why you hated his guts and probably don't mind the fact he's dead, but how you happened to find his body without your actually slicing and dicing him. All that."

My eyebrows must have raised a mile. I felt a combination of amusement, amazement, and relief.

Esther Ickes might look aged and frail, but despite her senior-citizen gargly voice, she sounded like a young, with-it defense lawyer.

Surely everything would work out okay.

But I couldn't count on Esther, wonder-lawyer though she might be, to fix everything.

I decided to make a stop on my way back to HotRescues. Well, not exactly on my way.

I headed for Pacoima.

On the street outside the place I'd last been days earlier, when it overflowed with abused dogs and puppies, I stared. The worn picket fence around the property gave it a seedy atmosphere, but there was no overt sign of the horror that had gone on there.

Even if I'd instead driven my car onto the narrow lane perpendicular to this one and focused on the storm drain, I'd have no sense of the torture those puppies and adult dogs had suffered. But I knew.

I'd learned that the Shaheens did, indeed, live here. And they, like Efram, had been released on bail after their arrest.

I realized that I shouldn't confront them on their own turf. That I should have an armed bodyguard watching my back, or at least be somewhere public.

But here I was. I'd been known occasionally to do foolhardy things to take care of animals under my guardianship. This time,

152

the purpose of my foolhardiness would be to protect myself.

I got out of my car and approached the front gate. Unlike the Animal Services folks, I had no authority to enter without invitation. But my anger at what had happened here before ignited my fury all over again. The animals were gone. Well cared for now, thank heavens.

But their abusers might be lounging at home.

Seeing a doorbell-like button, I shoved it with a finger released from my fist. Near it was a worn metal gadget that looked like an intercom. In a minute, I heard a staticky female voice. "Yes, who is it?"

I hadn't come up with a cover story. Maybe I could play the role of another reporter. Would they allow the press to interview them again about their side of what happened?

That might work. "I'm Lauren Vancouver. I —"

"I know who you are, Ms. Vancouver. Efram talked about you. He hated you, and you killed him. So what do you want here?"

"To talk to you. I didn't think much of him, either, but I didn't kill him. And — Look, could I just come in and talk to you for a few minutes? I'll explain it then." If I could come up with a good story fast. Why hadn't I prepared on my way here?

Maybe because I kept telling myself what a bad idea this was. I still thought so.

To my surprise, the voice said, "Well, all right." I heard a click, and the gate started opening. I stared at it. Most likely, I should run. Why were they letting me in?

They could have been the ones who'd killed Efram. Were they planning to get rid of me, too?

I made a quick call to Matt Kingston. Told him where I was and what I was doing.

"Stay right there, Lauren," he said. "Don't go in. I can be there in . . . half an hour."

"Too long," I said. "I'll tell you later how it goes."

"No!" he shouted. "Wait! Why the hell did you even call?"

"Talk to you soon." I headed inside.

Worst-case scenario — I hoped — I'd be able to tell the Shaheens the truth: a captain with one of the local law enforcement agencies knew exactly where I was.

CHAPTER 11

Fighting my legs' unsteadiness, I walked nonchalantly through the open gate and along the brick path — to the building where, a few days earlier, I'd observed so many abused puppies and their parents.

Having Matt know my location filled me with relief. Even so, my insides churned, as if I were being sent psychic signals from the dogs who were former prisoners, warning me to stay away and reminding me how miserably they'd been treated.

Well, the Shaheens were not likely to lock me into a tiny wire crate and leave me there. I'd be fine.

Although if they were angry enough, they could stab me as they might have done with Efram.

Where was that relief I'd tried to convince myself about?

Patsy Shaheen waited at the front door. I tucked my disgust for her deep inside. Who knew? I might even be wrong about her and her husband and their roles in what had happened.

That was as likely as each of the puppies found here marching through the gate to speak up on behalf of the humans accused of torturing them. If I was honest with myself, all I actually remained unsure about was the Shaheens' role in Efram's death.

"Hello, Lauren," Patsy said, as if she knew me. Oh, right. We were good buddies now, after having both been involved in the rescue the other day. Of course, we were on opposite sides, but did that matter?

Maybe not to her.

"Hello, Patsy." I might as well pretend friendship, on the off chance acting nice got me the information I sought.

She was about my height, five foot six, although I preferred my build — not skinny, but not overweight, either. Patsy had a gut that she displayed with her snug jeans and tank top. The sneer beneath her smile might be her normal expression, thanks to a severe overbite. In other words, she was homely.

That might just have been my skewed impression, of course. I couldn't imagine anyone who tortured dogs being beautiful.

She again looked familiar now, close up — and not just because of all the news coverage of the puppy mill ugliness. But I surely hadn't met her before all this . . . had I?

"Come in." She preceded me through the door. I took a deep breath and followed, unsure of what I'd find — including the reception I'd receive from her husband.

The place was much as I expected from the outside — rather Spartan, the look of a not particularly exciting office building.

The door led into a small entry dressed in a tight-weave brown carpet. A glassed-in directory hung on the pale green wall. As far as I could see, there were only two entries — Shaheen Enterprises and Plentiful Puppies, both with room numbers in the one hundred range. Nothing indicated an apartment on the second floor, nor any other businesses.

"Nice building," I exaggerated. "Do you own it?"

"Yes," Patsy said. "And before you ask, Bradley and I live in an apartment upstairs. Our sweet dogs were never without supervision. We checked on them often." She sighed, regarded me with dampness in her eyes, and said, "We miss them." Her round chin wiggled as if she was about to sob, but then she seemed to compose herself — or maybe she'd been acting with her supposed

157

tearfulness. "Please come with me. I'd rather you also talk with Bradley."

We followed a narrow hall with recessed lights above and dingy walls beside us broken up only by a few doors. At the last one on the right, Patsy turned the knob, pushed the door open, and motioned for me to precede her inside.

Was I about to be attacked? Shot? Photographed in the compromising position of even being here?

Did I ever mention that I have an overactive imagination? Well, I do — or at least I tend to dream up worst-case scenarios. It helps me survive whatever actually occurs, since little can be worse than what I wind up anticipating.

Except . . . although I'd vaguely considered killing Efram, not doing it yet being a suspect felt a lot worse.

I walked into a room as drab as the hallway. It contained a rectangular table surrounded by a half-dozen chairs. Bradley Shaheen sat in one across the room, nearest the bank of institutional-looking windows, regarding me with his head cocked.

I'd glimpsed him while he and Patsy argued with an Animal Services person on the day of the rescue. Since then, I'd seen both of them on the news.

Bradley was portlier than his wife but nevertheless more attractive, with a rough-and-ready smile that displayed white, even teeth, welcoming eyes beneath straight brows, and a full head of dull brown hair.

Oddly, he, too, looked familiar. But I'd surely have remembered it if I'd ever before come in contact with these despicable people who hurt dogs.

"Hi, Lauren," he said. "So good of you to come." As if they'd invited me. "Please sit down."

My mantra inside had been to keep reminding myself that Matt knew where I was. But I suddenly didn't feel threatened.

Stupidity on my part, or was my insight true?

Guess I'd find out.

I decided to start with truthfulness. I could always braid in some fibs if that later made sense. Patsy had taken a seat opposite me, beside her husband. "Thanks for agreeing to see me," I said.

"What can we help you with?" Bradley asked.

Confessing to murder and eliminating me from the suspect list, I thought. But what I said was, "Let me start by getting something on the table that I'm sure you know anyway. I despise puppy mills. What I saw here the other day made me sick. Those poor animals . . ." I let my sentence taper off while I forced myself to cool down. Becoming too angry and accusatory wouldn't get me what I needed to know.

Later, though, I might permit myself to vent more, depending.

"We can understand that," Patsy said. "We can't talk much about this, you know. That's what our lawyer said."

She leaned toward me, and I felt glad the table separated us, especially after her next words, said with all sincerity — obviously feigned. If I'd been closer, I might have done something I'd eventually regret.

"But, really, Lauren — we love dogs. Puppies, especially. We want to share them, and that's how we got into trouble. All of our dogs received individual attention, I swear it. And we did all we could to keep them from soiling themselves when we couldn't keep them close. Honest."

"Exactly," Bradley confirmed — also falsely. He reached out and held his wife's hand on the table. How sweet. Togetherness, in the face of adversity . . . consisting of an enraged animal rescuer facing two damnable abusers. "And you talk about abuse . . . Look, like Patsy said, we're not supposed to discuss any of this. But I figure you, of all people, will understand. That Efram guy. We never should have associated with him. He did nothing but get us into trouble."

Very convenient, I thought, now that Efram was dead.

At their hands?

"What did he do?" I asked, interested in hearing more about their perspective — true or not. "You know, he volunteered at HotRescues to atone for some possible cruelty to a dog he claimed was his. I'd thought he was making progress."

"Maybe." Patsy stood, clasping her hands in front of her extended gut as she paced behind her husband. "He seemed to care about the puppies here. He volunteered for us, too. Well, worked for us, since we paid him a little, when we were forced to help make ends meet by selling little ones now and then to pet stores so they could help them find new homes."

That sounded so good, like they really weren't just money-grubbing jerks making a living from selling badly treated puppies. They'd no doubt professed that before, maybe in the same words, to friends and neighbors. And to their lawyer. And probably to media sorts — although they'd apparently limited their interviews. After the initial flurry, I hadn't seen much of them on TV.

Patsy continued, "Efram helped give the doggies attention, feed them, clean up after them. I had no reason to believe he would ever hurt them."

"We've had arguments with one of our neighbors, Lauren," Bradley said. "She claimed she didn't like the noise from here, although the woman has a child daycare facility a few doors down, and you talk about noise . . ."

"She's the one who called Animal Services about us," Patsy continued. After claiming they couldn't talk, they sure were saying a lot. But if they thought they'd win me over to become a character witness they could manipulate — that wouldn't happen. "We heard about it before they arrived, and were shocked. Upset. We didn't know what to do."

"Except to tell the truth," Bradley went on.

They made a good tag team. I wondered if they'd testify the same way when they were prosecuted for animal abuse. At least I *hoped* they'd be prosecuted for that, at a minimum.

"Efram was here while we were waiting," Patsy said. "He knew we were concerned and that he'd be accused right along with us of whatever the neighbor claimed we were doing. He said he'd take care of things, and next thing I knew he was yanking some of the puppies from inside their crates, taking them outside. I figured he was going to try to hide them someplace safe till this blew over . . . but when I went out to check, he was throwing some down the storm drain. I screamed and was about to call the cops to get him to stop, but that was when Animal Services arrived and started accusing Bradley and me of all that nasty stuff. But we aren't guilty, Lauren. Honest. As an animal lover, like you've got to be to run a shelter, you have to understand."

What I had to do was to avoid throwing up, but I didn't tell them that. "I do understand loving animals," I said. "And I agree that if Efram tossed those puppies down the storm drain, he deserved to be thrown into jail and put on trial — by the official system. I, for one, felt betrayed for thinking I'd helped him learn to take good care of animals. You, too?"

"Well, sure." Patsy had grown quieter now, and she sat back down facing me, beside her husband.

"He'd started accusing you, though, not only of abusing those puppies but also throwing them into the drain. Made you mad, didn't it?" I watched their faces for reactions. Far as I could tell, they both felt unjustly wronged. Sad, and maybe a little scared.

Or they put on a damned good act, which was more probable. All we needed was the crescendoing sobs of violin music in the background, like in movies.

"Yes, Efram made us mad for lots of reasons," Bradley finally said. "I assume what you're leading up to is to ask if we killed him. We can ask you the same thing. From what the news says, you were there when his body was found — at HotRescues, your place. So . . . did you kill him, Lauren?"

"No," I said, "I didn't."

"Well, we didn't, either."

Oh, the look of sincerity on both their faces. It made me want to rub doggy excrement into their false smiles. I kept myself in check. No feces were handy anyway.

We gabbed a little more about animals and Efram and even justice and injustice. So where were those violins?

I left without any certainty about whether the Shaheens had sneaked into HotRescues with Efram and killed him.

They hated him enough to. I was sure

about that.

I felt lots of relief as I opened the gate and left the Shaheen property. I also remembered the small sense of relief I'd tried to talk myself into when I got there — that Matt Kingston knew where I was.

But when I checked my watch, I discovered that more than the half hour he'd said it would take for him to arrive had passed. Apparently he hadn't come after me, like a knight in shining armor, protecting the fair young maiden.

He did wear a uniform — Animal Services. But not armor, shining or otherwise. And I was far from a fair young maiden. Nor was I still naive enough to believe in fairy tales.

Even more, I didn't really want anyone butting in on whatever I was doing, even to theoretically save me from my own folly.

But I nevertheless felt irked. The guy had seemed to give a damn about the puppies. The adult dogs. Even me. Had he been so mad that he'd decided to let me suffer the potentially grim consequences of my election to confront the puppy mill owners?

Well, the hell with him.

Only — when I got back into my car, I remembered that I had turned my BlackBerry off in case Matt decided to call me at a crucial time in my talk with the Shaheens.

I turned it back on — and found he'd left three messages.

I smiled. And then I listened to them — each containing irritation, worry, a traffic report indicating it was taking him longer to get here than anticipated, and orders to back off.

"*You* back off, Captain Kingston," I muttered.

Only then did I see a familiar Animal Services car drive up and screech to a halt beside the curb. Matt jumped out.

As he reached my driver's side window, I cracked it open. "Everything's fine, Matt," I told him, waved my fingers at him, then drove off toward HotRescues.

CHAPTER 12

While I was on my way back to HotRescues, Matt unsurprisingly called me again. I
answered on my BlueTooth. I didn't give
many details of my conversation with the
Shaheens, but I did thank him for showing
up. Even if I didn't like his attempts to issue orders, his apparent concern about me
was rather sweet.

Unlike what I felt about the Shaheens. The
more I thought about it, the less inclined I
felt to take them at their word — which
wasn't saying much, since I hadn't believed
them in the first place. They'd certainly put
a creative spin on the barbarity of their
puppy mill.

They'd admitted to despising their sometime employee, Efram, but had sworn they
hadn't killed him. Yes to part one. I'd
continue to reserve judgment on part two.

There was still an irritating barb scratch-
ing inside me that I'd met the Shaheens

before. Where? And when?

I also received a call from Nina. I told her I was on my way — and mentioned, without elaboration, where I'd been and why.

Our welcome room was full when I got to HotRescues. Two family groups and a young couple had arrived at the same time. It was late afternoon. The kids had probably just gotten out of school for the day. Nina had her hands full, but at least Bev was there, too. Our senior citizen volunteer was working with one of the families.

Maybe their questions had been answered, since all three groups started toward the shelter area, apparently to see if any of our inhabitants made them spring right into adoption.

Nina accompanied the people outside, and I could hear her giving directions. One of the families and the young couple apparently had their hearts set on middle-sized dogs. The other family apparently seemed to be more cat-inclined.

When Nina and Bev returned inside, both looked tired. "Were any of them serious," I asked, "or did they just want to visit some animals?"

"Hard to tell," Bev said.

"If I were to place bets," Nina said, "I'd say that only one of those families was really interested. The others just had time to kill today and wanted to show the kids some doggies and kitties."

"I'll go keep an eye on them," Bev said. "Whether or not any of them are really interested, I want to be sure they don't tease the animals or hurt their feelings."

Nina and I smiled as Bev hurried out the door.

"So," Nina said, "how did your confrontation go?"

"Confrontation? *Moi?*" I placed my hand to my chest in an affronted gesture, so my fingers touched the HotRescues logo on my shirt.

She laughed, which caused me to drop my façade and join her. "Okay," I said. "You got me. Those two . . . Well, I doubt they said anything accurate other than that they hated Efram." I motioned for Nina to join me at the table. As we sat down, I gave her a blow-by-blow of all that had happened. I ended with, "I sure wish I knew if I'd ever seen either of them before, and if so, where."

"I'll Google them for you," Nina said. "And — hey, let me check one more thing, too." She whisked herself behind the reception counter and onto the computer there. In only a minute, she said triumphantly, "Ha! Come look at this, Lauren."

I joined her — and saw she had opened a file with a list of people who had relinquished their pets here, at HotRescues.

The name Shaheen wasn't on it, but the names Bradley and Patsy Shane were! Over a year ago, people with that similar name had brought in a pair of bichons frises. They had claimed they were moving out of the country and needed to have their beloved dogs rehomed. They had left them that very day.

Were they the Shaheens? Maybe. We had done our standard check to confirm what we could about these dog relinquishers. The address and phone number had checked out, so we'd been able to take in the relinquishments — although now, when Nina Googled the address, it appeared to be a private mailbox service, and the phone number was no longer working. Our standard veterinary exam at Carlie's clinic had yielded that those two bichons were younger than their relinquishers had claimed. The female appeared to have given birth more than once and her reproductive equipment seemed worn out. Both needed some medical attention including a respective spay/neuter, but they'd come out of it fine.

At the time, we'd suspected they had been puppy mill parents. If so, the Shaheens could have been dumping more adult dogs that could no longer be bred at other shelters, too. But by then we'd been unable to find the abandoners again to confirm it. Fortunately, we'd found the dogs a wonderful new home with a middle-aged couple — empty nesters who had recently lost their pet to cancer. Happy ending!

But if they were the Shanes, the Shaheens were definitely liars. Murderers, too?

Could be.

Another thought struck me. "Nina, could you check to see if Efram happened to be here that day?" If so, it could have been how he'd met the Shaheens in the first place.

We always kept records of when our volunteers were here — whether or not they were here voluntarily. Sure enough —

"Yes, he was!" Nina exclaimed.

Which made the scenario even more interesting.

As I got ready to head home, I got a call on my BlackBerry from Esther Ickes. I had programmed her number in, not that I wanted the lawyer to become one of my best friends. But having it readily accessible was a lot more practical than looking it up all the time. This way her name showed up on the screen when she contacted me.

Standing in the parking lot beside my car, I answered. My heart was revving up like a drag racer. Had she learned something awful? I was supposed to meet with her tomorrow before heading to the police station to be interrogated again.

What if they planned to arrest me that night? The best I'd be able to do is tell the cops that the Shaheens admitted they hated Efram.

"Hi, Esther."

"Hi, Lauren. I have some good news — at least for me."

What? That I was under arrest so she'd have an excuse to double her legal fees?

"What?" I held my breath.

"Detective Garciana has some business near my office tomorrow, so we've made arrangements for him to question you here this time. I hope that's all right with you."

Calling the whole thing off would have been better, but being in my lawyer's office, in territory that, if not neutral, at least favored me more than some stark room in a police station . . . "That's fine," I said. "Same time?"

"Yes."

I was collecting a lot of hours of sleeplessness these days. I wondered if I'd be able to make any of them up when the truth about Efram's death at HotRescues was known, whatever it was.

But of course the answer was no. I'd still be busy with the job I loved — and all the animals I protected.

At home, though, I felt nervous despite living in a gated community. The security at HotRescues hadn't protected either Efram or me. Anyone could get inside my residential complex. Not that I considered my life in danger. But Efram's death had made me a lot more aware not only of how fragile life was — and not just the lives of pets — but also of how any feeling of safety was as false as believing in immortality.

For now, I lay down on the sofa I had chosen when the kids were still at home, a blue upholstered thing with lots of fluffy pillows. I'd bought it relatively cheaply at a chain store that mostly carried items from Nordic countries. I put my head down on a knit throw given to me by a friend and watched a talk show way into the night.

My television was fairly new and state of the art, thanks to my son Kevin's pushiness about it. When he came home, he watched it with me.

That night, I hated being alone nearly as much as I usually cherished privacy. My mind kept turning to my first husband Kerry, whom I'd lost so many years ago. He'd scolded me lightly now and then for being so opinionated and having a temper. But if he were alive now, he wouldn't believe I had harmed Efram. He'd stand by me and defend me just like he did during our marriage.

The sorrow over my loss made my mind veer in another direction: again, to missing having a pet around. Someone to talk to and sympathize with, even if she didn't completely understand.

I'd mostly convinced myself that I had enough pets around every day, at HotRescues. But that still wasn't the same as having my own, probably a dog, who'd never even think of accusing me of murder but would love me no matter what, as long as I was good to her.

Heck. This was getting too maudlin. I turned down the TV's volume and soon felt myself nodding off.

Eleven o'clock in the morning. Back in Esther's offices.

This time, we were in a conference room big enough for half a dozen people. It reminded me of the room where I'd spoken with her the other day, mostly because it was lined with shelves containing a lot of law books.

I'd mellowed about Esther as quickly as a Google search. So what if research material was available online these days like everything else? Senior-citizen Esther might just be more comfortable with a hands-on approach. If she used it to my benefit, all the better.

She'd greeted me in her reception area on my arrival, and we'd chatted in her office for a short while about what to expect. She sounded so comforting and sure of herself that I felt certain I'd made the right decision by trusting in Kendra's referral. Esther's age — and, therefore, experience — now seemed a real plus. She wore a pretty, black suit with a white lacy blouse, dressy and lawyerlike.

I'd worn a suit jacket, too, for the occasion, but I'd put on nice slacks, the easier to change when I returned to HotRescues. Since the meeting was here and not at the police station, I was hopeful it wouldn't end in my being arrested.

Esther preceded me into the conference room. I felt almost lofty behind the rather stooped lawyer — especially when she appeared to slump even more as we entered the room. I caught the expression on Detective Stefan Garciana's face, as smug as if this interview would be a piece of cake. He'd be able to run roughshod over the pathetic efforts of this frail old attorney.

I knew better. He soon learned.

"How are you today?" the detective said as we took our seats. He, too, wore a suit — funereal, as if designed to warn me to mourn my freedom. The concerned expression on his face pretended he gave a damn about making sure my attorney didn't keel over because of her age.

She wasn't that old, anyway — especially these days. People often lived into their nineties and even beyond. I'd already guessed Esther to have achieved her seventies. I also figured she was shrewd enough to play the age card as long as it was to her advantage.

Esther had asked her staff to bring coffee, so I sipped on a dark, bitter brew as I also contemplated dark, bitter answers to the detective's questions. The most important thing was not to contradict what I'd said before — assuming I could remember everything.

The reason for this latest interrogation? "We've come across new evidence," the detective claimed. Something else that could point to my guilt? Or something manufactured in the hopes that I would get nervous enough to disgorge something against my own interests?

"Suppose you tell us what it is, Detective," Esther said calmly, sitting beside me with a yellow legal pad in front of her.

"We got an anonymous tip. The caller said you had threatened Mr. Kiley in front of an entire group of people, Ms. Vancouver. Is that true?"

"Hmmm," I responded. "Could that be when I yelled at him for participating in that horror at the puppy mill, like I told you about before, Detective? Or maybe when we went outside then, and I accused him of throwing those poor puppies down the storm drain — as I also mentioned to you." I put my finger to my chin in mock pensiveness. "Or — I know. My reaction when he came to HotRescues and threatened not only me, but my employees and the animals there . . . as, oh yes, I've described to you."

"She's got you there, Detective." Esther's smile ironed even more creases onto her face. "Unless you could be more specific — one of these, or did someone manufacture something else?"

The detective consulted a notebook he'd brought along. "Then these were the only times you threatened Mr. Kiley, Ms. Vancouver?" He looked at me as if his gaze were a drill that could extract different answers.

"I wish I'd brought a pack of playing cards," Esther said. I aimed a sideways glance toward her, wondering about the non sequitur. But then she added, "The kind my grandson has. He just loves a game of Go Fish. And I enjoy playing with him. But he's only six years old. I think we're all too old to be playing Fish here, Detective."

I didn't even attempt to hide my grin.

"So are we done?" she continued. "I need to prepare for a late-day court appearance." Her tone had changed from light and frothy to hard and lawyerlike. I loved it.

The detective, scowling, attempted to save face by asking a couple more questions, none of which particularly bothered me. He soon left.

When he was gone, I asked Esther, "Fishing or not, he's not going to quit till he makes an arrest, is he?"

"Unfortunately, I'm pretty sure that's his game. I've seen it before."

"And he's hoping I'll be the one he arrests. In fact, he's planning on it."

Esther put an arm around me and gave me a hug I'm sure she thought was comforting but only made me realize even more the tenuous situation I was in. "Could be. But

178

we'll thwart him, dear. Don't worry."

Right. As if I wouldn't worry that my relatively happy life, as I knew it, might be about to change into a disaster.

As I drove back toward HotRescues, I thought even more about how I couldn't rely on the official legal system to find the truth. I hadn't learned enough from the Shaheens to pin Efram's murder on them.

I always like to feel in control of circumstances, but right now circumstances seemed in control of me.

CHAPTER 13

"Everything okay, Lauren?"

As I hung up the phone, Nina peeked in through my office door. She'd been upstairs in her own small office when I'd gotten back from Esther's. At least that was what Bev, who was staffing the welcoming area, had told me.

Nina's face looked drawn, as if she was the one who'd just been raked over the coals by a detective itching to make an arrest. I wondered if I appeared as frazzled. I hoped not.

"Everything's fine." The fib rolled over my tongue as if it were a smooth latte. "Come in and sit down for a minute." When she'd settled into one of the chairs facing my desk, I asked, "Are you doing okay?"

"Sure." The word was belied by the droopiness of her smile. "Well . . . not exactly. I don't know how you stand it, Lauren."

"Stand what?"

"The taint around here. Efram's death. The cops asking questions. Do you know . . . Well, they seem to want me to tell them you lured Efram here that night so you could stab him."

My blood must have stopped pumping through my veins, since I immediately felt full of icy shards that formed a blockage. "I see. So . . . what have you said to them?"

"That you couldn't have. They're barking up the wrong tree if they suspect you." This time her smile was a little less ghastly, and I joined her.

"Thanks," I said. But I doubted whether her support would make even a tiny change to Detective Garciana's opinion. "I didn't do it. Period. And now all I have to do is prove it."

"But you're supposed to be —"

"Innocent until proven guilty. I know that. But that's only in court, or so I gather from some of the crime shows I watch. It doesn't deal with popular opinion. And it certainly doesn't mean a cop won't keep accusing you till you get a jury to acquit you. Rather, me. So — well, you've known me long enough to realize I'm not the kind of person who'll just sit here, wringing my hands and petting the dogs till I'm arrested, tried, and convicted." When she didn't say anything, I stared pointedly into her face. "Right?"

"Yes, but what —"

Before she could finish her sentence — which I assumed would be something like, "What the hell can you do to stop them?" — I turned the computer monitor on my desk so she could see it.

I'd been Googling Efram. Maybe knowing more about him would help me learn how to get the cops searching elsewhere for his killer.

"I haven't found much on Efram," I told her. "He had a Facebook page, and he'd posted some pictures that were taken here, ones with him playing with dogs. Guess he was trying to build a good, if false, image for some reason. In real life, when he wasn't pretending to take good care of our animals, he was an air-conditioning repairman, so he also has pictures up of wielding tools near an air compressor."

"So maybe someone whose air-conditioning he ruined followed him here and killed him," Nina surmised. "I suspect he was as good a repairman as he was an animal caretaker."

I smiled grimly. "You're probably right. About his skills, I mean. But who'd have followed him here to kill him, for something like that, at least? Although . . ."

Her mind must have gone in the same direction as mine did. "Hey, I haven't checked out the application and other forms he filled out to become a volunteer here," she said. "Have you?" At my headshake, she continued. "That should at least tell us where he lived, give a person to notify in case of emergency. That kind of thing."

I'd looked over his form when he'd started helping but hadn't paid a lot of attention to it since his presence was a result of our legal settlement. We hadn't even required that he take a class for volunteers — a must for everyone else. But his application should have been one of the first things I thought of to learn more about the guy, even before Googling him. At least I now had another way to research him besides going to the meeting I'd scheduled via a phone call I'd made a little while ago.

"Has the information been put on the computer?" That was our standard procedure. I turned my monitor back to face me and began to open our online personnel files.

"Probably." Nina edged her way behind me.

Efram's background had been added to our database. I found it right away. I quickly printed the page, which contained his former address, his employer's information, and the person to notify in an emergency: a woman named Mandy Ledinger. His girl-friend? But who'd have chosen to be that friendly with Efram?

I would find out soon who Mandy was — and why Efram had included her.

"If you'd like," Nina said, "I could continue the search you started and give you anything else I find on Efram, both through the Internet and our records."

"I'd love it. But first why don't we cheer ourselves up by visiting our residents?"

A big smile smoothed out Nina's pinched face. "Lead the way."

We were outside in the shelter area less than five minutes later. I started down the row of barking dogs, taking pleasure in my usual greeting of each one after encouraging them to quiet down. Their placement had been reorganized a little, at my direction. We'd gotten a couple more adoptions started, and having all our enclosures filled near the entrance usually made a bigger impact on potential adopters. It emphasized how many animals needed a new home. Besides, changing vistas now and then enriched the dogs' lives.

"Lauren, hi!" Si Rogan had just turned

the corner at the far end of the row and motioned toward us with one hand. The other was occupied with a leash attached to a Great Dane mix — Hannibal. "Come here. I want to show you how well Hannibal is doing."

Hannibal was a large and rambunctious one-year-old whose owner had dropped him off a couple of weeks ago in a relinquishment. Another victim of the economy, the twenty-something owner had lost his job and house and was moving in with his parents — into an already small apartment, in a building where pets weren't allowed.

For the best chance at a good adoption, Hannibal needed to be a lot better behaved. Si, great trainer that he was, had willingly taken on the task.

Forgoing my usual cherished petting of each dog along the way — for now — I hurried toward Si. So did Nina.

"Let's go into the rear visiting area," I suggested. It was at the far side of the storage shed, a place where we always had potential adopters meet with the animals they'd chosen to see how they got along in a location of less stress than the enclosures. We also took advantage of it for other uses — like now.

Nina and I let Si and Hannibal precede

us. I watched as the big dog moseyed quietly at the trainer's side, heeling as if he'd been brought up from puppyhood doing it. *Yay, Si!* I thought.

I'd have hurled a lot more "yays" at him, too, if I hadn't worried about breaking Hannibal's concentration a short while later. The visitors' area was charming and park-like, with a small grassy area along one side — one that didn't take a lot of water to maintain in drought-stricken Los Angeles but was large enough to permit abbreviated doggy games of chase the ball. The rest was paved but contained a picnic area with benches and a table.

Nina and I took seats on a bench while Si put Hannibal through his paces — sit, stay, down, roll over, heel, and speak. Nothing unusual or outrageous, but the formerly rambunctious large dog was clearly eager to please his trainer. Surely he'd be even happier to obey a new, loving owner.

"That's so great!" I told Si when the demonstration ended. Nina bent to give equal congratulations to Hannibal. "You've done a fantastic job."

"Thanks." Si looked down toward the walkway almost modestly, then turned his gaze back at me. "You know you're welcome to watch me give lessons here, or at my own place. I can teach you what I do. It's not hard, especially for someone who loves animals the way you do. Anytime." His tone was calm and bland, but there was almost a pleading in his expression.

"I appreciate it, Si. But with all your wonderful work, I don't need to become an expert at training animals. I can spend my time figuring out how to save more."

My turn to lavish attention on our new star Hannibal. But I could feel Si's hurt as I turned away.

"Hey," I said. "Maybe Nina would like to learn. How about it?"

"You'd teach me how to train animals? Would you really, Si?" She sounded so enthusiastic that it was contagious.

"She could help work with the ones you both train when you're not around, Si." I grinned at him.

His smile wasn't nearly as eager as ours, but he said, "Great idea. Next time I'm here, we can work out some lessons."

"Thank you!" Nina rushed toward him and gave him a hug.

I wondered why I hadn't thought of it before.

I couldn't help feeling a little smug as I headed back toward my office. I saved animals. That was my life's work. All I'd ever wanted to do.

But besides being my second in command, Nina had seemed a bit unfocused here. Maybe she could have a whole new direction by learning to be a trainer.

Later that afternoon I sat in my office staring at the computer, wondering where to look next. Not here, though. I'd been following links to news sites that discussed Efram's death and the ensuing murder investigation.

My name appeared a lot.

I'd just walked through the shelter area again. Wanted to do it once more. The animals' company made me feel better.

Maybe I should take lessons on training from Si after all.

I realized then that I was succumbing to unfortunately familiar emotions that I totally hated, a growing sense of despondency and resignation. I was a murder suspect. How could I take control and fix that?

The worst-case scenario part of my mind had taken over.

I'd felt equally helpless years ago, during my second marriage, when I wasn't sure what to do.

But I'd decided then to make a change,

retake control over my life. End that fiasco of a marriage. Yet nothing as relatively controllable as a divorce could help me now.

What could I do?

I minimized the latest news page on the computer, one taunting me that it was just a matter of time till I was arrested. My computer wallpaper appeared — a photo of the first dog who'd been adopted from HotRescues: Carlie's dog, Max, part cocker spaniel and all adorable. Around Max, the icons on my desktop glared up at me like a bunch of irritated kids demanding attention.

Icons that included shortcuts to HotRescues' online business folders.

Folders I'd started years ago, as a result of the plan I'd developed to impress Dante so he'd choose me to be the start-up shelter's chief administrator.

I suddenly stood, my legs casting my chair backward, as I stared at all those icons.

I needed the equivalent of an investigator's business plan! A way to take control of my own search for Efram's killer.

I'd start with an organizational chart, then determine what kinds of information I'd need on potential suspects, how to approach and gather it . . . and how all that knowledge, studied and digested, should surely lead to the murderer. Or at least give me enough ammo to get the cops looking another way.

My BlackBerry rang, and I picked it up from my desk where I'd laid it after making some calls.

Carlie. I was never a believer in out-there things like ESP, but she often called when my mind was hyperventilating — and even more when she was the focus of some of my thoughts.

"Hi," I said. "I was just thinking about you. Or at least about Max."

"Yeah?" she said. "He sends his regards — his barks, rather. So . . . how's your murder investigation coming? Have you solved it yet, saved your own hide, and gone on to bigger and better things?"

That was Carlie — always intuitive, always to the point.

"I'm just getting started," I told her. "By the time you get back here, I'll have my strategy all put together. It'll knock your socks off!"

CHAPTER 14

It was late, but I was eager to begin.

First, I went through some files, both computer and paper ones, to locate the original HotRescues operation plan that I'd created more than six years ago.

Putting together a strategy for figuring out who committed a murder wasn't exactly the same thing as devising a business plan for opening a well-funded no-kill private animal shelter. But the concept was similar: define the goal, then write down, in detail, all matters that had to be accomplished to reach it — after researching the items that were necessary.

Goal: Find the person who killed Efram Kiley.

Rationale: To ensure that I was no longer a suspect.

Method: Determine all other persons, or at least as many as possible, who had the means, motive, and opportunity to kill

Efram. I'd already begun a nebulous version of this one in my mind, but I needed to get more organized about it, including making detailed notes on each person I checked out.

Short-term strategy: I started on the list of all the steps I'd take to reach that elusive but utterly vital goal.

Best-case scenario: The police would solve this murder right away — correctly eliminating me as a suspect.

Worst-case scenario: I'd be arrested, unable to follow up.

Overall strategy: Being the kind of person who always assumed the worst would happen, I had to keep telling myself that, if I worked hard, I'd achieve what I needed to. The best-case scenario might sound good, and hopefully it would occur, but relying on the possibility would be foolish — and foolish wasn't the way I worked. I had to keep going to ensure that the worst-case scenario didn't happen.

For each person I thought could be guilty — beginning with the Shaheens from the puppy mill — I would create a new page in my file and jot down everything I knew that made them suspects.

Unfortunately, nothing stuck out at me as being the irrefutable answer. But there were more potential suspects to come, more blanks to fill in, until I had all I needed to solve the case.

That night, I learned that both my kids were coming home that weekend. And both were really concerned about my latest bit of notoriety as a possible murder suspect.

I admit I felt rather misty when I poured myself a beer after dinner, sat down in front of Kevin's big TV, and thought about seeing them. I'd certainly done one thing right in my life: bringing them up to be loving, wonderful people — and to give a damn about their mother.

Then again, maybe they really just wanted to see this aging YouTube star in person.

I also learned I was invited on Friday to go see the rescued puppies at that unopened shelter in the Valley. While I was still seated on my couch, Matt Kingston called to let me know. And to ask how I was doing. To see if I'd recuperated from my visit to the Shaheens. And to surreptitiously inquire if I'd been arrested yet.

Well, maybe not the last one. I just chose to read things into his questions. He sounded concerned, but I knew he was being nosy, too.

I did the appropriate thing and questioned

him right back. He'd probably have chosen a different location if he'd been the one to kill Efram, but he had nearly as much of a motive as I did. Matt loved animals. Efram had tortured animals. Matt had arrested him, but Efram got out on bail. I wasn't sure when he would have been scheduled for trial, but there was always the chance that a jury would bog down in an unsupportable theory of "reasonable doubt" and acquit him. Though I felt certain Efram had thrown those pups into the storm drain, there could be a convincing argument that it was, instead, the Shaheens.

Matt could have waited for months for Efram to be put on trial, then expend hours testifying and worrying about the verdict — and still not get Efram punished.

All of that still made my blood boil, even though it was now impossible. And I wasn't one of the good people who'd had a hand in arresting Efram. But Matt was.

It was a reasonable motive for him to kill Efram.

I just wished, if it was him, that he'd done it somewhere other than following Efram to HotRescues. But just in case, I'd add a file on him to my suspect collection tomorrow.

"You think I what!" Matt shouted into my ear. Guess I'd been thinking aloud — accidentally on purpose.

I smiled at the phone, then said into it, "That makes as much sense as my killing him."

"Yeah. Right."

I heard him stewing, which made my grin broaden. "Anyway, I'll look forward to observing for myself how the pups and their moms and dads are thriving. See you Friday." I hung up.

I knew I was elasticizing reality so I could develop and expand my brand-new suspect files, but if I wasn't creative, I'd never learn who killed Efram. I couldn't rely on the police to determine the truth with someone as handy as me locked in their sights.

Which was why I showed up at the law office of James Remseyer bright and early the next morning.

I'd called yesterday to set up this appointment. But I knew better than to come in as myself and try to talk to the attorney who had represented Efram in a situation where I'd been involved as an opposing party.

My name, to get me into the office, was Laura Brown. In fact, Lauren Brown had been my maiden name, before I'd married my dear Kerry Vancouver. Ah, the nostalgia . . . But no time to dwell on it.

The law office was in Northridge, not very far from HotRescues in Granada Hills. I walked into the reception area and gave my name to the young lady behind the desk. She told me to have a seat, which I did, and looked around.

A minute later, an even younger lady wearing a very short skirt came through the inner door and said, "Laura Brown?" I rose, and she motioned for me to follow. "Come with me, please."

We walked down a narrow hallway and turned a corner. "Right in there." She pointed to a door.

My intent hadn't been to impress the lawyer, but I figured looking somewhat professional wouldn't hurt, so I'd worn a no-frills shirt tucked into a skirt, and low heels. I'd change as soon as I got back to HotRescues.

I entered the moderate-sized but otherwise unimpressive office. Seated behind the unimpressive desk was James Remseyer. And, yes, he looked unimpressive, too. At least until he opened his eyes wide and glared at me.

"What are you doing here, Ms. Vancouver?" His tone could have stabbed me if he'd been throwing the ice in it in my direction. "Ah, yes, I see. I'm expecting someone named Laura Brown. Would that happen to be you? And if so —"

"Yes," I interrupted calmly, breezing forward and planting myself in a chair facing his desk. I remembered that the guy liked the sound of his own voice, since he'd kept using it nonstop when we all met to settle Efram's ridiculous claims against HotRescues, Dante, and me. "I figured you wouldn't see me if I told you who I really was."

He had apparently not wanted to display all his lawyerly splendor to the woman he thought Laura Brown was — odd, since she could have been a potential client. When we'd all gotten together, including Dante and Kendra, he'd worn a dark, expensive suit. Now, he was clad in a dressy white shirt without a jacket but adorned with a red-striped tie. I wasn't sure of his hairline's contours, since he'd shaved off his hair. I did note a five o'clock shadow, though, way back on his head.

"Of course I wouldn't have admitted you. It's unethical. You're on the opposite side of a matter from my client, and you're represented by counsel."

"But your client is dead, and so is the matter you represented him on. And I'm not represented by anyone about that situation now." No need to mention that I'd had to take on another lawyer because I was a murder suspect. He'd figure that out, though, if he hadn't already. "I came today to talk to you about Efram Kiley. I assume you know what happened to him."

"Yes, I know about Efram. I also know you're a suspect in his murder. So why are you here? I'm sure it's not to express sympathy."

"In a way, it is," I lied, trying to stick earnestness on my face as I assumed he did when he argued a client's untenable position in court. "Did he have any family? Friends? I'd like to contact them, let them know how sorry I feel about their loss." Which could, in fact, be true. I knew what it felt like to lose someone I cared about. The difference was that those I'd lost, like Kerry, had been good people, worth the emotions I'd spent on them. If there'd been a lovable side to Efram, I certainly hadn't seen it, but others might have.

"He had a girlfriend but lived alone, which made your stealing his dog even worse. And you know —"

"Like I said, that matter is over," I said. "But to again set matters straight, I didn't steal his dog. Someone found it and brought it to another shelter first. When it got to

HotRescues, I took appropriate steps to try to learn where the poor, obviously abused guy came from."

Never mind that I'd worked my way around the system, since HotRescues isn't supposed to take in strays. And I'd chosen not to see if he had an ID chip.

"He became one of our rescues, and I found him a new, loving home. That's all. But look," I said as the lawyer opened his mouth, apparently ready to start spewing his client's side of things again. "All that doesn't matter now. We settled it without a lot of hassle. Efram volunteered with HotRescues as he was supposed to. He didn't comply with all the conditions, but since he's gone that no longer matters, either." Unless he had heirs and Dante chose to try to recoup some of the money Efram didn't earn from them.

Oops. That might be a reason this lawyer wouldn't give me any information. Did he automatically represent everyone in Efram's family?

"So he did comply, at least in part?" Despite his shaved head, Remseyer did have eyebrows, which rose as his face took on an expression that seemed paradoxically innocent on a lawyer. "And I assume, with a deep pocket like Dante DeFrancisco on your side, that he was paid as agreed."

Interesting comment. Wouldn't he know for sure? Or maybe Efram would only have told him if he hadn't been paid.

A question sprang to my mind and dived from my lips before I thought it through. "Did you receive your fees from Efram, James?"

Innocence segued to a glower. "That's not your business, Lauren." Ah. He'd called me by my first name — my real first name — as I'd been doing with him. Before, he'd stuck with the formal Ms. Did that signify anything?

My assumption, right or wrong, was that it did. We were now communicating. Unless it was a device he was using to throw me off guard.

But wouldn't he have told me immediately if he had been paid? What would have been the harm in that?

"Maybe not." I lowered my head, pretending his chastisement had been effective. There might be other ways to find out whether James had been paid. "As I recall, he was an air-conditioning repairman when he wasn't helping out at HotRescues. Do you happen to know what company he worked for?"

"Yes," he said, "I do. But I don't know

what you're looking for, Lauren. Your giving his friends and acquaintances sympathy is a bunch of bull. You're a suspect in his murder. I'll bet you're trying to get as much as you can about him so you can blow a lot of smoke into the investigation. Am I right?"

"Not exactly." I still tried to sound humble. "Not smoke. Just information. As a lawyer, you must know you can't believe everything you hear on the news. I didn't like Efram, but I didn't kill him. If I can give the police other suspects to look into, maybe they'll figure out who really did it. I know you don't have to tell me anything, but I'd really, really appreciate it. Where did he work? Who were his family? His friends?"

"You can't always discount all you hear on the news, either, Lauren." He shot me a patronizing grin that looked like he was sure I was the killer. "But what the hell. I won't give you anything that's privileged information, but if you do more digging on your own you'd probably figure out his job and family and all."

He turned to the computer on the desk to one side of him and played with the keyboard. Then he pressed a button, and I heard the printer on a shelf behind him start to work.

He soon handed one page to me and

remained standing — my invitation, no doubt, to leave. "Here's all I'll give you. But you can be sure I'll make a record of our discussion. If anyone whose names I've given you is hurt in any way, I'll tell the cops what we've talked about."

Sounded like butt covering. Big surprise. He was a lawyer.

I glanced at the list. Three names, and he was making such a fuss? They were better than nothing, at least, and might lead to further information.

I wondered, though, as I left the office, why James Remseyer, attorney at law, had given me any help at all.

Could it be a form of misdirection, so I wouldn't look too hard to see if *he* could be Efram's killer?

He'd have a motive if Efram hadn't paid him — which he hadn't confirmed. Or denied.

A dead Efram couldn't pay him, either . . . unless the lawyer could get something from the guy's heirs.

Guess what, Mr. Remseyer, I thought as I entered the elevator. *You're now one of my suspects.*

CHAPTER 15

As I reached my car, my BlackBerry rang. The screen told me HotRescues was on the line, but not who was calling.

"Hello," I answered as I slipped into the driver's seat.

"Lauren, it's Nina. Are you heading here anytime soon? We have someone here who's eager to adopt one of the kittens. The credentials sound good to me, and I'd like you to meet the people before they leave, if you're going to be around."

"On my way. Should be there in half an hour or less. Will that work?"

I heard a murmur, then Nina got back on the line. "Perfect. See you soon."

I checked the time, then drove toward Granada Hills. I wondered which kitten was involved. Who its prospective new owners might be, and what they were like.

Whether I'd okay the match.

Years ago, I'd been accused of micromanaging. My not-so-darling ex had hurled that criticism at me a lot. He'd been talking then about how I juggled raising the kids, working as a veterinary technician, and dealing with my relationship with him. Everything had to mesh perfectly. Any veering from the schedule needed to be examined and reexamined so it wouldn't happen in the future. I had to approve every activity in advance.

All that was necessary when I was a full-time mom and full-time breadwinner, as well as a full-time wife.

The kids came first, of course. And since I had to support them — he wouldn't — my job came next.

Charles didn't like being a distant third. Not that he did anything to help out so I'd have more time for him.

So, I'd had to tell him what we could do together and when. Micromanagement? Perhaps. He certainly threw that at me a lot.

Back then, I'd felt hurt. Claimed he was wrong.

I eventually learned that he used his criticisms as an excuse to himself. My micromanaging supposedly justified his sneakiness, his using money that I earned to treat himself to extracurricular activities when I was busy with scheduled priorities.

Activities like taking his lovers out for a good time before screwing them.

I was excruciatingly happy to micromanage our divorce, including his reimbursement of all he'd stolen from me.

Now, I proudly admitted that I was a micromanager — at least, at HotRescues. I'd eased up on scheduling, but I was still, always, in charge. No animal got rehomed without my approving it. And that was notwithstanding the adopters' filling out their forms perfectly, answering all questions well about how their new pet would be treated, showing photos of their homes, bringing existing pets in to see how they got along with the potential adoptee, and passing muster with our resident shrink, Mona.

If I didn't like the match, it didn't happen. End of story.

Fortunately, this one looked like a winner. As I walked into the reception area, I saw the prospective adopter, a middle-aged lady, standing in a corner of the room talking with Mona. The kitten had been born here, thanks to an irate man who'd discovered that the family cat was pregnant and dumped her at HotRescues for her effrontery. Never mind that he could have prevented the situation in the first place by having the cat neutered.

The kitten was a little white charmer, a female we'd temporarily named Princess. She had a flat face and a way of looking at you that said she truly was royalty.

Where was little Princess as I entered the room? Snugged tightly against her prospective subject's heart, peering at me haughtily, as if daring me to say no to her rehoming.

I didn't. I checked the paperwork, including a lot of photos — she'd called before coming here. I talked privately with Mona. Talked publicly with the lady who wanted — badly — to take the kitten home with her.

That wouldn't happen, but I did tell Princess's prospective new mama that we'd expedite our approval process. I liked the woman and her interaction with Princess, so if all went as we believed it would, she could come back tomorrow or the next day. I'd let her know.

I was smiling when I went into my office, until I pulled the sheet of information from my purse that I'd gotten from James Remseyer.

So Efram had had a girlfriend. Her name, according to James, was Shellie Benudo. That wasn't the same person he had used for his emergency contact here at HotRescues, Mandy Ledinger, who was also on the

206

list but not identified.

I wanted to talk to both of them, especially Shellie. Even if I didn't ultimately create a suspect file on her — which I probably would — I was curious. Why on earth would she have been attracted to a man who hurt animals? Was she an abuser, too? Or simply unaware . . . before. Unless she was a hermit who shunned all technology and other news sources, she had to have seen him in the media after the puppy mill rescue. Before that, wouldn't she have wondered why he was suddenly volunteering at HotRescues?

What had she thought when Efram's dog, whom he'd called Killer, had disappeared? Had Efram told the same set of lies to her, or a different set, when he'd learned that Killer was now Quincy and had a new home?

Then again, who was Mandy?

Enough of this useless speculation. I had a mound of paperwork to complete, especially logging in the information about Princess's new home.

Better yet, I'd have Nina do that, and I'd just double-check it. I could also have Nina do Web research on Shellie Benudo and, if she hadn't already, on Mandy Ledinger. Instead, though, I decided to start the research myself.

I turned to the computer and plugged Shellie's name into the first search engine that came up.

I found someone with that name first thing on Facebook. The right person? I opened the Web site and looked at the photographs.

I was staring at them when Nina knocked on my door and entered. I looked up from the computer and glared at her for the interruption.

"Everything okay, Lauren?" Her stressed features grew even tauter with concern about me, which made me feel as awful as if I'd accidentally stomped on a miniature pinscher's paw.

"I'm fine," I said, waving her to a chair. I considered asking her to work on closing the Princess file. Instead, I started telling her about my meeting with Efram's lawyer. Talking about it might help my thoughts to gel better for inclusion in my file on Remseyer. "They apparently didn't get along well, and I suspect it's because Efram stiffed him," I concluded.

"So he's a possible suspect in Efram's killing." Nina sounded pleased, as if she really cared about my future exoneration.

"I'd like to ask you a favor," I said. "Remseyer also gave me information about Efram's girlfriend. Could you do an Internet search?"

Her face lit up. "Absolutely! And I did look up Efram's emergency contact on his application to 'volunteer' here — that Mandy Ledinger. I didn't find her on the Internet, but I gave her a call. She was his stepmother. And, well, I wasn't sure whether I should tell you about it, but . . ." Nina looked at me and swallowed, looking suddenly uncomfortable.

"But what?" I prompted.

She took a deep breath as if steeling herself to continue. "She demanded that I identify myself. And when I told her I was with HotRescues, she started screaming at me. Said she would get the bitch who ran this place and who killed her dear boy. That kind of thing."

I felt my face redden. I opened my mouth to say something, but nothing came out . . . at first. Then I found myself smiling. "The best defense is a good offense, right?" I'd thought that a lot lately. "I think I'll pay a visit to Ms. Mandy Ledinger. Efram wasn't exactly the lovable sort. Maybe she accompanied him here herself, to do away with him somewhere that she wouldn't be blamed. What do you think?"

"I think you're amazing, Lauren." Nina

grinned. "And innocent, of course. If I can do anything else to help you clear yourself, name it."

"Thanks." I'd keep her offer in mind, since I knew I was going to need all the help I could get.

I assumed that Mandy Ledinger wasn't inclined to talk civilly to me, so I decided I'd be the one on the offensive. Through Googling, Nina had learned that Mandy was a secretary at a medical office in Thousand Oaks.

I first took another walk through the shelter area, spending extra time with the cats in the center building, since I was sure they all meowed so pathetically because they missed Princess — or were jealous that she'd found a new home first. Then I left, heading first south, then west, on the freeways.

The address I had was on the main drag of East Thousand Oaks Boulevard. I parked in a lot at the side of the five-story building and just sat there.

Did I like confrontations? Not especially. But I could hold my own in one. And I was undeniably prepared for this one.

Look out, Mandy Ledinger.

She wasn't on the directory by the elevator, but I knew the number of the office where she worked. It was on the fourth floor. I felt full of energy and might have been better off using the stairs, but decided to store that dynamism inside me in case I needed it later.

Some of my adrenaline must have been obvious, since two people on the elevator with me kept hazarding glances in my direction, then looking away. Hopefully, they didn't recognize me from the news. They both got off before I did, leaving me alone once more. Thinking . . .

The door opened. I strode out and pulled open the door to the doctor's reception area. It appeared peaceful . . . for now.

A couple of women in colorful medical smocks sat behind the front desk. Neither resembled Efram. So what? Mandy was supposed to be his stepmother, not a blood relative.

As the nearest smiled at me, I glanced at her nametag. Not Ledinger. "Do you have an appointment?" she asked pleasantly.

I'd considered how to approach this on my way here and decided on a modified version of the truth. "No," I said, "I was a friend of Efram Kiley's. I heard that his stepmother, Mandy Ledinger, works here, and since I was in the area I thought I'd stop in to offer my condolences."

Another woman, similarly dressed, had just come into the enclosed reception area, her arms laden with files. She gasped, and the things she had been holding fell to the floor as if someone had kicked them, or her. One of the other people immediately stooped to pick them up.

The woman who'd dropped them looked old, maybe just in her sixties, but an air of defeat made her appear ready to accept the end of her life. Until she looked at me.

Suddenly, she turned into a shrieking harpy, the lines in her face exacerbated by the hurtling of rage-filled accusations in my direction. "You murdering bitch! Why did you kill my Efram?" She launched herself at me. Good thing the desk was in the way.

"Hello, Mandy." I kept my tone grave and quiet without suggesting confrontation, as hers did. "As I said, I'm here to offer condolences. But I also want to talk about Efram."

"Are you nuts?" demanded someone beside me. I looked over and saw that a younger woman with a baby in her arms, probably a patient, stared at me with amazement. "Get out of here before she gets any closer."

Too late. Mandy had catapulted herself

over the desk and reached for me. A sexagenarian? Septuagenarian? Couldn't tell it by her spryness.

I ducked, making sure that the lady and her kid were out of the way. "I didn't kill him!" I shouted. "I'm just trying to find out who did." Someone with a temper like hers? She had just earned her file on my computer. "I need your help. I'm sure you want the truth, too." Unless, of course, she was Efram's killer.

That seemed to get her attention. Or maybe it was the people, also in medical garb, who now held her arms. One wore a white jacket that suggested he was one of the doctors. Maybe she would listen to her employer and not maim me enough to require a physician's care.

"I saw you on the news!" she spat from between her teeth. She shrugged off the hands grasping her, and I readied myself for genuine self-defense — not the murderous kind I'd been accused of in Efram's death.

"I'm not surprised." I shook my head sadly. "But you must know how the media is. They sensationalize everything and make unsubstantiated accusations to lure more viewers. Not everything you see on TV is the truth."

Mandy continued glaring into my face.

"You didn't kill him?" She sounded doubtful, but her voice held a lot less passion than she'd hurtled before.

"No. Please, could we sit down and talk? Maybe we can help each other." Or not. She wouldn't consider it helpful if I discerned something that I could take to the police right away and make them lean on her instead of me.

She didn't appear thrilled, but she nevertheless motioned me toward an empty corner of the waiting room. The people who had restrained her didn't follow. We sat down perpendicularly to each other, our knees almost touching, which worried me. If she got upset again, she'd just have to thrust out her leg and trip me to keep me from escaping.

On the other hand, I could do the same to her. And if anything she said indicated she'd killed Efram and framed me, I'd be delighted to trip her up . . . in more ways than one.

"I can't talk long." She glanced at the watch on her bony wrist. Close-up, when she wasn't in the role of an insane harpy, she actually looked like a nice, nearly senior citizen. Her face was round, her chin pointed, and her hair an elflike cap. Her eyes were punctuated with a lot of lines running

214

from them toward her hairline. I had the impression they might even be laugh lines. When she wasn't thinking about Efram.

"I understand," I said, and proceeded to encourage her to talk about her stepson. She'd married Efram's divorced father about ten years earlier, and they were still together.

I wondered why Efram had included Mandy, not his dad, in his emergency contacts.

Efram had been a diligent son, helping out when his dad suffered a heart attack. Maybe Efram, too, had a heart after all, at least when it came to human beings who were his relatives. Or maybe his dad had changed his will when he remarried, and it was in Efram's financial interest to stay on Mandy's good side.

That was all speculation on my part, derived from how Efram had feigned niceness while sublimating his actually cruel nature, for money. No matter his rationale, Efram's caring had endeared him to Mandy.

"I saw him for the last time a couple of weeks ago," Mandy finished. "He had supper with us at our house. He talked often about helping out at your animal shelter. He really liked it."

I was sure it made better dinner conversation than his assisting in torturing dogs at the puppy mill.

"I was shocked when I heard he was dead." Her eyes teared up. "And his dad . . . I was afraid he'd have another heart attack. I couldn't believe that someone would murder such a sweetheart." She stopped talking and stared as if she was trying to look way deep into my soul to determine if it had, in fact, been me.

I wished I could read her insides the same way. But nothing she said made me certain she'd killed him . . . or that she hadn't. Things weren't really that perfect between them, were they?

"Did you know Efram's girlfriend, Shellie?" I asked gently.

"That bitch!" Mandy was suddenly on her feet once more. Fortunately, my legs weren't extended, so I didn't trip her, though I'd been taken by surprise by her action. "If you didn't kill Efram, I bet she did. You know what she wanted from him?"

"No, sorry, I don't." I hoped she'd tell me.

"Money. She wanted him to leave his job as an air-conditioning repairman and start his own company. Hire her to help. And how would he get the money to do that?"

I shrugged. "She'd lend it to him?"

"Hell, no. He'd started a campaign to get his dad, my husband, to lend it to him. Lend? Hell, he wanted a gift. If we had that kind of money, do you think I'd be working here?" Her eyes widened, as if she just heard what she'd said. She looked around. I didn't see anyone watching us, but that didn't mean they weren't listening. She must have thought so, too. "Of course I love my job. These people are great. But if I had a lot of money, I'd retire early and move to Arizona, to one of the really nice senior communities there. That would be so good for my dear husband — Efram Kiley Sr. He's still a little frail after his heart attack." Which might explain why he wasn't Efram's contact. "I didn't change my name when we got married."

"I see. And did Efram Jr. get what he wanted?" I assumed not, or he wouldn't have kept up the sham of "volunteering" at HotRescues to get Dante's stipend. Although, judging by his association with that horrible puppy mill, the guy might have been greedy enough to exploit all potential money sources at once.

"Not from us," Mandy said proudly. "And he didn't really push it. Efram was such a sweet boy. That Shellie was just a terrible influence on him."

We talked a little longer. I got the impression that Mandy wasn't an animal lover, that whatever abuse Efram might have committed on dogs or others wasn't of particular interest to her. If I'd been considering her as a friend — which I wasn't — that would have been a huge mark against her.

She'd helped me in my investigation, though, by verifying that I needed to talk to Efram's girlfriend Shellie.

I inquired as subtly as I could whether she'd ever visited HotRescues or knew anyone who did — mostly to see if Shellie or she had followed Efram into the locked facility the night he was murdered. She claimed she hadn't, and neither, to her knowledge, had Shellie.

Even so, with what Efram's stepmom had told me, I'd soon add not just one, but two new people to my suspect files.

CHAPTER 16

Back in my car, I inhaled deeply, ignoring the smell of eau de parking lot and trying to calm the synapses in my brain that flashed among relief and anger, indecision and determination. Guess I hadn't been as cool inside about the nasty and accusatory Mandy Ledinger as I'd pretended. Did she buy it? I'd no idea.

My BlackBerry rang. I pulled it from my pocket and saw the caller ID. "Hi, Carlie."

"Hey. I'm back in LA at last."

"You didn't warn me you were coming last time we talked."

"I wasn't sure. So what's going on?"

I'd want to hear all about her trip but, at this moment, had even more of a desire to vent to a friend.

"Nothing much. I just visited the loving stepmother of the guy murdered at HotRescues. She recognized me from the news and attacked, claiming I was his murderer. When she calmed down, I tried to get her to admit she killed her stepson. That's all."

"Just another boring day in LaLa Land." LA, of course. "So, is the strategy you mentioned working? Did she confess?" Carlie was never fazed by anything, no matter how bizarre. I suppose she had to be that way, as a veterinarian. Even more so, as the star of her own TV show.

"No, but she gave me a reason to check with Efram's girlfriend." I leaned back in the driver's seat. I'd a feeling this could be a lengthy conversation, and I didn't necessarily want to use my BlueTooth.

"You mean someone actually hooked up with that ruthless freak?"

"I haven't talked to her yet, but that's what I gathered."

"Eeew. What miserable taste that woman must have."

"My sentiments exactly," I agreed.

"So when will I be able to do a show around the puppy mill and Efram's death?"

"What does that ugly situation have to do with pet longevity?" I asked. That was the focus of her TV show.

"The puppy mill aspect, of course. I can get into how people who breed dogs over and over can kill not only the parents, but also subject resulting puppies to major health problems from the ugly conditions, inbreeding, and all. I've done shows warning people to check out puppies from pet shops carefully, since so many get the animals they sell from puppy mills or similar places for kittens."

I'd seen at least a couple of those shows. I'd been a fan of Carlie's since I met her and she adopted Max. "You'd focus on the potential health problems?" I asked.

"That's what I do, kid."

"Sure, but the puppy mill has been shut down. The owners are still around, but I doubt they'd talk to you since they were arrested for animal cruelty. And I haven't exonerated them in Efram's death."

"Have the police?"

"I sure hope not, but they seem to love me as their top suspect."

"With your involvement, I'd have an inside track on this story. Could turn my little show into —"

"A tabloid clone." Carlie was one of my best friends, but sometimes she went too far in her zeal to turn a great topical show on pet health to something with a bigger audience. Which meant more controversial subjects.

Like murder investigations? I hadn't seen that on *Pet Fitness* before, but there was always a first time.

"Hey, I'll do anything to call the public's attention to animal health problems and save lives. So, when can we get together for an interview that I can use on the air?"

"Not till they've arrested someone else for killing Efram."

"But maybe I can help."

And maybe I could figure out how to use her show, as I worked further on my organizational plan . . .

"I appreciate the offer, Carlie, but let me think about it."

"Which means no."

"It just means not yet. Are you pouting?" I asked.

"I deserve to," Carlie responded, then laughed.

It was past time to turn the conversation in a different direction. "So how are you doing?" I asked. "And tell me about the show you were just filming. You were gone nearly a month."

"Don't I know it? But I got some great stuff — mostly about products manufactured by an outfit in New York that specializes in items for disabled dogs."

"Things like ramps to help them get into bed?"

"Exactly. And wheels that can be attached

to hindquarters if the dog loses limbs or is paralyzed, harnesses to help them stand up, that kind of thing."

"I assume you knew about this equipment before."

"Sure. Vets get all kinds of promotional material from companies like this. But our professional focus is on preventing or curing diseases. This episode will be more about how to turn a bad situation into something more livable both for the pup and its owner."

"Sounds wonderful." Someday, I might need things like that for residents of HotRescues. We generally saved only healthy animals from high-kill shelters whose lives were threatened because of overcrowding of the other facilities. Once or twice, we'd rescued animals with minor disabilities — and in those instances, I'd taken them to Carlie to get them back on their feet, figuratively and literally.

I'd had to forgo saving other animals — a heartbreak — when not adoptable because of a more major disability. But maybe some could be rehabilitated with products that Carlie would feature.

"When will that show air?" I asked her.

"It'll be several episodes, starting next

month. We need to get together long before then."

We arranged to talk again soon to work out meeting for a drink or dinner. I said goodbye with a smile on my face.

Time flew by while I drove to HotRescues and mulled over the possibilities suggested by the contents of Carlie's upcoming shows.

I pulled into my space at HotRescues and entered the welcome area, smiling again at how kitty Princess had found a loving new home earlier that day. How I wished for a happy ending like that for all our charges — present and future.

"Hi, Lauren." Nina looked up from the computer. "Everything okay?"

"Fine." That was at least half true. "How about here?"

"It's been quiet. Ricki had to leave early to go to an orientation this evening at the school she's going to attend, so I'm out here for now."

I glanced at what Nina had on the computer as I passed on the way to my office. It appeared to be a local news site — which made me shudder.

"One good thing is that the furor about Efram's death seems to be dying somewhat — pun intended — at least for the moment." Nina was obviously aware that I was looking over her shoulder. "Till something breaks in the case, maybe. Another good thing is that HotRescues shows up even more on the Internet than before, in positive ways. I've Googled it, plus I have a Google Alert set to send me notices of when the HotRescues name appears online. Yours, too, by the way. There are a lot more mentions of HotRescues than there used to be before you got involved in the puppy mill rescue, and most don't mention Dante."

That was definitely a change. HotRescues was one of lots of private rescue organizations. What made it stand out was that Dante was its chief benefactor. For a guy who chose to stay out of the public eye, he was certainly in it a lot.

"Thanks for checking," I said. "Be sure to let me know if you see anything new that I should know about."

Nina nodded, and I patted her lightly on the shoulder as I headed into my office.

I stowed my purse inside a drawer. Then, making sure the door was closed and the blinds drawn, I quickly changed from the dressy clothes I'd worn for my in-your-face meetings into the casually official HotRescues outfit I always kept here.

I sat down and glanced at my old computer that enticed me with its dark screen. I could turn it on, or I could go outside and visit our inhabitants. Guess which won.

As I rose, though, my BlackBerry rang. I quickly sat again, yanked open the drawer and rummaged through my purse until I found my little high-tech companion. The number on caller ID was unfamiliar.

"Hello?" The word came out somewhat belligerently. "Lauren Vancouver?"

"Yes. Who's this?"

"My name is Shellie Benudo. Efram Kiley was my boyfriend."

The last sentence was redundant. I knew who she was.

"Oh, yes, Shellie. I'm very sorry for your loss." I kept my tone funereal and sympathetic. I actually did feel compassion for her, at least a little. I didn't know yet if she was aware of what kind of creep her guy had been.

My good attitude quickly disappeared, though, as if she'd wadded it up into a ball and kicked it into a seething mass of boiling tar when she responded. "Yeah, I bet you are, you bitch. If you gave a damn, you wouldn't have killed him."

I curled my hand that wasn't holding the phone into a tight fist. Yet again, I thought of the phrase about the best defense being a good offense. If she'd been in Efram's life,

226

she must have had some idea what a heartless jerk he was. Why not kill him and blame someone else? Like me.

I didn't accuse her, though, despite what she'd said to me. Instead, I kept my tone mild. "So you've been watching the news? Not true, of course, but interesting. I discovered Efram's body, that's all. He was trespassing, but I didn't even know he was around until I found him on the ground." *Did you come here with him?* I wanted to ask . . . but not yet.

She beat me to it. "I suppose you're going to ask if I killed him and then ran off. I know you've said that to his stepmom. Mandy called to cry on my shoulder."

Interesting. I apparently hadn't been as subtle as I'd hoped in my query about whether Mandy or Shellie had ever visited HotRescues. Plus, Mandy had said she hated Shellie. So why had she called her immediately?

I'd also not accused Shellie . . . yet. Apparently Mandy told her I had.

"You've even blamed Efram's lawyer," Shellie continued. "James Remseyer called, too, and warned me that you're out there making unfounded accusations."

So they'd both contacted Shellie. Were they all conspirators protecting one another

— and framing me?

I was allowed some degree of paranoia. I was, after all, an utterly innocent murder suspect.

How should I play the rest of this conversation to take control of it? I decided on honesty . . . somewhat. "What I'm trying to do, Shellie, is to find out what really happened. I'd like to meet with you, tomorrow or the next day. I'll tell you my side of things, you tell me yours. Neither of us will accuse the other. Maybe we can even become allies in finding out who killed Efram."

"But you hated him!" She shrieked into my ear, and I yanked the phone away. *Keep cool,* I told myself. Did I really expect her to become an ally? No. But I might learn something useful if we did chat somewhere, in neutral territory.

I took a slow breath to maintain my patience, then said, "I didn't like what Efram did to animals, Shellie. If you've watched the stuff on TV, you're aware that he was at that puppy mill. He may have told you about the disagreement he had with HotRescues and me, about his dog, Killer. Right?"

"You stole Killer." The accusation shot coldly in my direction.

"I helped to find the dog — his name is

Quincy now — a new home. I didn't know who his owner was when he was brought here, but he'd clearly been abused. If I'd found his owner then, I'd have turned him over to the authorities for prosecution, but things didn't work that way. Instead, Efram threatened to sue, and we worked out a compromise that was supposed to teach him how to treat animals better. Apparently, it didn't take."

"That's *your* story."

Too bad the young woman wasn't here so I could shake some sense into her. Or maybe it was just as well. If I laid a hand, or even a glare, on her, she'd scream to the world that I killed Efram.

But maybe I'd have a better sense of her innocence or guilt.

"Yes," I said, "it is. So — can we get together to sound each other out?"

"No," she said. The next thing I heard was a beep that told me she'd hung up.

I closed my eyes, willing myself to start breathing normally again. Tension had turned my respiration shallow, and I felt almost light-headed.

I also felt like I wanted to cry. Talking to three potential murder suspects who wanted me to take the rap for Efram's killing, all in one day?

I liked to think I was a calm, sane, rational person. Not prone to crying jags. But for this moment, I wanted to break down.

No. What I wanted was to find the truth. No matter what it took.

For now, I squared my shoulders. It was time, at last, to go see my beloved charges outside in the shelter area.

Nina was getting ready to leave for the day. "Are you going home?" she asked as I passed through the reception area.

"Soon," I told her.

"I had Ricki and some of the others working on the Princess adoption. Everything checked out."

"Great! I'll call tomorrow to get things finalized." Most of the time, adoptions we approved took days, or even weeks. Our last few had been surprisingly easy and fast, thanks to my current flock of diligent assistants. "Meantime, have a good evening."

"You, too." She studied me with her usual worried frown, and I made myself smile to counter it.

"Are you volunteering at a city shelter tonight?"

"Absolutely," she said.

A minute more, and I was outside. Some of the dogs were barking. Surprise!

I almost laughed as I greeted each by name, despite how choked up I felt. And then I realized what I truly needed. Hugs.

First, though, I headed into the center building and looked in on the cats and the rest of our animals. I didn't see Pete or any volunteers. They must be back in the shed, grabbing food — a good thing. I went back out, sneaked around the corner to one of the side paths, and opened Babydoll's enclosure. The shepherd mix stood on her hind legs, greeting me enthusiastically. I bent, braced myself, and threw my arms around her, basking in the doggy kisses she rained on my face.

I actually laughed. The first time that day, and maybe for many days before.

Jazzed, I gave her one final hug for that moment, then went out to engage in similar affection with a couple of the other dogs who'd been there awhile, including Honey, the Westie mix. Good for them, and especially good for me.

I took my time but eventually headed back toward the main building. Pete Engersoll caught up with me.

"All the animals have been fed," he said. "Our last volunteer of the day just left, too. Okay for me to leave?"

"Sure," I told him.

"You look happy," he accused.

"I am," I said. In case he doubted me, I gave him a big hug, too.

He looked startled but hugged me back. "You sure you're okay?"

"I'm great," I told him. For a murder suspect.

I watched him head toward the exit near the back shed, then returned to the main building. And was startled to hear a knocking on the opposite door, the one visitors entered through. My heart beat a heavy cadence as I approached. It couldn't be the killer. Whoever it was would hardly announce him — or her — self that way.

The cops? Was I about to be arrested?

"Who's there?" I called out, trying to sound confident and in charge.

I'd been right about one thing. The person outside was one of the authorities.

"It's Matt Kingston, Lauren. May I come in?"

CHAPTER 17

I half expected, after the day I'd had so far, that Matt had surged his way in this direction so he could brandish his official capacity at me, as an officer of Animal Services. He was wearing his official uniform, standing tall, his height declaring his authority. Maybe someone had dared to call in a complaint about how we treated our inhabitants.

Remembering the canine hugs I'd just participated in, I'd disagree loud and strong with any ridiculous assertion like that. I'd nearly convinced myself I didn't want to see Matt, and was marshaling reasons not to admit him, when he said, "I'm glad you're here, Lauren. I've been really looking forward to my tour of HotRescues. Is now a good time?"

I pondered the question. It actually was a good time. The animals had been fed, their enclosures cleaned one last time for the day, and it was past the time we allowed people to check the facility out for a new pet. All the staff had left, but I wouldn't need help showing Matt around.

Besides, he was one good contact to keep in my back pocket — the captain in charge of SmART, D.A.R.T., and more. He might help if I ever needed a good word at a city shelter to rescue animals on the brink of euthanasia.

He was also kind of cute. Of course, I was ready to kick myself for feeling any kind of attraction to him. Work with him, sure. Maybe even see him socially a little, if we got along — dinner, a drink now and then, like friends enjoying occasional camaraderie.

But I'd been married once to the only good guy out there and my awful second marriage had cured me of considering another serious relationship.

I opened the door, nearly laughing at myself for such an absurdly long and twisted reverie. "Come on in." It wasn't as if I was committing myself to anything but a tour of HotRescues. "I thought I'd get to visit the animals saved from the puppy mill before you came here."

"Friday's only two days from now." That was the day he'd already invited me to tour the facility where they were kept. "But I was in the area and figured I'd jump the gun a little and drop in here today. I didn't think it would matter . . . Does it?"

"No problem." But my adrenaline caused by the unexpected knock was still painting my insides with energy I'd no way to expend, and I tried to slow my breathing.

Matt's brown eyes were fixed on mine, appearing to study them. "Are you okay?" He didn't wait for my answer before entering. He walked into the welcome room and moved till he was behind me. "Nice place," he said. "I especially like that cat motif." He nodded toward the leopard-print counter. "Are all those real pictures of adoptions?" He pointed toward the photos on the wall.

"Every one of them. We've more pictures like that upstairs. And a whole lot more we haven't hung on the walls." I grinned, feeling my pride in HotRescues drape around me like the embrace of angel wings.

"My kind of place." Matt stopped looking from one photo to the next and turned to face me. The warmth in his toast-colored eyes engulfed me even more, and I took a step back.

"Just wait till you see the rest of it." I locked the door behind him, then motioned for him to follow. "If you like animals, you're about to receive a treat."

"If you've any doubts about my liking animals," he said drolly, "then I haven't been doing my job right when you've been around."

I laughed as I led him outside to the shelter area.

Of course the dogs all started barking. We reached Honey first, and she leaped at the bars. Did she remember our hugfest of a short while ago? I certainly did.

Matt reached in and gave her a scratch behind the ears. "How ya doing, Honey?" He wasn't psychic. The label on the outside of the enclosure gave a précis of the inhabitant's most crucial information. Even so, I felt a trickle of warmth inside. Matt obviously knew how to approach and speak to a lonesome pup.

My most recent walk through here had been just a short while ago, but I enjoyed it all over again as I gave Matt a tour, explaining our reason for each item of bedding, toys, and equipment in the enclosures as he gave each pup individual attention. I took him into the center building, showing him the cats, toy dogs, and the few hamsters and rabbits who were our residents at the moment. Some of the friendlier kitties responded to his soft talk to them, and to my surprise and delight a few of the more standoffish ones, too, drew close and let him pat them.

All the better for their future rehoming.

I took Matt upstairs in that building, where our rudimentary health office was — the room where our veterinary tech Angie Shayde hung out when on duty. It contained first-aid necessities as well as basic examination equipment. Si Rogan had a small office here, too. Plus, there was a room that feigned being a den, where potential adopters could experience what it felt like to be at home with the pet they were considering.

Back outside, I showed Matt the rear storage building by opening the door and letting him glance inside. Although it contained our laundry facilities, it certainly wasn't as interesting as the rest of the place. I also walked him through our park area where adopters could also have a one-on-one with their impending new pets.

"That's it," I told him. "You've pretty much seen it all."

"Great place!" he said, smiling down at me. His eyes glimmered, and I noticed even more than before that he had a five o'clock shadow. Definitely all male. And sexy.

Irrelevant to someone like me, with little interest in becoming interested.

So why, then, when he asked, "How about joining me for dinner?" did I say, "Sure. Why not?"

"What kind of dog do you have at home?" Matt asked.

We sat across from one another at a nice Mexican restaurant about a mile from HotRescues, also on Rinaldi Street. I'd ordered a taco and a chile relleno, and Matt worked on an outsized chicken burrito. The lights were dim, and the mariachi musicians were between sets.

"I don't have a dog," I said. "How about you?"

"I've got a black Lab mix. Rex. I wouldn't have figured you as a cat person . . . at least not only cats. No dog?"

"No," I said firmly. "No pets of my own at all right now." Fortifying myself with a long sip of a margarita, I told him about losing Bosley, the family Boston terrier. "I've got an entire shelter of pets. Why would I need one that I'd have to leave at home a lot of the time? Who could get sick without my even knowing about it."

"Is that what happened with Bosley?"

To my annoyance, I felt tears flood my eyes. I stared down at my food as if I needed to memorize it before eating, until I got my

238

emotions back under control.

"Pretty much," I said.

"How long ago?"

"A few months." I saw his hand dart across the table before I felt it grab mine. I looked up at him. "It still hurts, damn it."

"So why not adopt another one?"

"It still hurts, damn it," I repeated, and made myself aim a pathetic smile toward him. "Bosley was mostly my kids' dog anyway. He was ten years old, and we got him before HotRescues was even founded. He was cute and small and seemed overwhelmed when I brought him to HotRescues, so I didn't do it much. That meant he spent a lot of time by himself. I wouldn't want to do that to another dog."

"Understood. I sometimes bring Rex to work, although I have to leave him with other personnel when we're called out for a rescue. Maybe if you adopted a dog from HotRescues, he'd be used to the place and you could bring him in more."

"I've considered that." I hoped my tone was abrupt enough to convey that I wasn't an idiot. If I got another dog — which I didn't want to do, at least not now — it would definitely be a rescue dog, probably one whose life I helped to save.

"Any favorite breeds?"

We got into a discussion then about personalities of various kinds of dogs. I happened to love the looks of Border collies. Australian shepherds, too. I also liked the enthusiasm and intelligence of both breeds.

"So if you happened to rescue an Aussie-Border mix, that's when you'd consider adopting." There was no question in Matt's tone, as if he simply reiterated the conclusion I'd drawn.

"No," I said. "I'm not looking for another dog. Not now, and not anytime soon."

"I get it."

He was willing to change the subject, fortunately. I asked how he had decided to work for Animal Services, and how he'd become a captain overseeing the elite rescue organizations within the agency. "I was a Navy SEAL a while back," he said. "Great job, but I didn't want to do it forever. When my enlistment was up, I decided I needed a different kind of challenge. Sort of different, anyway." He'd gotten out and joined a police force in a small Southern California town, gravitating to the K-9 unit. Eventually, he'd heard of an opening in LA Animal Services. It seemed a good fit, and he'd joined, doing well enough to be promoted to get where he was now.

He described it all with some modesty. I

liked that.

When he turned the tables and asked how I'd come to run HotRescues, I told him briefly, without much description. "I always loved animals, even as a kid. Becoming a vet tech was perfect, at least for a while. But when I heard that Dante DeFrancisco was about to start his own animal shelter, I applied to become its administrator. Dante and I got along fine, and he hired me."

End of story? No, but it was all I told. He didn't need to know the really personal stuff, about how I'd grieved when my dear husband, Kerry, died. How I'd tried so hard to be a perfect single mother. How I'd thought it was in my own, and my kids', best interests for me to marry again.

How I'd hated myself for making such a terrible choice about who.

And how my divorce had been final just about the time Dante was looking for the HotRescues administrator, and I'd wanted the job enough to practically beg — but I hadn't had to. I made it clear to Dante how much I loved animals. How well I could run a business. How much I could contribute to the place. And how skilled I was at developing a workable business plan.

I'd finished eating. So had Matt. The server came over and asked if we wanted anything else.

Actually, I did. More time with Matt Kingston.

Which meant it was definitely time to leave.

I'd driven myself to the restaurant. I had told Matt I needed to stop to pick up coffee and soft drinks for the HotRescues people kitchen, and there was no need for him to waste time shopping with me.

Even so, when he walked me to my car, he asked if he could follow me. Make sure everything was okay at HotRescues when I got back.

His concern made me feel a bit warm and fuzzy inside, but I assured him that the security company was much more alert these days.

The fuzziness apparently mushed my brain, since I didn't back off when he leaned toward me.

He clearly wanted to kiss me. My instinct was to turn and open the car door and leap inside.

My libido won out over my instinct.

The kiss was a good one, as spicy as the food we'd just eaten. But I knew I shouldn't read anything into it. We'd had an enjoyable meal together. This was the extent of dessert.

"Thanks for dinner," I told him, trying to swallow my breathlessness.

"You're welcome. You know, I'd feel a lot better if I accompanied you back to HotRescues."

I'd thought we had resolved that. "Very gentlemanly of you, but unnecessary. Thanks again." And then, not wisely at all, I planted one more brief kiss on his mouth and hurried into my car.

I didn't want to overthink that dinner with Matt, or either of those kisses. But I hadn't been lying to him. I stopped to pick up supplies at the local supermarket on my way home. Choosing the same old coffee and sodas didn't fill my brain with a plethora of important decisions, so I found myself rehashing all the things I'd directed myself not to angst over.

I gained no further insights — surprise.

A while later, I finally pulled into the HotRescues parking lot. I yanked the recyclable grocery bags and my purse from the floor and got out of my car. I glanced around. No sign of the security patrol. But even if they were doing their job right, that didn't mean they'd be here at every moment.

I walked up to the entry gate and performed the magic that got me inside without tripping the security system. Inside the welcoming room, I stopped before going to the kitchen. A few dogs were barking outside, in the shelter area. Just a sociable conversation, not the loud warning to each other and any nearby humans of an intruder stalking the area. Or maybe someone had heard me come in and was telling the others, without making a huge fuss about it.

I should have felt pleased. There was nothing unusual about that kind of exchange.

Instead, a feeling of disquiet tingled over every inch of my skin. Why? I had no idea. Maybe it was just a continued reaction to my having found Efram's body a few nights back. Or leftover uneasiness from the conversations I'd had that day with people I considered to be real, live suspects in his murder.

As I've said before, I'm not into woo-woo kinds of experiences. If I felt anxious, there was a reason for it, even if I couldn't explain it to myself. The dogs' voices, some sound only my subconscious had heard, who knew? But I wasn't about to ignore it.

I dropped the grocery bags on the table and headed for the shelter area.

It was past dusk, so the low security lights

were the only illumination. Hearing me, the dogs started to bark louder. "Hi, guys," I said, doubting that my voice was audible to them over their own cacophony. "What's happened here since I've been gone? No one else on two legs has been around, right?"

They didn't quiet down, nor did they answer in a manner I could interpret.

But as I began to walk down the path, I realized immediately that something was very wrong.

Even if a staff member had returned, no one would have adopted out a dog in the amount of time it had taken me to have dinner. No one would have adopted out a dog at all without getting my approval.

So why was Honey missing from the very first enclosure?

CHAPTER 18

My heart slammed on the brakes before restarting and accelerating beyond its usual cadence. Where was she?

"Honey?" I yelled, barely hearing myself among the clamor from the dogs who hadn't disappeared.

I considered calling 911. But what would I say? I looked around, seeing no evidence of any intrusion, dognapping, or other illegal activity.

Only a missing pup.

I dashed down the path, looking for her. How had she gotten out? Had I done it? I'd snuggled Honey in my arms earlier that day. Later, Matt and I had come by and said hello. Had the gate been unlocked then? Had we somehow knocked it loose? Had someone else left it open? No matter how it had happened, I should have noticed. By not doing so, I might have carelessly endangered Honey's life, potentially as much as if

I hadn't swooped her out of one of the high-kill shelters at the last minute. She'd apparently slipped out of her kennel, and could even have gotten away from HotRescues altogether.

I was always so careful, obsessively so — or that's what I'd always thought. But now, I seemed to be losing it. Stress was no excuse.

But no sense browbeating myself now. I could do it later just as well. At this moment, I would devote all my thoughts, all my actions, to finding her.

But was I observant enough to do it alone?

Hey, someone should have been observing. I pulled my BlackBerry from my pocket, my hand quivering. I called the security company. "A dog disappeared?" The dispatcher sounded incredulous. "Just a moment."

"Ms. Vancouver!" This was a different male voice. "I've been monitoring your facility from the cameras. I didn't see anything . . . Oh, yes. Is that you on the path, there?"

"That's right. Look, I have to find the missing dog. Call me if you see anything helpful in the pictures." I hung up.

I considered phoning Nina for help. She was volunteering at a shelter tonight. Should

I interrupt her?

Better yet, Matt. He might not be too far away. It had been less than an hour since we were together at the restaurant.

Or . . . Heck, I was the head administrator, and I was right here. I had to shrug off all the emotions that were paralyzing me, including the self-blame pouring over me like boiling wax.

I would look for Honey myself.

"Honey, come," I wanted to shout to her. I was used to giving commands around here that were obeyed.

As if she'd listen to me now.

"Okay, guys," I said to the other dogs, keeping my concern leashed inside. Most were finally quieting down. "Did you see where Honey went? Give me a clue."

Some had seen Efram die here, sliced by a knife, and none had disclosed who did it. They were just as unlikely to rat on their buddy, Honey, who had escaped her cage as most of them probably longed to do.

Rounding corners, I continued to walk the paths outside the enclosures, staring into each in case Honey had somehow burrowed her way into someone else's domain. A couple of the dogs stuck their noses through the chain-link fence enclosing them as if in support of what I was doing.

I checked the gates and other exits from the shelter area. They all seemed secure. Honey couldn't have opened them — not herself.

But if I hadn't simply been careless, some human could still have entered the way Efram had the other night — he and his killer. The security system had been set then, too, and the security company had supposedly been on duty, although maybe not as diligently as now. The cause was irrelevant at this moment. I'd figure it out later, when Honey was safe.

Shouldn't they have noticed Honey's escape on pictures from the nearest camera? It would have been the same one that Efram had covered, but when I checked I saw nothing obstructing it now. I'd been farther down the path before, though, when I'd talked to the guy at EverySecurity, so he'd seen me on a different camera.

I walked around the entire maze of dog enclosures, still calling Honey's name. As I proceeded, the dogs I passed urged me on with their loud voices, but I still didn't find the missing pup.

I searched through the center building, both upstairs and down. If she was there, she did a superb job of evading me.

I'd seen no sign of her in the administration building, although I hadn't exactly looked for her there. But instead of retracing my steps, I decided to go somewhere I hadn't been that night: the storage building at the rear of the property. If I were a dog who'd escaped my cage, I might sniff the air, determine where my food was kept, and hurry there.

I unlatched the door and pushed it open — one indication that Honey couldn't be there. I doubted she could climb in a window, and they were kept closed anyway. But Honey wasn't a large dog. Perhaps she'd found some other means of entry that a human wouldn't think of.

I flipped on the ground-floor lights and peered into the laundry room. "Honey?" I called, not expecting to hear anything . . . but a muffled bark responded.

"Honey!" I shouted. "Where are you?"

Another bark. It sounded far away, but I was sure it originated somewhere in this narrow, two-story structure. I crossed the entire first floor, passing ladders, pooper scoopers, and other gear, including equipment sometimes used to modify the sizes of the enclosures. Not to mention the large metal toolbox that the cops had examined and left here. The one filled with the knives we use to slice open food bags — like the one used to slice open Efram.

No Honey.

Beyond the hardware area was where we stored the largest bags of food. I didn't find Honey there, either, but she started barking more forcefully. From upstairs.

I climbed the stairway as fast as if I used it for exercise, hurtling my way to the second floor.

"Honey, where are you?" I yelled again, flipping on the lights here, too. I was gratified to hear more woofing from the end of the storeroom farthest from the stairway. "Keep talking," I shouted. She did.

There she was, at last, way down at the end of the room. But how had she gotten trapped there, among piles of various sizes of dog and cat food bags? It almost looked as if someone had built her a prison cell. The stacks behind her were as tall as me. Those nearer the aisle, although piled lower, were unscalable by a dog her size.

"There you are, sweetheart," I crooned, moving some of the bags away from the front.

Only then did I notice the leash attached to her collar. The tether disappeared into the food stack against the wall.

My concern began shifting to ire. Someone had brought her here, trapped her.

Maybe endangered her life, if all those bags became unsteady as she pulled on the leash.

I finally got a row of bags in front out of the way and was about to unhook the leash from her collar. She started to yank her way toward me, though. "Sit!" I commanded, unsure whether she knew even rudimentary commands. Even if she did, she was too excited.

As she pulled toward me even more, I heard the rustling above me — just as the pile of food toward the back began falling. Followed by another. An avalanche.

Only then did I notice that one of the largest bags from downstairs was right on top — and it catapulted downward, toward my head.

That's when I saw the knife.

CHAPTER 19

Honey leaped at me from the other direction, all excited, as if she thought we were playing a game of doggy tag. I tried to block her with my body. Getting buried by large packages of dry dog food — what were the big ones doing on top of that unstable pile? — would probably hurt like hell as they fell on me, but they could kill her. Not to mention if that damned knife plunged into her. Sticking out ominously, the knife was one of the largest we had. It appeared to be attached to one of the bags in a way that would hurtle it, treacherous point first, toward whoever was in the bag's path as gravity and momentum catapulted it downward.

I grabbed Honey and attempted to run, but I tripped on some of the bags that circled us on the floor. I sprawled out, careful to release Honey so I wouldn't squash her.

The graceful maneuver didn't get me out of the knife's path. As the bag of food whomped me, I felt the blade slice my calf, through my pants, as easily as if I was a cake and this was someone's birthday.

"Ow!" I screamed.

"Ms. Vancouver, where are you?" yelled a voice from downstairs, startling me even more. I bit back further noise, inhaling my pain. Was it someone from EverySecurity, checking in since I'd called? Or was whoever did this still here, ready to finish what he'd started?

I lay still, my leg shrieking and my mind reeling. How could I protect myself and Honey?

Honey? Now where was she? I'd released her as I'd fallen, and now I didn't see her.

I didn't dare call her and give my location away until I knew who the person downstairs was. But the person who'd done this obviously didn't care about hurting a dog. Maybe that was even a major part of his plan — kill a dog and a human, and enjoy every moment of doing both.

I heard barking from the opposite end of the warehouse — still upstairs, I thought. Which meant Honey was still alive.

It also meant the excited little pup was

divulging to the intruder where we both were.

I was in no position to sneak toward her and muzzle her. I was in no position to do much of anything . . . except maneuver my aching body in a circle, trying hard not to move my leg too much. Trying even harder to ignore the small, but growing, puddle of blood that looked so much like an expanding red ameba from a horror movie, ready to morph into something even more dangerous.

I heard footsteps growing closer. My back was now aimed in that direction, and I curled up even tighter, trying to protect myself.

"Ms. Vancouver, are you all right?" demanded an unfamiliar voice.

I lunged to my feet, ignoring the pain . . . and holding the knife that had sliced me as my own weapon of self-defense. I'd fortunately been able to wrest it from the food bag.

Fortunately, despite my haziness and fear, I only wielded the thing as a means of protection without having to use it.

The person who stood there was Ed Bransom, the guy from EverySecurity company.

Sure, he could have been the fiend who'd done all this. The security force had better access to HotRescues than anyone else but my staff and me. But I didn't think so.

In case I was wrong, I kept the knife aimed at him until I heard a lot of noise from downstairs. "Up here!" I shouted, and it was only another minute before some other guys in security uniforms appeared.

And Matt.

"Are you all right, Lauren?" he demanded. One of the security men had him by the arm, but he wrested it free.

"I will be." I turned and placed the knife on a remaining stack of dog food bags. "I wish I hadn't had to touch this, though. It might have been a helpful way of determining who set this up, although I'd be surprised if he left fingerprints on it. That would violate TV Cop Show 101."

"You're bleeding," Matt said unnecessarily, but he was looking at my stabbed leg.

So was I. "No kidding." Leaning down, I unpeeled the dissected fabric from my skin. Bright red wasn't my favorite color, and I scowled at its abundance right around the wound. Fortunately, the cut didn't look very long or deep. I'd live. I turned back to Matt. "What are you doing here?"

"Exactly what we asked," said the security guy who'd previously had Matt's arm. His nametag said he was Clifton.

"I got a call." Matt's tone was oddly expressionless for a guy who'd seemed so interesting and interested only an hour or so previously. "Did you try to reach me? It came from the HotRescues number, but when I answered no one was there."

"It wasn't me," I said.

"Sure you got a call from here," Clifton said at the same time. Was that sarcasm? What did he mean?

Matt glared at him, then turned back to me. "Why don't you sit down?" This time, he sounded as alive as when I'd eaten dinner with him.

He rearranged some of the pet food bags into a seat, then helped me onto it. Not exactly a soft, upholstered chair, but at least it kept me from keeling over where I'd stood. I suddenly felt woozy. From loss of blood or stress? Most likely, a combo.

I remained aware enough, though, to discern the unspoken battle raging between Matt and the people supposedly here to protect HotRescues.

Where had they been before? If the only problem had been Honey getting loose on the grounds, I couldn't hold them entirely responsible — although I still wanted to know why they hadn't seen anything on any security camera, assuming that was true.

Someone had been around and set this thing up. EverySecurity had been hired to protect HotRescues' grounds, as well as our residents. They'd failed. Again.

I'd fire their butts right out of here, but not immediately. I needed their cooperation in looking into who'd done this.

Besides, I'd need Dante's okay. He was the one who'd hired them.

"Did the HotRescues silent alarm go off before?"

"You're sure it was set?" Clifton countered, which gave me the answer. It hadn't. So who had turned it off?

Or had I forgotten to set it? Surely I hadn't.

Of course, Efram could have shown his killer how to turn it off.

"Did you or any of your guys see someone sneak onto the HotRescues grounds while I was out?" I asked him next. Maybe someone on patrol would have picked up what the cameras apparently didn't.

"No way," he said.

"We'd have grabbed 'em," seconded Ed. "This guy, though." He nodded toward Matt. "He was lurking around outside. I saw him as I drove by on patrol. That's why I stopped and radioed for backup, then I got a call that you'd phoned the office. I didn't like this guy's story, so I left him with my men, came through the fence, then heard you."

"I see." I looked at Matt. I didn't ask why he'd been there. He'd already claimed he'd gotten a call from the HotRescues number.

Claimed? The security guys didn't believe him, and I realized I considered what he said rather far-fetched, too. I'd been the only human here. I hadn't called him.

The only explanation I could think of that might corroborate his story was that the perpetrator had hung around after setting his trap and called Matt.

Possible? Sure. Probable? Not really. Why would the sadist imperil himself by hanging around that long?

While I was musing about this odd scenario, and hurting all over, the cops and EMTs arrived.

Despite the late hour, I made the EMTs wait to examine me until I called Nina and told her what happened, asked her to come to HotRescues and keep an eye on things — particularly Honey. The little Westie mix stayed near me now, mostly because I held on to her leash once I got the security folks to bring her to me again. She seemed fine, if a little excited. But I also told Nina to call my friend Carlie if Honey seemed at all hurt. Carlie's veterinary skills were unrivaled, and she was back in town. Besides, I always used her animal hospital if any of our HotRescues animals needed medical attention, even if she wasn't there to do the work.

Then I had to contend with the medics. I told them I was fine. Just needed bandaging, plus some low-dose painkiller. Antibiotics? I'd use an over-the-counter antiseptic salve on the wound. We even had most of that in our first-aid cabinet here at HotRescues, for situations where our personnel scraped their arms or got nipped. That would be good enough.

But they dug in their white-soled shoes and insisted that I needed to see a real doctor, at a real medical facility, right away. I'd already done all the fighting that night for which I could muster any energy, so my arguments sounded lame even to me.

I felt tearful as I shambled like a creature in a monster film while returning Honey to her kennel. "Someone will be here to keep you company soon," I promised, and gave her another hug before securing the gate — and checking it again.

Then I let the EMTs have their way with me, shuttering me into the back of their emergency vehicle. At least they didn't blast the siren.

I'd half hoped that Matt would come along, a shoulder for me to lean on while I kept weight off my leg. But since I first rode in an ambulance, then in a wheelchair, I didn't genuinely need that kind of support. Just support of the moral kind . . . and I wasn't sure Matt could provide any just then. He was still being questioned when I left HotRescues.

Once I arrived at the hospital, the wait in the emergency room seemed interminable. Even worse, I spent most of the rest of that night similarly to one I'd endured nearly a week before — undergoing another heartless interrogation by Detective Stefan Garciana, who found me there.

He insisted on shooing me into a corner to talk while I waited. My injuries weren't life threatening. My irritable mood was — to Garciana's life, not mine.

"I thought you were a homicide detective," I hissed at him at one point, keeping my claws sheathed. I sat tensely in an uncomfortable hospital waiting room chair, glaring and trying to ignore the buzz of activity in the vicinity. A lot of people must have gotten sick or injured that day. "No one was killed."

"I just figured this situation could be related to the homicide I'm still investigating," he said mildly. "The one that also occurred at HotRescues." As if he needed to remind me.

Despite the late hour, the guy looked wide awake. His dark eyebrows were raised, as if he gave a damn what I said to him. His black, wavy hair looked recently combed, and he again — still? — wore a formal-looking suit. The epitome of a police detective. Not that I wanted to know the best characteristics of a quintessential interrogator.

"So, tell me what happened."

I did so briefly, without mentioning that I'd dined earlier with Matt or that he'd shown up at HotRescues, apparently during the time I'd been frantically searching for Honey.

He knew about the latter, though. "And you'd called Matt Kingston from Animal Services to help?"

I could have said yes to protect Matt. But he worked for a government agency involved with law enforcement, too. He should be perfectly able to take care of himself.

Besides, the seeds of doubt had started inching their roots into my thoughts. I'd no theory why Matt would have set up Honey and me that way. I didn't genuinely believe he'd done it. But the facts were that he'd been around HotRescues, and he'd claimed it was because of a phone call that only I had been in a position to make — and I hadn't done it.

I felt trapped in a living conundrum.

Presumably Matt had caller ID on his cell and could see that the number had been HotRescues'. His phone records would confirm it — or not.

If he'd received that call, and not from me, then maybe whoever set the trap had wanted to send a message. Frame Matt. Make things even more confusing.

My thoughts were definitely engaged in unrelenting somersaults. But I didn't tell the detective any of that.

What I did tell him was the bare-bones truth. I'd left HotRescues for a while. When I came back, one of our residents, Honey, was missing, and I'd looked for her. When I'd found her, she had seemed like the bait in a trap set by an unknown perpetrator for an unknown reason.

He didn't ask if I'd been interrogating people from my own suspect files that day. I didn't volunteer it, either. But that was the only thing I could think of that would cause anyone — one of those very suspects — to try to hurt me, possibly warn me from conducting another day like this one.

Maybe they'd succeeded.

But how had whoever it was avoided the security patrols and camera? If it was Matt, he hadn't eluded both, since the security patrol had captured him. But apparently neither he, nor anyone else, had shown up on the camera.

How would I deal with this in my organized computer files? Add a file on Matt? Yes. But would this help me identify the killer?

At the moment, I'd no idea.

I, therefore, asked Garciana a question of my own. "Do you really think this was connected with Efram Kiley's murder, Detective?"

"We can't rule it out," he said grimly.

Neither could I.

Then I really pushed the envelope. "If so, that should at least convince you I wasn't the killer," I said, looking right into the detective's cool brown eyes.

"Maybe," he said. "Unless you did this all yourself to try to throw suspicion somewhere else."

I felt almost as if that damned knife was stabbing me all over again. Maybe, this time, in my gut. "I didn't!" I exclaimed.

"That's what I intend to find out," he responded.

So I wasn't off the hook — or knife blade — yet.

CHAPTER 20

I was fine. I was released from the ER.

I was ready to get back to HotRescues.

But I had no transportation, and it was too far to walk, even if my leg hadn't been aching.

Detective Garciana was long gone by then, which was a good thing. I was so glad not to be in his presence anymore that I wouldn't have asked him for a ride even if he offered to chauffeur me in a posh limousine.

Not that I aspired to posh limousines.

Nina might still be at HotRescues. Even if it hadn't been so late — around midnight — I wouldn't have called to lure her away from there, even for a short while.

Carlie was a definite maybe. As a veterinarian and TV personality, she kept odd hours anyway. But my curiosity led me to try someone else first: Matt.

Was he still with the cops?

And was my mind still twisting like a whirlwind in fog for even considering suggesting that he come and get me, putting me alone in his presence? He was a suspect in the trap set for Honey and me. I couldn't completely exonerate him, despite how remote I thought the possibility of his guilt.

The thing was, I liked him. Wanted to talk to him, hopefully to minimize my own suspicions about him.

But even if he was guilty, I doubted he'd do anything to follow up right now, while he was in the cops' radar — at least for that night's attack on Honey and me.

Standing outside, on the curved sidewalk beside the ambulance driveway, I called him. He answered on the first ring — a good sign that he wasn't, at that moment, undergoing a tough interrogation.

"Where are you, Lauren?" he demanded. "*How* are you? Is your leg all right? The rest of you?"

My smile, which I was glad he couldn't see, was full of irony. He cared . . . or did he? "I'm okay, but I'd be a lot better if I were at HotRescues right now."

"Then, where are you? Can I pick you up?"

"I thought you'd never ask."

He got there in about twenty minutes.

Meantime, I sat outside the emergency room on a bench in an intense glow that suggested people's ill health could be cured if they were greeted by brilliant artificial lights. I'd done what I could, before coming out here, to wash some of the blood off my slacks. They were deep blue in color anyway, so the stain wasn't as obvious as it would be if I'd worn something lighter. But I'd temporarily repaired the slit with the only mending material readily available at the hospital: white surgical tape. It wasn't exactly invisible.

Matt pulled his Animal Services vehicle up to the curb. I stood and hobbled toward him. He leaped out and helped me to the car. All gentleman . . . maybe.

Once I was settled in, he got back into the driver's seat. "I'll take you home so you can rest," he said, his eyes moving from my face downward.

I figured I looked as bad as I felt. Good thing I wasn't trying to impress him. "HotRescues, please," I contradicted.

"But —"

My steady, challenging glare must have told him I'd argue with him, no matter how bad I felt. "Okay. HotRescues."

He pulled slowly from the hospital, driving as if he feared that any jostling would catapult me into greater pain.

"I'm fine, Matt," I told him, as if he'd asked again.

"You don't look it," he muttered.

I laughed. "Are you trying to make me feel better?"

His turn to laugh. The tense atmosphere melted, replaced by the warmth of a late spring night in Los Angeles.

But congeniality wasn't exactly on my agenda. "What did the cops ask you?" I said casually.

We were stopped at a light, and he peered at me with suspicion, as if I'd made an official complaint against him. "They seemed to think I set the whole thing up at HotRescues, and that I even called my own cell from there so it would look like someone else was there, framing me."

"I don't suppose there's any truth to that."

"Lauren, why the hell are you with me now if you think I could possibly have done that?"

The light changed, and he accelerated slowly, not looking at me.

"I don't. But I'd like you to tell me you didn't."

He was silent for a long time. I didn't think it was an admission of guilt, but I squirmed a little nevertheless.

"I didn't do it," he finally asserted. "Satisfied?"

"Yes," I said firmly, unsure whether I was fibbing. "No need ever to mention it again. So, I really appreciate your coming to pick me up. My leg is sore but it's bandaged, I'm a little bruised, and I have painkillers. No need to mention that again, either. Nina is waiting at HotRescues. I asked her to make sure that Honey is okay. You can just drop me off there. I won't be alone."

We'd turned onto Rinaldi and were only about a minute away.

"I want to go home and get some sleep," he said. "But don't argue with me when I say I'm walking in with you."

I didn't.

I was both delighted and scared when I saw Carlie there waiting with Nina, both sitting at the visitors' table in the welcoming area. "Is Honey all right?" I asked immediately. Why would a vet be there at that hour except to take care of an injured animal?

"She's fine," Carlie assured me, rising. "I was waiting for you." She eyed Matt, and I introduced them.

I hadn't seen my closest friend for a while. She looked as attractive in her jeans and "Pet Fitness Forever" T-shirt as if she was ready to be filmed for a show. Carlie was about my age, wore her highlighted blond hair shoulder length, and looked as youthful with her softly chiseled features and bright violet eyes as if she'd had plastic surgery — which she hadn't.

"You're on that animal health show on LVC, aren't you?" Matt asked.

They chatted for a minute as I sidled toward Nina. "Everything okay?" I asked.

"I hope so," she replied. My second in command looked pale and even more drawn than usual. "I was really frightened when you called, both for you and for Honey. I called Carlie when I got here, just to be sure. She says Honey's fine. Are you?"

"Definitely."

Matt and Carlie ended their discussion and looked across the table at Nina and me.

"Looks like you're in good hands," Matt said. I noticed then, in the inside lights, that he appeared as exhausted as I felt. It harshened his features, made him appear more masculine, and maybe more handsome.

I should have been too tired to notice.

"I sure am," I told him.

"Good. I'm leaving." He approached, took me into his arms with all other eyes in the room on us, and gave me a kiss. A brief one, to be sure. But it felt like more than a pleasant contact between friends. "Let's talk tomorrow." He said goodbye to the others, then left.

"So why didn't you tell me about him?" Carlie demanded, motioning for me to sit down. She joined me at the table.

"Is it okay for me to leave now?" Nina asked from behind the counter.

"Sure. One question first, though."

She slung her purse over her shoulder and looked down at me. "What?"

"Were there any animals that you learned are scheduled for euthanasia first thing tomorrow when you were at the East Valley Care Center this evening, before you came here? Any we can rescue?"

"Oh. Well, I wound up not going tonight."

She hadn't mentioned that before. "Everything okay?" I asked.

"Sure. I just . . . I mean, I checked and they had enough other volunteers tonight, so I went home."

I didn't know where the thought came from, but I realized that Nina could easily have sneaked onto the HotRescues property and put Honey into the storage building under those awful circumstances. She'd have no trouble lifting those bags, attaching the knife. She might have known I'd been

272

with Matt and could have called him. Set him up.

I'd demanded answers from him, but I was too tired to get into it with her.

Besides, I had no idea what her motivation could have been.

Throwing her onto the pile of suspects had to be an offshoot of all the insecurity floating in my brain. A result of painkillers gone awry. Whatever. But when I wasn't so tired, I just might type up a page on her for my Efram files.

"Thanks for checking on Honey and everything," was all I said.

She bent and gave me a quick hug, then left.

"So you're really okay?" Carlie eyed me critically, as only Carlie could do, with her veterinarian's appraising glare.

"More or less." I could be honest with her.

"I've checked on Honey more than once and taken a peek at the rest of the animals," she told me. "Everyone appears fine. Time for you to go home and get some sleep."

"I agree."

"You up for lunch tomorrow? I want to interrogate you about this whole situation."

"You and the cops," I said with a doleful shake of my head.

Carlie reached across the table, rested her

hand on mine. "Number one: no matter how miserable that Efram slimeball was, I know you didn't hurt him. Number two: whoever did kill him probably is now out to hurt you; hence the incident tonight. Number three: you're too tired now to be coherent, but tomorrow we'll discuss your plan of attack to make sure whoever is doing this is caught."

"Number four," I said, smiling faintly. "You're a hell of a good friend."

I allowed myself to sleep in a bit the next morning.

When I woke, I ached all over. First thing, I called HotRescues and learned that Nina wasn't there yet, either, but Ricki, the volunteer who answered the phone, assured me that everything was fine. "Pete Engersol came in early as always. He and I are holding down the fort."

As long as the fort included the entirety of HotRescues, that was great. I dressed quickly, ate a quick bowl of cereal so I wouldn't take my painkillers on an empty stomach, and hurried there.

I did my first walk-through right away. Honey was right where she belonged, cute as always, and I entered her kennel to give her a hug.

"I'm going to concentrate on finding you a new home," I assured her. "I doubt anything else bad will happen to you here, but you deserve someone who'll pamper you all the time."

The possibility of taking her home myself darted through me. But I wasn't the right person for her . . . even if she'd been the right dog for me. Which she wasn't.

I contacted EverySecurity. Spoke with Ed Bransom, who'd come in early, too, despite his late night. He said they still didn't know who had gotten into HotRescues last night but were looking into it, checking out the camera feeds, et cetera.

Of course they were. We paid for services that I'd considered adequate . . . before. Now, they had to prove they weren't completely useless — and I suspected that would be as impossible as ensuring that every abandoned pet in the LA area had a loving home by tomorrow.

But even if I wanted to fire them, I would need Dante's okay. He was good buddies with their CEO at their corporate headquarters in Chicago.

Next, I thought about calling Matt. Instead, I phoned Carlie and arranged to meet her for lunch at a restaurant specializing in pies, located halfway between her veterinary clinic and HotRescues. I wasn't after dessert, just a salad. Same went for her.

We both arrived on time. "So," she said after a server had taken our order, "you're doing better today, right?" She gave me a critical once-over again. She was dressed pretty much as she'd been last night — casually. I knew she wore a white veterinary jacket while seeing patients and also, often, on her show. Right now, she was off duty. But that didn't mean she was off my case.

"Well enough." I knew better than to try to convince her everything was perfect. Besides, the knife wound still hurt.

"Then tell me everything — but keep it brief and to the point."

I did, describing the rescue from the puppy mill, my reason for being there, how much I'd wanted to strangle Efram . . . and how I'd found him at HotRescues without harming him myself. "There's a homicide detective who seems to think otherwise, though." I sighed.

"You're not just letting life batter you around that way, are you?" She looked at me shrewdly. We'd learned a lot about each other in the six years since she'd been the first adopter of a pet from HotRescues and we'd become friends.

"Not hardly." I told her even more succinctly about the unofficial investigation I was conducting on my own behalf.

"That's my girl!" she exclaimed. "I'll want to see those organizational charts and files one of these days, in case I can give you any helpful ideas."

"We'll see," I said as our lunch was finally served.

Carlie was definitely insightful, and her input might be helpful.

Though I always preferred taking care of things myself, I wasn't above seeking assistance when I needed it.

And in this situation, I definitely needed it.

CHAPTER 21

I returned to my office. Discussing the whole mess with Carlie had inspired me to leap right in and update my written plan to unearth the killer. I sat down at the computer and began creating the new electronic files I'd been considering, including one for Matt.

I also started a separate new file for last night's incident. I tried to analyze what had happened — and what the perpetrator's motive could be.

My initial guess? I must have spoken with whoever it was since Efram's murder — a thought that both made me shudder and cheer inside. All I had to do was figure out who it was — out of my ample list of suspects.

That person might now believe that I knew he or she was the killer and that it was just a matter of time until I proved it.

As a result, that person tried to thwart me

by harming me in multiple ways.

First, potentially hurting one of my pet charges at my sanctuary. Which especially riled me.

Second, hurting me. I could live with that . . . as long as it eventually led to answers.

Third, setting things up to appear as if I had created the whole scenario myself, as if in an attempt to get the cops to focus their suspicions on someone other than me — and also making it look as if I'd botched it. That would only make the cops more certain I'd murdered Efram.

The whole thing made me furious. Sure, it was complicated — which made it all the more likely that the cops would buy into the ludicrous plot and continue to suspect me. How else could last night's fiasco have happened, especially with our security company on high alert? Once more, I'd been the only one around that they knew of, thanks to their ineptitude. Except, maybe, for Matt.

A knock sounded on my door. Before I could drag my eyes from my computer screen and respond, Nina popped in.

"Hi, Lauren," she said. "How are you doing today?"

I took a deep, calming breath before

responding. No need to confront Nina with my anger . . . or concern. "I'm okay. My leg's healing well — hardly hurts at all. So — how are you doing?" Like, why did you come in so late this morning?

I didn't ask, though. She was probably exhausted, too, after last night.

When I glanced her way, Nina looked as miserable as if she was one of the dogs sometimes brought in off the street: abused-looking and forlorn. The ones we particularly hated to turn over to a city shelter in compliance with the terms of our operating permit. Dogs like the one Efram had claimed to own . . .

"Everything okay?" I repeated.

"Sure." She lifted the edges of her lips as if she were a marionette with a sad clown's face, being controlled by a puppeteer. "What are you up to?" She walked in and looked over my shoulder at the computer.

I didn't try to minimize the screen. She was a lot more tech-proficient than me. Maybe she could help. "I'm working on my plans to figure out what happened to Efram," I told her. "What happened here last night has to be connected. I'm trying to analyze everything I can about all possible suspects. If you have any other ideas, let me know."

I prepared to show her exactly what I'd done so far, when I heard a strange noise, like a sob. Facing Nina once more, I saw how distorted her face had become. She was crying.

"What's wrong, Nina?" I stood and took her arm, leading her gently toward one of the chairs facing me.

"You . . . you need to add me to your list," she gasped out.

I stopped, staring at her. "What do you mean?"

She sat and looked at her hands in her lap, obviously avoiding my gaze. "I was late today because that detective who's questioned you — Garciana?" I nodded but she couldn't have seen me with her head bowed. "He was asking me questions again about Efram and you and —"

"He's still questioning you about whether I killed Efram?" I felt as horrified as if he was badgering my kids about whether they thought I could murder someone I loathed. Nina wasn't my child, but she was my subordinate here, which had its similarities.

"Well, yes. But it was more than that." She looked up at me with flooded waiflike eyes. "They really suspect both of us, Lauren."

Not just me, then. "Why do they suspect you?" I asked softly.

"Efram . . . I didn't tell you, but he threatened me after the puppy mill rescue." Her voice was a quiet siren's wail of a moan.

"Why?"

"Because I'd told you about it and you were there, and you said you'd have Dante DeFrancisco stop paying Efram for his work here at HotRescues. I was scared. The first threats . . . well, they were anonymous and general, and I thought they were from my ex . . ."

Her abusive ex-husband. No wonder she was a cauldron of emotions now. I didn't recall her being particularly emotional between the time of the puppy mill incident and Efram's death. Even so . . . "But it wasn't him, it was Efram. How did you find out?"

"They were e-mails from an address I didn't recognize. I think Efram knew about my past. Maybe someone here had mentioned it when he was around. I don't know. But he was playing games with me at first. After sending a couple, he called me. Said it was him, and wasn't this a fun game? I hung up on him. But then he called back and said if I didn't listen, if I didn't fix things with you and with Dante, he'd do even worse things to me than my ex did. I was considering whether I should call the cops, or at least tell you . . . and then Efram was found here dead. I felt so strangely happy that someone so evil had died. I also felt scared. His death was mysterious, and I was afraid I'd become a suspect. But . . . but if I'd spoken up earlier, maybe no one would be suspecting you." She broke into sobs again.

Interesting. But even if she hadn't told the entire truth before, I still couldn't bring myself to start pointing fingers at her as being my number-one suspect in Efram's death . . . yet.

"Nina?" She looked at me again, her pallor even whiter than I'd ever seen it before. "Two questions."

She didn't react.

"Did you kill Efram?"

"No," she rasped.

"Did you set Honey and me up last night?"

"No!"

I stood and approached her. She cringed, as if she thought the next abusive person in her life would be me. Which made me want to cry, too.

Instead, I knelt, put an arm around her. "Okay, then. You didn't do either. I didn't do either. I still have work to do to figure this out. We'll help each other. All right?"

"Lauren, you're the greatest." She turned

and hugged me tightly.

When she left my office a little while later, I knew she wouldn't think I was so great if she knew what I was doing.

I'd considered it before, but now I did it: I created a page on her in my list of possible murder suspects.

It almost seemed preordained — synchronicity or whatever — that Matt called while I was putting the finishing touches on the notes in my file on him. Of course he had said that we'd talk today, after he drove me to HotRescues last night. Why not now?

Last night. That kiss . . .

So what?

"Are we on tomorrow for your visit here to see the animals rescued from the puppy mill?" he asked.

"I'd love to," I said, meaning it. We set up a time, and I smiled at my phone as I hung up.

Then I frowned at my computer screen. All of what I was sticking there was interesting, but would it really help me zero in on Efram's killer? I wasn't a detective. I knew nothing about investigations except what I saw on TV cop shows, and, as I'd considered before recently, I knew from everything I'd read that they were all about drama and nothing about reality.

I needed information. Guidance.

Even if I didn't explain why I needed it.

I lifted the phone once more, took a card out of my top drawer — one I'd stuffed in there, never intending to look at it again — and called Detective Stefan Garciana.

CHAPTER 22

Detective Garciana worked out of the LAPD's Devonshire Division. I arrived at the Devonshire Community Police Station, a low brick and concrete building on Etiwanda Avenue, at exactly the time he'd agreed to see me, three that afternoon.

I was shown by a woman in uniform — probably a rookie, judging by her apparent age — into a room no larger than a closet, with nearly all its space occupied by a large table. Used to seeing interrogation rooms on TV shows, I looked around. Sure enough, there was a camera. Would I be recorded? Probably, but I didn't intend to say anything incriminating. I was there to learn all I could.

Detective Garciana entered a minute later, wearing — of course — a suit. A dark one. He looked even more rested than the last time I'd seen him. Maybe more intimidating, too.

But I wasn't intimidated easily. Although I might allow him to think so, if it made it easier to get what I wanted from him.

"So," he said, "did you come here to confess, Ms. Vancouver?" His Hispanic features seemed more pronounced than I'd seen before, here under the artificial bright lights. His eyes glowed, too, as if in anticipation. Or glee. If he really thought I'd ventured here to confess to something — Efram's murder or feigning the situation with Honey at HotRescues last night, or both — he'd undoubtedly feel pretty cocky, as if he had won a game that had been in play for over a week now.

"Actually, no," I replied. "I'm here for advice. Research, really. One of my kids is doing a paper at college on law enforcement and asked me to do some research at the LAPD." I'd considered how to approach this and decided that some semiwhite lies were in order. Garciana would certainly not be pleased to tell me how I could do his job since he obviously wasn't doing it right.

"Do you always do your kids' work?" His tone was dry, and the pleasantness had all but disappeared from his expression.

"Only when it sounds interesting to me. What I'd like to find out is the kinds of things you look for during a background check on a suspect. Also, which of those things are the red flags that make you believe you've found the perpetrator."

"Those are pretty broad questions." He'd been leaning toward me over the table, but now he moved back and crossed his arms — his body language pronouncing his lack of enthusiasm over how this conversation was going. Maybe because he wasn't controlling it . . . or me.

"I know. But my child will really appreciate any input you can give me." I shifted in my seat, too — not because I was uncomfortable with our discussion, but because my injured leg hurt.

"Your child . . . or you? Are you trying to figure out what makes me so sure you're a primary suspect in the Efram Kiley murder? I'll bet your lawyer wouldn't be happy to learn you're here. You shouldn't feel happy to be here, either."

"I'm not. But I'm looking for information anyway. So . . . what makes you decide someone's a viable suspect?" A lot of possibilities came to my mind. Would he confirm them?

For example, opportunity had to be high on his list. Efram Kiley died at HotRescues, and I happened to be there that night. I figured that's why he'd zeroed in on me.

That, plus I'd been arguing with Efram — motive.

I wasn't going to voice my thoughts aloud, though. I wanted the detective to tell me what was on his mind — hopefully, beyond the obvious.

"You know, I took time from a busy afternoon to talk with you. I'd hoped we'd make some progress in the Efram Kiley situation, if not the incident in which you were hurt last night. You don't strike me as stupid, Ms. Vancouver. I think you know why you're an obvious suspect. The basics of police investigation — motive, means, and opportunity? You could learn them all on the Internet or TV. In both of these matters, you had them all." His voice grew louder and more irate the more he talked. Obviously, he was practicing those intimidation techniques of his on me, just as I wanted to use him to practice my inquisition skills.

Neither of us was getting anywhere.

Then he finally said something helpful. "You want to know how I conduct an investigation? Very methodically. By the book." He leaned closer again. "I also think a lot about it *not* by the book. My SOP isn't exactly like the standard operating procedures of my fellow detectives."

"What do you mean?" I suddenly felt as confused as if he'd sent me home with a free pass, deleting me from the suspect list.

"I like to think way outside the box. Even as I'm focusing on the most probable suspects, I also spend time doing the same analysis of the least likely. Just in case, I spend nearly as much time and energy looking into their backgrounds, their MM and O, and anything else I think could be helpful in each case."

"Really? That's fascinating," I said, meaning it. I jotted notes on a memo pad I'd brought along, ostensibly for my kid working on a paper. This was something I could use in my own computer files on everyone I suspected.

"But you know what?" I had a feeling Garciana was about to burst the little balloon of possibilities he'd just inflated in my mind. "That's all just an exercise to keep my mind open as long as it needs to be. Because . . ."

He paused dramatically. I was fairly sure I knew what came next.

"Because?" I prompted anyway, waiting for the theoretical knife stab that might feel nearly as bad as the real thing.

"Because reality is almost never like the garbage you see on TV or read in books, where the cop, or viewer, or reader, doesn't really know till the end who did it. Reality is that the person most likely to have done it, judging by their motive, means, opportunity, and attitude, is the actual culprit."

His fiery expression segued into blankness — except for his eyes, which seemed to reach over to pinch me.

"Like you think I am," I said very softly, not actually wanting him to respond.

"Like I know you are," he responded with a grin.

I returned to HotRescues both exhilarated and disheartened. I liked Garciana's way-out-there concept of an investigation. But if, in his experience, it was mostly an exercise in futility and eliminating false possibilities, how could it really help me save myself?

For it was clear that, no matter who else he looked at, how deeply he considered unlikely murder suspects, I was the one he intended to arrest eventually for murdering Efram.

Which made my own probe even more critical.

Volunteer Ricki was our greeter this afternoon when I returned to HotRescues. A good thing. I didn't want to run into Nina while I was in the middle of evaluating her position in my suspect files.

Garciana had said he put time and effort into the least likely suspects, just in case. To me, that included Nina. And Matt.

"Hi, Lauren," Ricki said as I came in. I glanced at the desk behind the counter. She'd been reading a textbook I knew from my days as a veterinary technician. She'd start school soon, and I heartily encouraged her. "Pretty quiet day today, although there are some phone calls for you to return. Also, a couple of people in the back said they're interested in maybe adopting a dog. Their answers to our initial questions sounded fine."

"Thanks. I'll go check them out in a minute." First, I stopped in the office and exchanged the blouse I'd worn to my thought-provoking discussion with Garciana for a blue employee HotRescues shirt that contrasted with the yellow volunteer one Ricki wore. I also checked the wound on my leg. It was still bandaged but was healing well.

I soon headed into the shelter area. The folks who had come to visit had either circled back to the entry or hadn't gotten beyond Honey's enclosure in the first place. A twenty-something man and woman both knelt on the pavement, hands inside the fencing, petting the Westie mix. I noticed that Si Rogan watched from just outside the center building, a good thing. I preferred that a close watch be maintained on visitors, especially now. I was still knotted up inside after what had gone on the night before last.

Plus, there had been some news coverage — not a lot, fortunately, but I suppose something as offbeat as a landslide of dog food plus a knife injury got some tabloid sorts' adrenaline flowing. Honey hadn't been identified, at least, either by breed mix or name, so her involvement couldn't be the reason for this couple's interest.

Fortunately, I'd remained anonymous, too, this time — although HotRescues hadn't. People who'd seen earlier reports on the puppy mill rescue and on Efram's death might infer my connection anyway.

"Hi," I said to the visitors petting Honey. "Isn't she sweet? She was left at a high-kill shelter about six months ago. It's beyond me why no one has adopted her by now . . . although maybe she was waiting for you."

The young Asian woman rose. She had a glow on her face that suggested she'd had the same idea. "Maybe so. We . . . we didn't intend to adopt today. I need to check at our apartment building, make sure it's okay to bring a dog in."

"But we really like her," said the man with her, short and stocky and also of Asian heritage. "We'll be back just as soon as we can, if we're able to take her home."

"Sounds good," I said. "In the meantime, why don't you fill out the paperwork so we can check on some background things? That way, if you come back, we may be able to handle an adoption more quickly. And be sure to bring a copy of your lease to confirm whether you're allowed to keep pets. Photos, too, of where she'll sleep and get her walks." Were they on record in the system we used to keep track of animal abuse, or did they have other black marks against them? I suspected that wasn't the case here . . . but like in investigating Efram's murder, I had to consider all possibilities.

Including Matt Kingston. That was why I was doubly glad to show up the next day at the Animal Services shelter in the northern San Fernando Valley that was still waiting for funding to open — the one where the puppy mill rescuees were taken.

I'd fortunately slept well the previous night, since all adrenaline that had resulted from the Honey attack had worn off. I had even arrived at HotRescues a little later than usual, and left after lunch.

That Friday afternoon, Matt was there at the unopened shelter to greet me, as we'd planned. He now occupied a page in my file of murder suspects, and I intended to check out all details relating to his MM and O as carefully as I would someone I really wanted to believe was guilty.

But mostly, I was there to see how the puppies and their moms and dads were doing now, nearly two weeks after they'd been saved from that hellhole where they'd been living.

There weren't many cars in the parking lot in front of the smooth beige stucco facility that resembled a Spanish mission, with a peaked tile roof and arched, paned windows. The walkway was charming, decorated with poles on which pictures of dogs, cats, and horses were hung, and others had decorative bells on them.

When I reached the front entrance, everything appeared to be locked, so I called Matt. He came nearly immediately and held the door open for me.

"Glad you could make it." His smile reminded me why I found him one attractive example of masculinity when I thought about it. Today, he wore casual clothes, not an Animal Services uniform, and his knit shirt hugged a muscular build that I'd already figured let him scale cliffs and pull himself out of storm drains, all in the name of saving animals.

It would also make stabbing someone who tortured animals a lot easier.

"Me, too," I responded.

Matt led me along pathways between enclosures, most of which had no animals in them. We reached a populated area — one filled with a lot of young dogs of breeds that were highly familiar after the puppy mill rescue. Including little beagle pups.

"They're so adorable!" I exclaimed. I looked at Matt. "Are they all still healthy?" They looked it, at least.

"Like I told you, we didn't lose any." His proud smile made me grin in return. "Of the pups."

I felt my smile disappear. "The parents?" I braced myself to hear the worst.

"Most are fine. We've completed our photographs and documentation for the puppy mill owners' prosecution and started distributing adults to public shelters. A couple were already adopted. But a few here need a lot of medical attention. They may make it, or not. We've got them under veterinary care, but unfortunately, in a public facility, we may not be able to do all that's necessary to save them. Two are on the list to be put down, maybe in a day or so."

I grabbed his arm. "How bad are they?"

"I'm not sure."

"May I send a vet here to check them out?" Today, if Carlie was available. If not, I'd twist her arm so she'd come no later than first thing tomorrow. With me. Even though it would be Saturday and my kids were coming home from college this weekend. "If they're suffering, I won't get in the way. But if there's a possibility of saving them, giving them a good life ahead, I'd like to take them to HotRescues to get them the care they need."

"I was hoping you'd say that." To my surprise — and unexpected delight — he bent toward me and kissed the tip of my nose. "Let me introduce you to them."

CHAPTER 23

This was one of those days that I was thrilled I'd chosen to buy a Toyota Venza with its variety of dog-friendly accessories.

My gray crossover was attractive enough, but I liked it mostly because I had it equipped to be one of the most practical vehicles on the road for the chief administrator of an animal shelter on days that the regular shelter van was just too big.

It was Saturday morning. I had just pulled my Venza into the area behind HotRescues where deliveries were made. I glanced into the rearview mirror to look at the wire crates I'd positioned in the back, behind the removable pet barrier, after flipping down the rear seats automatically.

Inside the crates were the two dogs whom Matt had said were not well enough to be kept alive at city shelters. The little beagle and Boston terrier would require more individual attention than official care centers could provide.

I'd cried on Matt's shoulder yesterday afternoon, figuratively and literally, when he had introduced me to them. Then I'd made a frantic call to Carlie, who met me there in less than an hour, bless her. She had examined them and pronounced that, given lots of TLC, they could thrive well enough to be rehomed — most likely soon.

"You okay, Mom?" That was my son, Kevin, who sat in the passenger's seat beside me. He'd arrived home late yesterday evening, a blast of life into my quiet, too somber home. His university was only a couple of hours away, so he'd gotten here ahead of his older sister, Tracy, who was due into town from Palo Alto in about an hour. A friend was picking her up at Burbank Airport.

I'd assured them that I was surviving just fine as a murder suspect and dog-food-and-knife prank victim, but they'd insisted on checking themselves.

The thought of having both around as company . . . well, I'd been smiling a lot. Except when I'd seen the condition of the overworked parent dogs I'd just rescued from truly awful and unnecessary fates.

Fortunately, the other rescued parents hadn't wound up as fragile as these two and were not in imminent danger.

"I'm doing great!" I assured my son. Looking at him as we sat there, I smiled once more. How could I help it? Kevin was so like my beloved Kerry: tall and slim, with longish, unmanageable hair the shade of a deep red autumn leaf just segueing to brown. His brown eyes were intense beneath a straight brow line, and his mouth nearly always appeared ready to burst into laughter.

Smart kid, too. Otherwise, how could he be majoring in Science and Management at Claremont McKenna College?

How could I afford to send two kids to college at the same time? Fortunately, HotRescues had the most generous benefactor imaginable. Knowing my financial and social situation, Dante was my benefactor, too, giving me hefty raises and occasional bonuses to help cover tuition.

Which was another reason I had to get this whole Efram situation resolved as fast as possible. Dante had been completely understanding so far. But I was under no illusions. His largesse could evaporate as fast as it materialized, if he believed my resignation was in HotRescues' best interests.

I wondered if anything was happening with the Brooke Pernall/Cheyenne scenario.

Brooke had called to thank me after she'd heard from Dante, but hadn't given any details after indicating that things might be looking up. She'd sounded almost cheerful, and I hadn't detected any illness or despair in her voice this time. Plus, she hadn't relinquished Cheyenne to us, which could be promising. I'd check again someday soon.

Right now, Kevin and I both exited the car. I went around to the back and opened the rear hatch.

Two small faces regarded me from separate crates. The mama beagle's eyes were a massive amount more doleful than the breed standard. The brindle and white Boston terrier had her pointed ears up and moving, as if she listened to radio waves that told her whether to trust me or not.

"You may not believe it yet," I said to them, "but your lives are about to change a whole lot for the better."

"I'll say," Kevin seconded from behind me.

"Can you carry this one?" I asked him, pointing to the crate with the Boston, who was smaller and lighter.

"Mom." He drew the word out in the exasperation only teens were capable of. He wasn't quite nineteen, after all. "You take

301

the smaller one. I'll take the beagle."

I didn't argue. Not when I was proud of how much of a gentleman he was. I gently slid the crates down the pet ramp that I'd gotten with the car and put them on the ground. Then I closed and locked the car. Kevin waited by the back HotRescues gate, which was locked. I got the key out of my purse and opened it.

Almost immediately, when we went inside toting the crates, Pete Engersol met us, his well-worn features brightening. "Are these our first rescues from the puppy mill?"

"They sure are," I responded with pride, setting the crate I held down on the pavement. The nearest dogs became sentinels and barked a greeting and warning to the newcomers, soon taken up by other residents. I watched as the Boston cringed, then noticed the same with the beagle as Kevin put her crate down.

The Boston. The beagle. If they'd had names before, no one had passed them along to us. We'd give them new ones soon, even if they didn't stick.

"Have you gotten a place ready for them?" I asked Pete.

Pete, as our all-around go-to guy, was the first one I checked with when we had an out-of-the-ordinary situation to deal with.

He'd vowed to make sure our usual temporary hospital quarters inside the center
building were in good shape to take on these
newcomers.

"Absolutely."

He bent down and opened the Boston's
crate, lifting her out and slipping a collar
around her neck, then attaching a leash. He
hugged her. "Hi, little lady. Welcome."

Kevin got the beagle out and put on
another similar leash that Pete had brought.
We both followed Pete along the path to the
center building. The two dogs apparently
weren't used to tethers and balked at first
but soon appeared to decide it was easier to
go along with us than to feel more pressure
around their necks — not much, of course.
Kevin and Pete were careful not to choke
them.

Inside, Angie Shayde, our veterinary
technician, waited along with Si Rogan. It
was too soon for Si to have much contact
with these rescuees. Making sure they were
pampered with all the care they needed to
restore their health was the number-one
priority. Retraining would wait for the future.

"Let me see those babies," Angie said.
One under each arm, she took them both
into the infirmary set up on the second

floor. I followed and motioned for Kevin to join us. Pete and Si came along as well.

We watched as Angie did her magic, examining them. I handed her some paperwork that Carlie had given me, with her diagnosis and prognosis and suggestions for care. Angie read them over. "Great!" she said. "Pete, we're going to put them on a special diet for a while. Can you run to the HotPets store and pick up the things on the list I'll give you?"

"Sure will."

Of course there was a HotPets not far away. That was one of the criteria for picking this location for HotRescues — near one of Dante's official retail outlets. This way, the food supplies could be dropped off by delivery vans going to the HotPets in Chatsworth, about a mile from here.

These two would be in quarantine for at least a week to ten days, as we did with all our rescue animals. That minimized the possibility of their passing diseases to other residents. Even a veterinary exam didn't always discover all problems. Of course the humans who'd visit them would always use antibacterial hand cleanser before and after touching them. We all did that before and after touching cats, too, since they seemed more prone to catching things from one another than dogs did.

Right now, knowing the dogs were in excellent hands, I motioned to Kevin, and we walked downstairs. I needed to go to my office and start the official files on these two rescue animals.

It would help, though, if they had names.

I said so out loud as we exited onto the walkway and started toward the main building, with the dogs whose enclosures we passed barking their greetings all over again.

At the last kennel, I looked in at Honey and stopped for a pat — as did Kevin. Were those people who seemed to fall so hard for her yesterday coming back to adopt her? I hoped so, for her sake. But I'd miss her.

"How about Missy and Sweety for the dogs' names?" said Si. I hadn't realized he had followed us from the infirmary area. "For now, at least."

"Not bad," I said. "For our use, anyway." Had he been the one who'd named Honey? I couldn't recall for sure, but it fit.

We'd reached the main building, and I shooed Kevin through the gate, making sure that none of our inhabitants were loose and ready to sneak through. Then Si held it for me. I assumed he was staying in the shelter area, but he joined us on the other side, obviously cautious to ensure no one followed us out.

We went into the welcome room. My intent was to make a few notes to start the new rescue file on each of them, then turn it over to Nina. She was there greeting visitors. So was Ricki.

Matt Kingston was one of those visitors.

"What are you doing here?" I asked him.

"I wanted to make sure you got those two dogs you picked up here okay, see how they're being treated, that kind of thing." I suspected that the real "kind of thing" was to check on me, see how I was handling these two new residents whose former ill-treatment had been such anathema to me. I'd certainly cried about them yesterday — all over Matt.

Not especially the image I'd wanted to portray of the calm, collected, and organized shelter administrator who'd seen it all and would do anything to prevent it from happening again.

"They're doing as well as can be expected," I told him. "Our veterinary tech is getting them acclimated to the area where they'll stay for now."

"Sounds good. Will you show me?"

Whatever his intentions, he wasn't going to give up until he had seen those two dogs.

"Why not? Kevin, why don't you tell Nina

all the information she asks to start up our files on . . . Missy and Sweety." I glanced my thanks at Si, who nodded. "By the way, Matt," I said. "This is my son, Kevin." That ought to do it for any semblance of attraction Matt might think he felt for me. A mother of a teenage kid? Not exactly a hottie.

They shook hands, and then I took Matt back to visit with the dogs. Si stayed behind to talk to Mona, who'd just come in.

When Matt and I returned, there was a visitor in the reception area — someone who looked vaguely familiar. I realized who she was when I saw that there was a guy outside the window who held a large video camera.

She was a reporter for some tabloid show on TV.

I'd been fairly lucky so far, all things considered. I was a murder suspect. I'd also been the victim of a nasty crime that resulted in being stabbed — never mind that I was suspected of doing that myself. Unfortunately, it had all made the news, but I'd managed to stay pretty much off camera after the first wave of YouTube.

I didn't always discourage the media. The more publicity HotRescues had, the more visitors and, hopefully, the more adoptions we'd experience.

But I didn't think that was why this reporter was here.

"Hi," she said. "My name is Corina Carey. I'm here to ask you a few questions, Lauren. I'm with *National NewsShakers.*"

"How nice to meet you, Ms. Carey," I lied, noticing that Matt had disappeared. Obviously he didn't want to meet her, either. "Would you like a tour of our facilities? We have some really wonderful animals who need homes, pets your viewers will fall in love with." I projected so much gushiness that she could have scraped whipped cream from my body.

"That would be fine," she said. "Also, if you could point out the dogs you just brought from the city shelter, the ones who were part of that puppy mill rescue the other day, that would be wonderful."

How had she heard so fast that they were here? No matter. Maybe giving Sweety and Missy some on-air coverage would help their futures — once they were given veterinary clearance for adoption.

Despite the way showing her around felt like anticipating nonstop torture, I managed to give Corina Carey a brief but — at least I felt — heart-wrenching tour of HotRescues. Including an introduction to our two newest inhabitants. All caught on camera by the guy with her.

She left soon after. I returned to the welcome area, where Kevin was working on the main computer. I guessed he was filling out the initial data himself.

Matt had reappeared and was looking over Kevin's shoulder, making suggestions.

Si, Mona, Pete, and Angie all followed me from the shelter area. Did everyone around here hope to be featured in whatever kind of media event Ms. Carey was going to derive from her visit?

"Okay, gang," I said. "I'm going home to spend some time with Kevin. Tracy should be there by now, too. Call me if anything comes up, and I'll be back for a while this afternoon."

"Can I see you for a minute before you go?" Matt said.

I hesitated. Was he going to bawl me out for going along with that reporter? Was he okay with how our newcomers were being handled?

The look on his face seemed more interested than angry, so I said, "Sure. Come into my office for a minute."

He did. Once we were alone there, with the door shut, I was astounded when he took me into his arms. So surprised that I didn't resist when he kissed me. Talk about surprise — I really enjoyed it. Even kissed him back.

"What's that for?" I demanded breathlessly, my voice low.

"For rescuing those dogs. And for running such a good private shelter. And —"

"And?" I prompted.

"Just because I felt like it." He smiled, opened the door, and left.

CHAPTER 24

I got a call on my cell phone that afternoon from James Remseyer, Efram's former lawyer. "What do you think you're doing, Ms. Vancouver?" he demanded.

"I think I'm having a pleasant afternoon with my family," I responded between clenched teeth. "At least I was."

I was sitting in my kitchen at the oval wood table, watching my daughter bake cookies. I'd taught her well. We'd bought the premade dough from the supermarket, and Tracy was slicing it on a cutting board on top of the tile counter and putting it on a cookie sheet before sticking it into the oven.

My daughter resembled me, as Kevin looked like his dad. She was moderate height and slender, and wore her dark brown hair shoulder length. Like me, her eyes were green.

Kevin was outside mowing the lawn,

wonderful young man that he was. The groan of the lawnmower harmonized with my unwelcome phone conversation.

"Have you seen *National NewsShakers* today?" Remseyer continued.

"No, but I assume, since you brought it up, that HotRescues is mentioned. A reporter came to visit us, and I spoke with her since I wanted to tell the world about all the charming animals we have there, waiting for new homes."

"Well, she talked primarily about the two allegedly from the puppy mill. She defamed my client, Efram Kiley, which is especially heinous since he isn't around now to defend himself. She also implied that his friends and family were as unsavory as she claimed he was. I'm calling on behalf of Efram's estate."

What? Efram had an estate? He'd left some money?

I'd assumed he had spent everything Dante had paid in compensation for his supposed rehabilitation.

Or maybe his "estate" was a euphemism for a claim Remseyer might make against someone for the defamation he was asserting. He all but confirmed the latter.

"You must understand, Ms. Vancouver, how upset Efram's stepmother Mandy

Ledinger and his girlfriend Shellie Benudo are. They both called me, aghast after seeing that untrue news report, and retained me to make claims against the news station and HotRescues and their respective personnel. I would suggest that you make certain that the newspeople retract any actionable statements."

"Actionable like what?" I noticed Tracy staring at me with concern and shook my head with a barely tolerant smile, as if what I was hearing was too stupid to worry about.

"You should watch the broadcast and see how they've quoted you. I won't attempt to restate anything, but you are cited as having alleged animal torture by Efram and everyone he ever knew, such as my clients. And me."

Ah. That had to be the crux of it. The lawyer was worried about his own reputation, at least among clients who might care whether animals were abused.

"I suspect I was misquoted," I said, "although frankly I loathe anyone who even tolerates animal cruelty. Do you tolerate it, Mr. Remseyer?"

"Heavens, no. But I suspect even those two dogs you brought to your shelter allegedly because they were too ill to make it in a public facility aren't as bad off as you made them out to be. I could have a veterinarian I sometimes retain as a consultant take a look at them."

"No, thank you."

"Are you with them now? Are you at HotRescues?"

"Like I said, I'm home with my kids now." But was he asking because he wanted to know if my charges were alone and defenseless, so he could sic the vet in his back pocket on them? Maybe make claims that we were abusing animals?

I might be stretching things, but I certainly had no reason to trust this lawyer.

I continued quickly, "I'll be back there very shortly, though. Joining my staff. And I'll be there late enough to ensure that our new residents do well on their first night at HotRescues. So will other people. You can be sure, Mr. Remseyer, that I'll watch *National NewsShakers.* If the reporter says I've claimed that Efram abused the poor creatures in the puppy mill, that's true. I'd also stand by any claims that, if his friends and family" — and lawyer — "knew about it and did nothing, they were nearly as guilty as him and deserve a fate like his. Being arrested, I mean."

I'd love for them to suffer additional punishment, too, but didn't want what I said to sound like they should fear for their lives — especially from me, and especially till I was no longer on the cops' list of murder suspects.

"So you're saying that even his employer at the air-conditioning company where he worked was as guilty as him?"

"Did he know about what Efram was doing?"

"He knew about the claims against HotRescues and you, and the settlement, since his volunteering at your shelter resulted in Efram's having to take some time off work."

"Is he your client, too?"

A brief silence. Then — "I can't get into that at the moment."

In other words, this shyster liked the idea and was probably going to go solicit Efram's former employer as a client. Interesting. It also gave me someone else to look into for my suspect file in Efram's murder.

"Well, it really doesn't matter to me who you represent," I asserted. "I said nothing untrue. If it turns out I was misquoted, I'll take that up with the reporter and get a retraction, but nothing you've said so far worries me particularly."

Not exactly true, but I'd learned, throughout my life, to appear to put a positive spin on things — overtly, at least, no matter how miserable I felt inside. And how much I anticipated the worst.

"We'll see, Ms. Vancouver. And if you haven't already retained counsel, you might want to consider doing so."

As he hung up, I wondered whether I should contact Esther Ickes. Although she was my criminal attorney, I'd gathered, from things she had said, that she sometimes took on civil matters like bankruptcies. Claims of defamation? I'd have to ask her.

"What was that all about, Mom?" Tracy's voice was worried. She had paused with the cookie sheet in her hands, which were tucked inside large, quilted orange oven mitts. The mitts clashed with her cardinal and white Stanford T-shirt with the green logo of a redwood tree in the middle.

"The same nonsense that's been going on since that creep Efram Kiley died at HotRescues," I said, shaking my head. "Too much finger-pointing and not enough fact-finding. I suspect I've graduated beyond YouTube and am on TV now."

"What!" she shrieked. "Where?" She quickly put the baking sheet into the oven, turned on the timer, then hurried out the back door before I could figure out what she was up to. In a moment, the sound of the lawnmower died. Apparently, she'd gone to get her brother so they could both confront me. Oh, joy.

I was almost glad that my BlackBerry rang again. A distraction. Maybe a friend calling. But the number on the caller ID wasn't one I recognized.

"Hello?" I said cautiously, bracing myself for further misery. Good thing I did, since that was certainly what I got.

"This is Patsy Shaheen, Lauren," said a shrill voice on the other end. Great. Now champion animal abusers had my phone number. I might have to change it. "A friend called about that terrible *National News-Shakers* show and how they talked about Bradley and me and our babies. They said you've taken in some supposedly sick dogs. Can we come see them? The Animal Services people have forbid us from visiting any of our darlings."

"Sorry," I said. "We're still nursing them back to health."

"Are you with them now?"

"Close enough," I said. Would she demand that I send her a picture over my phone or something equally bizarre?

"Please, just give them a hug from us and tell them we want them to get all better soon. And if they have to go to some other

317

family, we wish them someone who loves them like we do."

Bull crap. But all I said to her was, "Of course, Patsy. How nice of you to care." And then I not-so-gently hung up.

My kids were back in the room watching me. "You okay, Mom?" Kevin asked.

"Just peachy," I said, then smiled. "Honest. But if you really want to help me feel better, stay with me while I watch that damned *National NewsShakers* show on TV."

Tracy turned on the oven light to peek in at her cookies. I assumed they must look all right since she joined her brother and me as we went into the living room. I perked my ears up so I'd hear the timer go off, in case she didn't.

I sat on the middle blue cushion on the sofa and patted the ones on either side of me, turning me into a Vancouver sandwich when my children complied. My leg barely hurt any longer. I used the remote to turn on Kevin's monstrosity of a large TV and found the channel with *National NewsShakers.* Would the show featuring HotRescues still be on? I clicked the directory. *National NewsShakers* had just started another hour of broadcasting.

And, yes, the same show must either be repeating or another one had begun that focused on my shelter. We started watching.

After only a few minutes, I grasped Kevin and Tracy's hands. I could see why anyone who knew Efram could be upset. *I* was upset — not because of the accusations against him and them, but because that reporter, Corina Carey, had somehow taken news clips of other people, her filmed discussion with me, and pictures of dogs like those just saved from euthanasia by sheltering them at HotRescues . . . and made it sound, via an overlaid narration, as though I was one sick, angry broad who'd do anything to save animals. Especially ones abused in hellholes like the Shaheens' puppy mill.

There wasn't a lot I could object to. Except for the sick part, it was true. But I hadn't named names when I was interviewed — except for a few of the dogs and cats at HotRescues. I hadn't directly accused any of the folks that shyster Remseyer had claimed to be representing in my answers to the reporter's questions. Not that I could exonerate any of them in Efram's death.

"Whoa, Mom," Kevin said as we watched and listened, and I grew even more concerned. "That's some nasty stuff you said about all those people."

"A bit of misrepresentation here," I said.

319

"I didn't say all the things that reporter claimed, or even very many of them, even if I thought them."

I wasn't particularly surprised when Detective Stefan Garciana also called me, making sure I'd watched the show. That spurred me to leave a message for my attorney, Esther Ickes, who was in a meeting that afternoon. I told her secretary to have Esther take a look at *National NewsShakers* — and to assure her that I wasn't quite as imprudent as the show portrayed me.

I'd want to talk to her, also, about whether I should put that reporter Corina Carey on notice that I'd like her to clarify my participation in what she'd used for her show.

But as I sat there pondering what to do, I realized that the sensationalism in this purported news story might actually work to my advantage. It certainly stirred the pot of any complacency that the people I believed could have murdered Efram might have been simmering around themselves.

Of course, I'd thought that the incident with Honey, the food bags, and the knife had resulted from the killer's anger about my inquiries. I'd have to be even more careful now.

I turned off the TV. Tracy had already gotten her cookies out of the oven. Chocolate chip — my favorite. I was good and only ate one, though. I'd promised to take them out to dinner at their favorite Mexican restaurant.

At dinner, I'd have preferred directing the conversation to getting a full rundown on how my children were doing at their respective schools. Fortunately, we did get into that some. Both were fine, even Kevin, despite this being his first year.

Mostly, though, we talked about how I was doing, what I was doing, and whether someone as dedicated to pet rescue as me could ever kill a guy — especially one who was as miserable an excuse for a human being as Efram, who'd continuously abused animals.

I assured my kids that I couldn't. I realized, though, that making that kind of assurance was as false as if I'd told them I couldn't kill anyone in defense of either of them.

On our way home, I stopped at HotRescues. I looked around and didn't see the security patrol, but maybe they'd just been by. I turned off the alarm and we all went inside.

Amid chaotic greetings from the rows of dogs, we went upstairs to the infirmary.

There, we took Sweety and Missy out of their quarantine enclosures and gave them some hugs and TLC.

Both seemed rather listless, as if energy was a landmark that they hadn't yet discovered. But they also seemed happy for the attention, so we gave them a lot.

We were in the building where most cats, toy dogs, and small animals resided downstairs, so I took my children to visit them, too. They even got some quality time with a few of the kitties who were willing to accept, with royal dignity, the attention showered on them by mere humans.

When we left, I purposely hurried the kids out. I didn't want them asking questions about where Efram had died or even demanding to see the place in the storage building where I'd been assailed by the food bags and knife. My daughter and son were full of intelligent curiosity — and I wanted them to direct it elsewhere, far from their mother's troubles.

Tomorrow was Sunday. I would spend as much of it as I could with them, since they'd both head back to school in the evening.

But my mind was swirling already on all I wanted to do on Monday. And it didn't involve just ensuring that all the inhabitants of HotRescues — except for our newest ones, who needed time to heal — were healthy and ready for new homes.

CHAPTER 25

I brought the kids to HotRescues for a short while on Sunday, too. Not particularly early, though. They were taking full advantage of the time off what they both claimed were rugged academic schedules.

Having once been a college student, then a grad of veterinary tech school, I realized that half their assertions were probably exaggerated. But it was all part of the learning process — learning to be adults, not just scholars in their chosen fields.

Because it was the weekend, we had an abundance of volunteers present at HotRescues, but Nina had the day off. Our most senior helper, Bev, seemed charmed by the opportunity to take Kevin and Tracy for a walk around the facility, giving them the VIP tour though they'd been here uncountable times before. They didn't seem to mind. In fact, I had the impression they enjoyed seeing the place through the eyes of someone other than their watchful, opinion-ated, and sometimes obsessive mother.

I did some paperwork — rather, computer work — in the office. Several volunteers had noted a couple of pages of messages from answering the main shelter phone, but I didn't want to take the time now to return the calls.

While I sat there, though, my BlackBerry rang. The caller ID wasn't one I'd pro-grammed in, but I recognized it: Corina Carey from *National NewsShakers.*

Never mind that I'd convinced myself that her approach to reporting about the puppy mill rescue and ensuing situation at HotRes-cues might be useful to me. That didn't mean I wanted to talk to her again.

But being rude might only make things worse. "Hello," I said without acknowledg-ing I knew who was calling.

"Hi, Lauren. Have you heard what's go-ing on? I'd like a statement from you."

Confused, I said, "I'm sorry, but I don't —"

"That dogfighting ring in South LA. The one where they're making all the arrests as we speak. You haven't heard about it?"

"No," I admitted grimly. "But I'll look into it."

"Can I get a general statement from you

about what you think about dogfights?"

The idea of being quoted again by Corina Carey made me hesitate before responding. I considered just saying "no comment." But I definitely had an opinion and, on reflection, didn't mind sharing it with the world. "They're another act of cruelty," I told her, selecting my words carefully. "Different from puppy mills like the one in the rescue situation a couple of weeks ago. But as with puppy mills, people guilty of that kind of abuse deserve to be punished. And as you know, HotRescues stands for animal protection."

I did a rewind through my brain. I thought it came out okay, not pointing fingers at any actual person but expressing my opinion as an animal advocate — while also putting in a plug for HotRescues.

"Thanks," Corina said, and then she was gone — probably off to add her recording of my statement to whatever her network was broadcasting.

Which I decided I needed to see. I didn't have a television at HotRescues, but my computer would do. I did a search and found *National NewsShakers*.

The details of the story made my blood roar in my ears.

As Corina had stated, there had been a

major raid of a place in South LA that was a dogfight venue. Dogs — mostly pit bulls, judging by the photos — had been taken into custody, as had the people responsible.

Dogfights were major, illegal acts of cruelty — all the more so because the animals bred and trained to battle were usually doomed to be euthanized, since retraining them to become manageable pets was so difficult.

Yet not impossible. There had been the case of an athlete a few years ago who'd been sent to jail and an animal sanctuary, Best Friends, had taken in the dogs. Many had been rehabilitated, thank heavens. But what would happen to the dogs here in LA who'd been caught today?

Impulsively, I called Matt. The Animal Cruelty Task Force was probably involved, but not necessarily the teams reporting to him, including SmART and D.A.R.T. Even so, he might know.

"Oh, yeah, I'm aware of it," he responded to my question. "I'm on my way there now."

"And the dogs? What will happen to them?" I cringed as I waited for his answer.

"As far as I know, they'll be taken to the South Los Angeles Care Center for evaluation. Then we'll see."

Which meant that, if they were too damaged, too vicious for rehabilitation, that would be the end of them.

As a private rehoming facility, HotRescues was not equipped to help in that kind of situation. The official shelters would not have the staff or mandate to do anything different.

I could only hope that another private group could step in to help.

Fortunately, the kids returned to the main office, which immediately cheered me — as long as I directed my thoughts toward them and not what I'd just heard.

They were joined by Bev and also by Angie, who'd come to check on our newest residents, and Si, who'd additionally dropped in. We had an upbeat conversation about how Missy and Sweety were acclimating to their non–puppy mill existence here, and how they seemed to be growing stronger already.

"They're not completely out of the woods yet," Angie cautioned, "but I'm really optimistic."

"I'm looking forward to the day they're ready to get out of quarantine and start some training so HotRescues can find them new homes," Si added.

I wanted to hug them all. But I didn't get

the opportunity to. My cell phone rang.

I excused myself and answered it. This time, the caller ID was clear. "Hi, Matt."

"I'm here now," he said. "Awful situation, but fortunately the dogs seem to be in good condition. Some are pretty young and I have the sense they haven't been subjected to much of the training yet. The older ones . . . well, we'll just have to see."

"How many are there?"

"Maybe a dozen total."

"Thanks for letting me know," I said softly. And then I looked up. I wasn't about to explain the conversation. Fortunately, no one asked. I stood. "It's time for me to drag Tracy and Kevin away from here. Or for them to drag me away. Same difference."

We headed for home.

The rest of my day was bittersweet. I had my kids with me until evening, when both left to return to their schools.

But before they did, we went through some old pictures, and the nostalgia nearly made me cry.

They'd grown up so fast. They were adults now, worried about their old mom and her new public persona.

As well as her private nonlife.

"What you're still doing at HotRescues is

really cool, Mom," Tracy said as we sat at the retro glass-topped table in the dining room, passing around old-fashioned photo albums. "But are you becoming . . . I mean, getting on YouTube and in the news about animal rescues and things that happen to you because of them . . . well, I'm worried about you. That's why I came home."

"Yeah," Kevin agreed. He'd always let his big sister be his mouthpiece whenever they were on the same page. That happened now and then, although not often.

"I'm fine," I reassured them. "The whole situation about Efram Kiley's death will blow over, and once the person who harmed him is caught and put on trial I'll feel a lot better."

"But he was killed at HotRescues. And you were hurt there afterward. Can't you go get a job at some other, safer place?" Tracy had stopped pretending to concentrate on the photos and was staring at me, her green eyes overflowing with tears.

That was the crux of why both of them had come home. I knew that, and I loved them all the more for their worry about me.

It reminded me of all the worry I'd lavished on them forever, especially since their father died.

"I like it where I am," I told them. "I don't

intend to make any changes in my life. HotRescues is part of who I am now. And I'll be fine there. I promise." I spoke in a tone that they hopefully recognized from their childhoods. Mom was issuing an edict, and there would be no contradiction.

I only hoped I was making a promise I could keep.

Apparently they decided to buy into what I said. Or at least they realized that any argument would be futile. Silence reigned at the table where we'd celebrated holidays and family events for years.

Then Kevin pulled one of the albums toward him again and started thumbing through it. I watched him, glad not to meet either one's eyes. He stopped and pointed at a picture. "There the three of us are with Bosley. He was a great little dog."

I smiled and pulled the album over. Sweety, the rescued Boston terrier now at HotRescues, resembled him. "He sure was," I agreed.

"Have you considered adopting a dog yourself, Mom?" Kevin asked. "I didn't try to figure out which one there now might be a good match, but I'll bet —"

"I'm fine with things as they are, at least for now." This sounded like an ongoing litany, nearly a repetition of what I'd said before. In this, though, I was a little less certain.

Did I want to adopt a dog?

It wouldn't be good for the dog.

But —

"How about taking on a bigger dog?" Tracy sounded excited. "A watchdog. A guard dog. You could take care of each other."

I smiled. "Maybe someday," I said, again a repetition of something they'd heard many times before, which always meant no. But in this case, it was a definite maybe.

The next morning, I awoke alone in my bedroom. My house.

My kids had left, and somehow I'd managed to sleep.

But the silence, and the knowledge that they were gone once more, squeezed my heart as if I wadded it in my hands to still its motion for a while.

They were young adults now. They would visit when they wanted to and could manage it. That was how it should be.

I had a life, too. I showered and dressed quickly, then headed for HotRescues.

Nina was already there, in the reception room. "You've done it again, you star, you."

Leaning over the leopard-print counter, I

stared at her. "What do you mean?"

"Your statement about dogfighting has been played a lot on *National NewsShakers,*" she said. The expression on her face wasn't particularly thrilled. I wondered why. I asked her.

"No big deal," she said. "I'm just a bit concerned about the kind of publicity HotRescues is getting lately, what with the puppy mill and Efram and the attack on you — and now this. Is it in the best interests of our animals?" I must have looked affronted, since she raised her hand and said, "I'm just asking."

"Like I told my kids, more or less, 'this too shall pass.' Most of it isn't negative publicity for HotRescues, and our being in the news tells people we're here and have animals waiting for adoption. The bad stuff will fade away with time — hopefully sooner rather than later."

"Right," Nina agreed, although enthusiasm seemed distinctly lacking in her tone.

She was right, though. So were the kids. The sooner things calmed down and returned to normal, the better.

I wouldn't give any more quotes to Corina Carey or any other media sort, even to publicize HotRescues.

And I'd be working harder on my files of

information to figure out who killed Efram.

I did my first walk-through of the day, stopping to say hi to each of the dogs and pet a bunch of them when they stopped barking. Then, into the center building to visit the animals there, including Sweety and Missy.

Finally, I secluded myself in my office — in time to take a call from Carlie. "Okay, news lady," she said. "If you're going to get yourself on TV, make it my show from now on, not that tabloid stuff."

"Got it."

I became so occupied with some potential adoptions — yay! — that the only thing I got around to doing regarding Efram's death was to follow up on a new lead suggested indirectly by attorney James Remseyer. I called Efram's former employer, the air-conditioning repair company.

His immediate supervisor was named Pedro Suarez. I donned a pseudonym to talk to him. He had a thick Hispanic accent but I had no problem conversing with him. My story: my air-conditioning was acting up, and I needed a repairman. I claimed that the last time, the guy who'd been sent was named Efram, and he'd done such a great job. Could they send him again?

Not talking to Suarez in person, I gleaned

no body language or facial expression. But he sounded sad, as if he genuinely mourned his employee, when he told me that Efram was gone.

"Oh, no!" I exclaimed. "What happened to him?"

"Long story," he said. "But he was murdered."

"How awful. What happened? Who killed him?" Like, did you do it?

"It had something to do with volunteer work he was doing on his own time." Sounded as if the guy was discreet.

"Then it had nothing to do with his air-conditioning repair work?" Like, once more, did you do it? "He did a good job at my place, but . . . well, you know, I thought I saw him looking into some of my jewelry. Could one of your customers . . . I mean . . ."

I allowed my voice to drop off, waiting for him to respond. He didn't immediately jump in to defend his subordinate. He also issued no criticisms of his own.

"Did anyone complain about him?" I prompted. "Did you think he did a good job?"

"I'm sorry, but I must get back to work. If you would like, I can send someone else to look at your air-conditioning unit. What did you say your name was?"

"Thank you," I said without answering, and hung up.

And added a page devoted to Pedro Suarez to my file of murder suspects. Where would he fit, in the order of most likely killer to least? Probably somewhere lower than the middle.

I decided to work late that night. I'd been spending too much time on my obscure suspect file, and I needed to work on some bookkeeping issues.

Nina popped her head in to say goodbye. So did Bev and a few of the others. I was distracted but managed, I hoped, to be cordial.

It was dark out by the time I left — but I was only away for a short while to pick up a salad that I brought back.

By the time I pulled my car back into its slot, no other vehicles were in our parking lot. My entire staff should be gone by now, and our security company should be on duty.

I turned off the alarm and walked through the main building at the entrance, wanting to go right into the shelter area and visit with our residents before I went back to concentrate on paperwork.

I went outside, onto the path where dog enclosures were on my left. Honey was still there, and she barked. Of course.

Other dogs nearby joined in. Also of course. Only . . .

I'd been around animals for a long time now. They had, if not a language of their own, certain nuances in how they barked or what other noises or moves they made. Somehow, this wasn't a normal greeting plus watchdog kind of bark that surrounded me.

It was more frantic. More of a warning. But of what?

I stopped walking, only one enclosure down from Honey's. Inside it was Hannibal, a Great Dane mix, whose loud, anxious bark sounded like a harbinger of something frightening. What was going on?

And then I heard it. A low growl, vicious and disturbing and very, very nearby. But where . . .

Suddenly, an animal emerged from behind our center building.

A pit bull I hadn't seen before ran toward me, teeth bared, seemingly prepared to leap on me, at my throat.

Ready to kill.

CHAPTER 26

"Hi, there, fella," I said in a soft, soothing voice that I might use on a shrieking human infant. "How did you get here? What can we do to get you calm?"

His growl only rose, like a revved engine. He stood half crouched, his forepaws stretched out with his head nearly to the ground. It was those rear legs I had to watch. He looked ready to spring.

"How about a treat?" I continued. "Are you hungry?" I glanced around from the corner of my eye. Fortunately, I didn't see any of our inhabitants running around loose. That rarely happened, but obviously one had managed to get out of his enclosure. Only, I didn't recognize this guy. We get a lot of pit bulls here, and pit bull mixes, but the dog facing me was nearly all white, with a black circle around one of his eyes. The only dogs of similar heritage I was aware of that were currently our residents had more black on them.

If this wasn't one of our rescue animals, who was he? How had he gotten here?

The same way Efram Kiley had been murdered and Honey, the Westie mix, had been set as bait for a trap in our storage building?

The same way someone had started to target *me?*

My imagination was running wild. But if fear and adrenaline could trigger offbeat ideas, I certainly had good reason for them.

The dog's growl had muted down to a whisper. Did that mean he was chilling out a little? I saw no collar around his neck to grab on to, but if I could get close enough to pet him, maybe I could steer him toward the nearest empty enclosure, about four cages down from where we participated in our current standoff.

I took one baby step toward him. His growl intensified again. I wasn't stupid. He'd perceive my coming closer to him as more of a threat. So, I couldn't move.

But this couldn't go on all night. At least I hoped not.

Were the security cameras on? Was help on the way? I couldn't count on it.

I didn't have my purse with me, and I hadn't stuffed my BlackBerry into my pocket, so I had no way to call for help. I was on my own here — just Mr. Vicious, all the other nearby but fortunately secure dogs, and me.

I tried to recall everything I'd ever heard about what to do if a dog seemed ready to attack. Don't make eye contact, since that's a threat. If necessary, assume a fetal position. Use pepper spray, assuming you just happen to have a container in your pocket.

None of that seemed particularly helpful at the moment. I decided to wing it.

I stopped looking directly at him, in case that made him nervous. Staring over him, I edged toward the cages. He turned a little, still growling yet looking a little confused.

Good. Confusion might be helpful — unless it led to fear and his excuse to jump me.

I inched along, my back touching the enclosures of Honey and her neighbors till I reached the empty one. So far, so good.

I opened the gate very slowly. The dog had turned, his back toward the central building, since I had moved into a spot that had previously been beside him.

I could do one of two things: lock myself inside and wait till morning or help otherwise arrived, with him growling at me through the wire bars — and perhaps endangering other dogs if he had escaped in some way that could be imitated. That would also potentially place my employees at risk, if he attacked whoever arrived first.

Or, I could take a chance on getting him inside.

No choice, really. Time to act. I stopped pretending not to look at him, stared him straight in the eyes, and growled as loud as his most vocal rendition. He bared his teeth and leaped toward me.

I screamed. Had I made a huge mistake? As he launched himself toward me, I turned, protecting my throat with one hand and using the other, plus one leg, to shove him as hard as I could into the enclosure.

I felt the skin of my arm rip as I swiped against the latch on the gate while avoiding his teeth, but I managed to get him inside and shove the gate closed. Panting and crying, I locked it from the outside.

I noticed pain then, from my new wound and the one in my leg from the knife, and my assorted bruises.

But I wasn't badly hurt. The angry dog, barking and hurling himself at the metal rungs, was confined.

Everything was under control.

No need to call 911. The danger was over. I

nevertheless double-checked the lock on that enclosure. The dog inside was starting to calm down. Once he realized he was trapped, he sat down and regarded me with fury in his eyes, as if I were his evil stepmother who had foiled his good time.

Poor thing. Now that he was no longer a threat, I had a moment to think. He was a dog. Dogs should be people's friends and allies, not their enemies.

This particular dog clearly didn't know that now. Had he ever? Would he in the future? I certainly hoped so.

I'd see what I could do to make it happen. But for now I decided to phone Every-Security.

The nearest camera might not pan far enough to pick up what had happened. Not so coincidentally, it was the same one that may not have been in working order the night Honey was moved into the storage building, and the same one that Efram had covered the night he was killed. I'd no idea, after the Honey incident, if it was even working. I had never gotten a straight answer about that from the security company, whose representative had claimed they would check out the camera feeds and get back to me. They hadn't.

The dog and I had certainly made enough

noise to tell them something was wrong now — sounds that would be picked up by cameras farther away. Shouldn't their patrol be here already to help? Maybe that was stretching things regarding their abysmally inadequate services.

They'd been of so little use recently that I hoped I would be able to convince Dante that they should be fired. This was the last straw from a hugely overgrown haystack. We hadn't had that discussion yet, but this time we certainly would.

Murmuring comforting words to the other dogs in enclosures along my route, I dragged myself inside the main building to my office. I collapsed on my barely comfortable desk chair, as exhausted as if I'd just completed running one of the marathons I sometimes entered to solicit more donations for the benefit of HotRescues.

Marshaling all my energy and ignoring my pain, I made that first call to EverySecurity. I didn't explain all the circumstances to the dispatcher who answered, just said there had been some trouble here and I needed help.

As if I trusted they'd be of any use at all now, especially since I had everything under control.

Next I called Matt Kingston. Animal

343

Services needed to take control of this dog . . . maybe. Vicious dogs did not belong on the loose, and holding a license to run a shelter gave me certain obligations to protect the public. Plus, we weren't permitted to take in strays, which this dog might be.

But I knew that the overworked, understaffed, and limited facility public shelter system would take the official position that there was only one answer to this apparently untrained dog: put him down, as they were potentially considering with the animals taken into custody from the dog-fighting location. Whatever Matt might personally think, that might be what he was required to say.

Or he wouldn't tell me, just take possession of this dog and do what he had to.

Good thing I only reached Matt's voice mail. So why did I feel so deflated about it? I left a message.

Better choice: I called Si Rogan. I needed him to come as fast as he could to assess how brutal this dog really was — and if he could be retrained. I never, ever wanted to be responsible for putting a healthy dog down, even indirectly, and this guy looked as healthy as any dog I had ever seen. Hopefully, Si would back me and help me figure out a way to save him.

I reached him immediately, and he promised to come right away.

For the first time that evening, I let myself relax a little.

But not for long. A backlit figure appeared at the door to my office, causing me to scream.

"EverySecurity," the guy ID'd himself, holding his credentials as he wedged his way inside. "I got a call that you've had a problem here."

He looked vaguely familiar, had probably been here before. He was moderate in height and weight and, of course, wore one of the standard dark green uniforms of the security company. His identification said his name was George.

I stood to face him. "You could say that," I retorted. "Where were you guys?" I proceeded to ream him for somehow allowing an apparently vicious, stray dog get into the premises without any notification to us. "He could have injured, even killed, some of the animals sheltered here."

"He *was* one of the animals sheltered here." I could see George's face, now that he wasn't backlit, and although his somewhat bulbous features appeared pretty much expressionless, there was an irritated gleam illuminating his small eyes. "Or he was about to be."

"What do you mean?" I demanded.

"I think you know . . . Look, let me talk to my supervisor. We'll get back to you." He disappeared as fast as he'd shown up to frighten me. I followed long enough to make sure he exited through the reception area door, into the adjoining parking lot. Then I returned to my office.

He thought I knew . . . what? *I* knew that *he* knew plenty. In fact, I wouldn't have been surprised to learn that he, or someone else from EverySecurity, had let that uninvited dog onto the HotRescues premises. But why?

My BlackBerry rang. I was back at my desk and dug my phone from my pocket before letting my legs collapse until I was seated again on my chair.

It was Matt. "I'm outside, Lauren. Just saw a security guy drive his car away. Let me in and tell me what happened."

Usually, I'd have reacted quite negatively to his ordering me around. I don't like anyone telling me what to do — not even Dante, although I tolerate it with him, since he has the ability to get the HotRescues board of directors to fire me.

Right now, though, I decided that obeying Matt was in my best interests, so I didn't tell him to stuff it. Instead, I agreed to let him in right away.

I went to the door to the parking lot and opened it. There he was. Talk about my acting uncharacteristically. I flung myself into his arms. I didn't even consider the fact that he might not want me there. I just held on.

Fortunately, those arms closed around me. "You okay?" he demanded.

When I looked up to assure him that I was fine, he kissed me. I kissed him back. Then, I decided it was time to get sensible again.

"Come in," I said. "I'll show you."

I locked the door behind him and preceded him through the reception building and out into the shelter area. Of course the dogs began their usual clamor of greeting. I smiled wryly, glad that they were all safe behind the gates of their enclosures.

I stopped in front of the cage where I'd tricked my unwelcome visitor into entering. He was standing now, and barking as loudly as his nearby compatriots.

"I don't know where he came from," I told Matt. "But he was loose here, and maybe scared. We had a standoff for a while." I didn't tell him about my disagreement with the representative of our security company.

Plus, I downplayed this visitor's aggressiveness.

"So he's a stray."

"Probably," I admitted sadly.

"And you don't know his background, whether he's been trained for dogfighting or anything else?"

"Unfortunately, no," I said. "I know Animal Services needed to be informed, so I called you. But I'm hoping we can take him in, and that he can be retrained. And speaking of that . . ." I smiled broadly as I saw Si Rogan approaching from the opposite end of the path. "Thanks for coming, Si," I said.

"So this guy attacked you?" Si sounded angrier than I'd ever heard him before. He didn't look at Matt or me but only at the dog. "Hey, fellow, who are you? What's your problem?" He turned toward us. "Please stand back." He reached to open the gate.

"That may not be a good idea," I cautioned him, then tilted my head apologetically. "Sorry. You know that better than I do."

He slipped inside the enclosure. I noticed then that he was wearing not his usual jeans and shirt from his dog training school, Rogan's Dog Obedience Studio, but leather-covered garments. If the dog bit at him, the

348

leather might get hurt but Si wasn't likely to.

He stared down at the dog, who'd crouched again as if ready to spring and begun growling as loudly as I'd heard him at his worst before. I'd recalled then that eye contact would only make an aggressive dog worse, but Si's expression, whatever it was, must have somehow registered in my prior foe's mind as belonging to someone even more alpha than he. The dog stopped growling and lay down on the ground submissively.

He'd met someone who could handle him.

That only made me smile. But I didn't want to break the mood by talking aloud to Si. I waited and watched. So did Matt, beside me.

In a few minutes, Si came back out of the enclosure. "If it's okay to leave him here overnight, I'll bring appropriate equipment tomorrow to transport him to my school. I think I can rehabilitate him."

"That's wonderful!" I smiled all the more, which earned a shy smile from the dog trainer. "*You're* wonderful. And that means Animal Services doesn't need to get involved, Matt."

"But this dog's a stray. Plus, he attacked you, didn't he?" I hadn't exactly said so, but Matt had undoubtedly seen the scratch on my arm. "I'll need to have him impounded for observation."

"No. We just had a minor disagreement."

"And I'll take personal charge of him," Si said. "That way, HotRescues isn't taking in a stray."

I thanked Si with a warm smile. "That's wonderful! I won't have to worry about anyone killing him for having a . . . bad disposition at times. Thanks for coming, Matt, but everything's under control now."

Si was grinning now, too. I suspected he liked the idea of winning out over Animal Services.

"Fine," Matt said. "I'll talk to you soon." His eyes met mine, as if he intended to remind me by his soft glare about how I'd greeted him before . . . with a kiss. But that had been in the heat of the moment, so to speak. I'd enjoyed it, as I'd enjoyed kissing him before, but it didn't mean anything.

Did it?

Didn't matter. Matt left. Si didn't.

"Do you know how the dog got here?" Si asked. "I mean, I was here earlier today and didn't see him. Did one of the staff pick him up somewhere? He doesn't seem the usual kind of animal cared for by HotRescues."

"You're right. And, no, I don't know how he got here. It's really strange."

Si nodded. "Well, I guess it doesn't matter, especially if I can make sure he can have a productive life from now on. I'll keep him isolated, of course, to watch for rabies and all. But was Animal Services already here to pick him up?"

"What do you mean?"

"I found one of these near the back gate when I came in." He handed me a piece of paper with the Animal Services logo at the top — one that appeared to be a memo from a commissioner to someone at SmART. Odd. How could that have gotten there?

Unless . . . could it have been in Matt's possession? Had he been at the rear gate sometime today?

Had he been the one to let the vicious pit bull mix inside?

He'd undoubtedly have access to dogs like that, especially after the dogfighting ring Animal Services had just broken up. But why would he do such a thing?

If he did, was it an indication that he'd been responsible for some, or all, of the other things that had been going on at HotRescues?

Like Efram's murder?

He was one of my suspects, after all. But not a serious contender — or so I'd believed.

"I'm leaving now." Si interrupted my thoughts, and I nearly blessed him for that. "If you're okay. I'll see you tomorrow, when I come by to bring this guy to my place."

"I'm fine," I told him, and walked him to the back gate. "Thanks so much for taking care of this, Si. I can't tell you how much I appreciate the fact that you're saving that dog's life."

"You don't need to." He smiled at me, then went through the gate.

I realized how sad that smile looked. The guy apparently was still attracted to me, but I felt nothing toward him but friendship. And gratitude.

Maybe someday I'd have a drink with him, make sure he understood why I just wasn't seriously interested, in him or any man.

Although if Matt weren't such an enigma . . .

I hurried back toward the front of HotRescues, observing all the inhabitants in the artificial light as I passed by.

And saw, as I reached the welcome area, that it wasn't empty now. Ed Bransom was there, the manager of our ineffective security company.

Not good timing. I didn't want to chew him out until I talked to Dante about this latest fiasco.

But I could make it clear how angry I was.

"Did your patrol guy George tell you what happened here?"

"Yes," Bransom said, "he did." I didn't like the belligerent look on his military-sharp face.

"Did he tell you I made it clear I wasn't happy that the dog got in here, that it could have harmed others?"

"He told me."

"Then what happened. Why wasn't your company doing its damned job?"

Bransom scowled even more fiercely, reminding me of the dog I'd faced before, partly thanks to his company's ineptitude. "We were doing our job, Ms. Vancouver. Can't necessarily say the same for you."

Shocked, I said, "What the hell do you —"

"Our guy doing rounds — George — did see someone bringing a dog into HotRescues earlier this evening. Not out. Nothing looked amiss. His assumption was that the person he saw was someone who belonged there. She certainly didn't appear as if she was engaged in anything improper."

353

Despite my rage, my brain seemed to narrow its focus onto one word. "She?" That would definitely abridge my suspect list.

"Here's the gist of what he told me: The person he spotted was in a unisex kind of getup, jeans and a hoodie worn so it obscured her face. Or his. He wasn't sure. But . . ."

"But what?" I pushed.

Bransom's eyes narrowed, even as his mouth edged up in what appeared to be a cruel and accusatory smile. "He's been around here before, when you've been present. He knows you, Ms. Vancouver. He's seen you wearing that hoodie. And he'll swear that the person he saw was you."

CHAPTER 27

Once again, it was really late by the time I thought about leaving HotRescues that night.

Once again, I'd suffered a wound — this time a scratch from a usually benign gate latch, not a falling knife.

This time, no one was insisting that I go to a hospital to make sure I was all right. Which was fine with me. I didn't like to be babied.

But I wasn't a fool. In all my many years of dealing with animals, I'd heard of a lot of minor wounds that turned into something really nasty and even life-threatening if they weren't taken care of adequately.

But not necessarily by a medical doctor in a hospital emergency room. I called Carlie. Despite how late it was, she was still at her veterinary clinic in Northridge.

The Fittest Pet Veterinary Clinic was on Reseda Boulevard, in a relatively quiet commercial area. The building was delightful, an animal hospital that looked like a medical facility people might aspire to. It was pink stucco and square, with treatment rooms along the outer perimeter. Test and care facilities lined the inside, and windows opened to a large Eden-like garden.

Dogs in good enough condition, including those being boarded while their owners were out of town, were treated to walks outside in the loving custody of the veterinary techs. Cats weren't leashed, of course, but they were nevertheless given the luxury of some pleasant crate time overlooking the lovely garden area.

Even if I hadn't been good friends with Carlie, I'd have made sure that animals from HotRescues that needed medical care were brought here. And, of course, when my own family's sweet little Bosley had been alive — and when his life was clearly almost over — this was the veterinary facility we had used.

It was long past office hours, but I walked up to the reception area and pushed a button to ring a bell inside. I heard it go off, and a female tech with a kind and concerned expression on her face responded quickly, opening the door.

The Fittest Pet hospital offered twenty-four/seven emergency care. When I identified myself to the tech, she smiled. "Dr. Stellan is expecting you." She looked down at my arm and shook her head. "That isn't the usual kind of emergency we see here. Are you sure you wouldn't rather go somewhere else?"

"If it was something life-threatening, absolutely. But I have lots of faith in Dr. Stellan's ability to perform first aid on a human."

"Me, too." The tech led me through the door into the heart of the medical center and into a room within the inner sanctum. "Here she is." The tech left me there.

Carlie was inside, dressed in a white hospital jacket, softly petting an unconscious collie mix.

My heart stopped, softhearted organ that it was. Carlie obviously saw my concern and smiled. "Just waiting for this fellow to wake up after successful minor surgery to remove a few coins that he decided to eat. They weren't just passing through as we expected, so I went inside to help."

I smiled back. "And are those coins helping to pay your exorbitant bill?"

"A down payment. Let's go next door and take a look at your arm. You'd think someone who spent as much time around animals

357

as you would know when to stay away from a dog who's lost his temper. And to stay away from vicious gate latches."

"Yeah, you'd think so." I'd told her enough, when I'd called her, to realize she was kidding. She understood the circumstances and seemed almost as outraged as me about my confrontation with Every-Security.

After calling for a vet tech to keep an eye on the sleeping dog, she sat me down on a seat reserved for patients' owners in the next-door treatment room. She washed her hands, then bathed my arm in a solution that I assumed was an antiseptic. She applied some clear ointment and bandaged the sore spot. My friend worked so efficiently and gently that I barely felt any pain. I also showed her the wound on my leg. It was still healing well and didn't hurt much.

"Okay, come on into the kitchen and we'll talk," she said.

The pet hospital kitchen, down the hall and around a corner, was a huge room filled with a variety of cooking and storage equipment — gas ovens and microwaves, refrigerators and freezers. I'd seen it before when Carlie gave me the hundred-dollar tour of the place, but I hadn't spent time in this area.

Now, she fiddled around with a coffee-maker, added beans for it to grind, and started a fresh pot. "I assume regular will be okay with you, even though it's getting late?"

I assured her that I looked forward to the caffeine. I'd probably need it to get home safely that night.

While it was brewing, she sat down beside me. "Okay, now, tell me all. You only whetted my appetite before. Some jerk of a security guy is accusing you not only of bringing a vicious dog to HotRescues, but leaving it loose so it could bite you? What a crock."

"Yeah, but this crock could turn into a boiling cauldron of trouble for me." I explained why I felt so anxious, in light of the other things that had happened at HotRescues. "The security guy claimed that the person was wearing a hoodie like mine — which was missing from my office. Who-ever came in could have grabbed it before bringing the dog in. Or the security guy could have done it himself. Or lied about it altogether. But if the police thought I was setting things up before, this just adds another suspicious act to their list. Especially considering the purportedly stellar reputation of that damned security company."

Carlie's usually brilliant violet eyes sizzled down to a deep and ominous purple. "What's really going on, Lauren? Not that I know what I'm talking about, but as an outsider looking in, it appears that someone is going to a lot of trouble to make you look bad in a lot of ways. The person who murdered Efram? But why all the rest of this?"

"I've wondered that, too." I sighed, glancing over her shoulder toward the counter where the coffeemaker seemed to be finished with its work for the night. I stood and so did she. She'd already put two blood-red *Pet Fitness* TV mugs out and I filled them.

She waited for me to rejoin her at the table. When I didn't say anything at first, she demanded, "Well, what's your conclusion. Who's doing this and why?"

"The killer at HotRescues, with ingenuity," I said, in a feeble effort to jokingly employ the format of the old board game Clue.

"Yeah, yeah. Okay, so I gather from your silliness that you don't have a clue."

"I have several, but none conclusive."

She laughed, then grew serious. "So what are you going to do about it?"

"Talk it through with you, of course."

I gave her a rundown of my latest effort at organizing my suspicions in computer files. "I keep moving my suspects around, since I'm trying to keep a running assessment of whom I think is most likely to be the perpetrator."

"Okay, but what else?"

"Well, here are those I have in mind so far." I gave her an abbreviated list of those I suspected, how much I suspected them, and why. I realized that Matt had moved up several rungs on my ladder of suspicion. I didn't want that to have happened, but it unfortunately made sense.

"So you think those damned puppy mill clowns are the most likely to have killed Efram?" Carlie demanded when I'd finished.

"Yes, and after them those other people he knew. His stepmother and girlfriend both had excellent motives."

"But the opportunity to do all the rest of this junk, right there at HotRescues?" I must have looked surprised, for she smiled and commented, "I'm a TV star, don't you know? So of course I watch some of the competition, like those shows where all kinds of characters, official or not, solve murders. I know all about the basics that are fed to the audience, including who, why, what, where, drama, opportunity, and sex."

My turn to laugh.

But seriousness washed her lovely face into a grave and worried expression. "Anyway," she continued, "I have lots of faith in you, Lauren. I know you're using all your ingenuity to try to figure this out, including how a stranger might be able to sneak into HotRescues. But I think some kind of kick in the butt is needed, something different. Something that will get your villain to differentiate himself from the other riffraff of suspects. Let's brainstorm, see if we can come up with something that will turn the tide here."

"I've been thinking about that," I admitted. "Something has come to mind. I've no idea if it'll work, but let me run it by you."

I did, and despite throwing in suggestions and concerns of her own, Carlie appeared to love it.

Which was a good thing, because the next day Detective Stefan Garciana appeared bright and early at HotRescues.

Although I wanted to tell him to get lost, I was the epitome of politeness and invited him into my office. He sat immediately in one of the chairs in my conversation area, motioning me to join him. I swallowed my irritation that he was giving me nonverbal orders in my own environment.

"I heard about what happened here last night," he said, his features even darker than usual, which tossed an urgency to run in my direction. "I was also in touch with the manager of EverySecurity. Do you know what he alleged?"

"Mr. Bransom and I are not exactly admirers of one another. He told me last night how much he suspects me of bringing that nasty dog here to attack me and make people feel sympathetic. Same thing about dragging Honey into the storage shed so I could use her as an excuse to get myself stabbed — again to elicit sympathy. And all of this so the world would assume that I'm so targeted and persecuted that I couldn't have murdered Efram — which he's sure I did. Is that it?"

"You've nailed it." Garciana's mouth lifted on one side, whether because he wanted to feign a grin or heartburn I wasn't sure. "It certainly would explain how whoever's been doing it all has gotten onto the property despite your having a security company on board."

"There are other explanations, like Efram showed his killer how to circumvent the system the first time and the method is still working."

"Maybe." Garciana didn't sound at all convinced. "Any idea who it could be?"

"You're the detective," I countered, trying to keep my tone reasonable instead of as explosive as I felt. "You should have figured it out by now and arrested the real bad guy."

"I hear that a lot from people who want me to think they're innocent. The problem is, ninety-nine percent of the time they're the bad guys themselves. How about you, Ms. Vancouver?"

"This is the other one percent, Detective," I assured him. But at the ironic skepticism he glared at me, I was sure my time to prove the truth to him was running out.

I'd have a lot of planning to do, but I intended to start on my hopefully last-ditch scheme to save myself right away.

CHAPTER 28

It had taken over a week to get this event together, but it was still one of the fastest I'd ever accomplished — and I'd put together a lot of them, all over LA.

With the help of my excellent staff and volunteers, plus a hint to that obnoxious reporter Corina Carey, I'd gotten out the word about the HotRescues pet adoption fair in memory of Efram Kiley — and worded it with the tact of a politician up for reelection, without rubbing his dead face in the fact he had been involved with a horrendous puppy mill.

No, I wasn't the world's most despicable hypocrite. I was using Efram for my own purposes, just as he had abused animals for his. My intent was to get each of the people I suspected of his murder to appear, to at least feign grieving, and hopefully to say something that revealed the truth and exposed him or her as the killer.

I'd gotten all required permission to hold the event in O'Melveny Park, one of the largest in LA, which happened to be in Granada Hills not far from HotRescues. My team and I had brought a dozen dogs and nearly as many cats, mostly in crates. They included Honey, since the people who'd expressed interest in adopting her hadn't yet followed through, poor baby. Or maybe it was just as well, if those folks were so unreliable.

The animals we'd carted here also included Sweety and Missy, from Efram's puppy mill. They were just exiting quarantine and doing amazingly well, thanks to Carlie and lots of TLC at her veterinary clinic and HotRescues. Soon, they'd be ready to rehome. It didn't hurt to display them to potential new owners now.

Naturally, the dogs didn't stay in crates. We'd constructed holding areas surrounded by portable fencing, so a few pups were loose inside — the better to put their noses to the barrier and look wistful enough to attract possible adopters. Plus, our volunteers displayed them, one at a time, by taking them for walks through this area of the park, like models flaunting their assets on a runway.

I intended to go on some of those walks

— later. Right now, I sat at a shaded table nearest the parking area, the better to see who joined us, at least from the area most likely to entice visitors. Fortunately, all my wounds had healed well enough by now that I barely felt them.

Nina was beside me. We'd brought along plenty of applications for people who were interested in adopting. Plus brochures that would tell them about HotRescues, our achievements, and our goals. We also had some bags containing pet food samples and other goodies from — where else? — Hot-Pets.

We had called on a lot of our regular volunteers to join us, so they could ask our standard questions of potential adopters. I still needed to personally approve each adoption. Although it happened sometimes at our pet fairs, none would be finalized that day. But we often had success in getting people to become excited about animals they met at this kind of event and start the adoption process.

"This is such a good idea, Lauren." Nina's pleasure was contagious. Or maybe I just felt really proud of myself, killing two or more birds with one of this park's stones. With luck, some of our residents would find new forever homes, thanks to this event.

And with even more luck, I'd get myself off the hook as a suspect in Efram's murder.

"Thanks," I said to Nina. "I just hope we're really successful." In all ways.

I decided to practice my intended routine on Nina. I did, after all, still maintain a page on her in my suspect file. Even though she was one of those I wanted in the worst way not to be guilty.

"I hope it's not too tacky making this a memorial for Efram," I said. I hadn't expressly discussed it with my second in command before. I'd just told her that this was what I intended to do, then expressed my desire for her to help with it. "But my hope is that it'll show what he himself never seemed to grasp: pets need to be taken care of, not harmed, and not left in shelters without someone to love them."

"That's what I thought you meant." Nina's face looked as bright and enthusiastic as I'd ever seen her. Her long brown hair was pulled back in a clip, emphasizing the leanness of her cheeks. Her curviness filled out her HotRescues T-shirt. I'd wondered often if she ever considered dating again. Despite my recent moments with Matt, I rarely did, and my miserable excuse for an ex-husband hadn't abused me.

"I've thought long and hard about who

could have killed him," I continued. "Of course murder's a heinous thing, especially since whoever did it is apparently willing to let me take the rap. But I can certainly understand why someone was angry enough with a man like him to wish him harm, don't you?"

She looked at me with a defeated expression that suggested she thought I was about to accuse her. Which I wasn't . . . directly.

"You know I do," she said quietly. "I hated him because of what he did to animals, and because he threatened me for telling you about the puppy mill rescue. I wasn't as sad as I should have been about what happened to him. But . . . I couldn't have done it, even if I'd wished I could."

"Of course," I said.

An older couple approached our table, which sent a wave of ambivalence through me. This conversation was over, at least for now. And although I realized that Nina could be lying, I didn't think so. I'd learned enough about her over the year she'd been working for me to get a sense of when she was fudging the truth.

I sent her off with the couple, who seemed emotionally overwhelmed about seeing so many homeless animals here. I had the impression they'd never visited a shelter.

Did they want a pet? Maybe they would now, even if they hadn't considered one before.

The area was crowded now with people who didn't stay on any paths but approached the dog enclosures and cat crates with oohs and aahs I could hear from far away. Surely some of them would fall immediately and madly in love — hopefully good people who'd pass our adoption scrutiny. At least the weather was on our side, which it usually was in LA. Not too hot and not too cold; just right for attracting people to stroll around and, hopefully, fall for the pets of their dreams.

Our animal shrink, Dr. Mona Harvey, was there, flitting from one enclosure to the next. I was able to chat with her along with our vet tech, Angie Shayde, giving them similar spiels to what I'd talked with Nina about. They hadn't liked Efram — or at least what he'd done — any better than I had. Admit here to killing him? Not quite.

I saw Captain Matt Kingston approaching from the side of our festival. He was another person I'd intended to sound out about how he felt about a memorial for Efram — and whether he could have been involved in the event that generated it.

He, even more than Nina, seemed to have

no alibi for the night Efram was killed, or for the ensuing dangerous situations at HotRescues. He clearly had despised Efram as much as I had. But kill him?

Well, someone had, and the thing I was surest of was that it wasn't me.

Matt had come in his official Animal Services uniform — khaki shirt, green slacks, and jacket with appropriate badge and patch.

He stopped long before he got to me and knelt outside one of the fenced-in areas. I stood. As I'd thought, that was the place that the animals from the puppy mill were now enclosed. I guessed he was doing his official duty and making sure they were well cared for.

Motioning to Bev, who'd just finished walking a sheltie mix, to take my place at the table, I headed toward Matt. He was still on his knees, his hand inside the enclosure where Missy and Sweety vied to sniff it. He turned his too sexy grin from them toward me.

"Glad you could make it," I told him. "There's been some interest in adopting those guys, but it's too soon. I'll let you know if anything comes of it."

"Great." He stood to face me. I'd noticed before how much taller than me he was, but he now seemed to marshal his height and stare down. "What's this really about, Lauren? A memorial for a guy you despised?"

"It's intended to send a message," I said coolly. "That even if he couldn't be rehabilitated while alive, at least there can be happy endings for some of the animals he abused. You know HotRescues would love to take in more of the moms, dads, or pups that were saved from the puppy mill, when Animal Services is ready for them to leave."

"Right." Matt cocked his head slightly, watching as if attempting to read what was actually inside my brain.

I could give him a hint . . . "Don't you think that might be what the person who killed him intended? I mean, to teach not only him, but others who abused animals a lesson." My turn to scrutinize him for a reaction.

"Sounds like a stretch," he said. "But even so, I hope you're successful here today."

Me, too, I thought — in both of my endeavors.

Matt's attitude and words had neither made him more of a suspect or less. I still had to mistrust him, for reasons including the Animal Services paperwork found near the back entrance on the day the pit bull had mysteriously appeared, but I didn't really want to.

A tall, thin guy in shorts and sleeveless T-shirt jogged up to us. His dog, too — a leashed and panting Border collie. "Hi," the guy said, addressing Matt. "What's going on here?"

Matt quickly explained the adoption event while I bent and petted his companion. She looked up at me, and I smiled back. This obviously was a loved dog, and I sensed she understood how much better she had it than her enclosed cohorts around here.

As the two loped off, I watched, then realized Matt was watching me. "Cute," I said. "And smart."

"Border collie," he responded. I nodded, hoping my wistfulness didn't show. There was something about that kind of dog that spoke to me without saying a word. If ever I were to adopt a dog again myself . . . but not now.

Matt began to walk away, glancing back as if he assumed I would follow. I didn't — mostly because I'd just spotted another of the people I'd hoped would be here that day, Ed Bransom of EverySecurity. He didn't look as if he was there in any official role for his company, since he wore an LA Dodgers T-shirt over jeans. Since I'd seen him most often in his dark green uniform, I was a little surprised to see that he had well-toned muscles. I supposed that made sense for someone who was in the business of keeping customers safe.

It also moved him higher in my suspect assessment. The knife that had killed Efram was sharp, but even so, the person who'd wielded it needed strength behind it. Plus, it had taken some strength to move those pet food bags around for the Honey incident.

Whatever his reason for being there, it apparently wasn't because he intended to adopt a pet. Nor had I called him to help with any security here.

"Hello, Lauren," he said. "What the hell is going on? I've heard from our main office that Dante DeFrancisco is considering other security companies for HotPets and your little shelter. Is that your doing?"

Yes, I'd finally had a conversation with Dante. Despite his long-term friendship with the EverySecurity CEO, he'd promised to consider alternatives . . . under the circumstances.

"I think it's a wise course of action," I told him. "You seem to have the idea that everything your company should have prevented at HotRescues was my doing. It wasn't. A parting of the ways is more than appropriate."

I still hadn't heard a viable explanation or excuse for the slipup in the Honey matter — except to blame me. Plus, Bransom also blamed me, vocally, for the unwelcome pit bull visit. Even if he was innocent of everything that had happened, he couldn't have been surprised that I wanted his company gone. But the fact that Dante so far was on my side and was looking at other options for his entire business empire? That might have annoyed this dismal excuse for a security advisor, more than a little.

Another reason for him to become an even weightier suspect. Yet why would he have killed Efram in the first place? Just because the guy had shown up at HotRescues in the middle of the night? Bransom didn't appear to care whether someone was abusing animals, unless he was paid to pretend to give a damn. But to protect his own butt, or his job . . . ?

He took a step toward me. Maybe I should have acted cowed and stepped back, but I didn't. I stared him right in the eye.

"You'd better watch what you say. We've had this account sewed up for a long time, and you're not going to ruin it."

"I think that you've managed to do that

yourself," I said, then turned and walked away.

And practically felt the daggers from his glare piercing my back like the HotRescues feed knives.

Oh, yes, this man was one person I definitely suspected.

I took a quick potty break and returned to the adoption area near the far side, where that very pit bull was in a nice, roomy crate — all by himself, of course. Si was near him, sitting on a folding chair. As I approached, he jumped to his feet.

"Lauren, I've been hoping to get you over here. I want to show you my progress with Perry."

"Perry?"

"I thought that Perry the pit bull mix would sound cute and not especially scary."

"Got it."

As Si bent to open the crate and leash Perry, I looked around. The park was still full of visitors. I crossed my fingers, hoping that Perry wouldn't attack anyone else. Including me.

I noticed Matt watching from a distance. He hurried in our direction as Si brought the nearly all white dog out. I appreciated Matt's concern. Was it for me or for everyone here, as part of his Animal Services responsibilities? Probably both. Whichever, it made me feel good.

Si noticed him, too, and glared. "Please stay back," he said. "Everything's under control."

And it was. Si put Perry through an amazing array of commands, from the usual "sit" and "down" to "shake" and even "beg."

"You did this in a week?" I said in amazement.

"He knew some of it. Whoever his owner may have been before, he'd apparently had some training. I've found that the more I work him out, the less aggressive he is. He's not for a household with kids or other pets, but he's a good candidate for adoption."

"One more test." I'm not usually wimpy when it comes to being around any kinds of animals, but Perry had been one nasty canine to me before. I approached him slowly, my hand out in a nonthreatening manner, but half expected him to go back into snarl and growl mode.

He didn't. In fact, his tongue flopped out of his mouth as I petted him.

As I stepped back, I smiled at Si and gave him a brief hug — making sure that Perry didn't take it as a threatening gesture toward his new master. "You're fantastic!" I told Si. "Don't you think so, Perry?"

The dog I'd feared so much previously just seemed to smile.

I visited the cat area next and was thrilled to learn from Nina and a couple of our volunteers that half of the kitties we'd brought here were likely to be rehomed, once I approved the applications. I wanted to hug them all in congratulations. But that was when I spotted two more people I'd hoped would show up that day, thanks to my e-mailed invitations: the Shaheens.

Patsy and Bradley looked bemused when I greeted them, then showed them the two parent dogs from their puppy mill. "We haven't found new homes for them yet," I told the couple I despised. "Too soon. But we will when it's appropriate."

Patsy again put on her act of loving them all and missing them. And blaming Efram for everything.

I again thought how convenient, since he was dead. Possibly at her hands, or her husband's.

We were joined then by Efram's step-mother and girlfriend, whom I'd also invited. Apparently the Shaheens knew Mandy Ledinger and Shellie Benudo. Maybe they'd met Efram's stepmother and girlfriend at his funeral, if not before.

Smiling a lot and keeping my digs at them ambiguous, I told them my reason for holding this adoption event in Efram's honor. Did they buy it? Maybe.

The Shaheens still seemed affronted that I would equate their actions with Efram's supposed really bad animal abuse in throwing puppies into a storm drain. After all, they'd merely tortured dogs and their offspring by untenable conditions.

Mandy and Shellie seemed to accept the situation with more grace, although they still maintained that Efram had done nothing wrong. Holding an event like this to help counter anything he had allegedly done was insulting to his memory.

Had any of them killed him? A definite maybe, considering their respective attitudes — although they seemed more angry with me than with Efram. Could any of them have tried to cover it up by the ensuing shenanigans that had taken place at HotRescues? Yes, if Efram had demonstrated how to get in and circumvent the security, including the cameras.

But no one yet knew where Perry had come from or how he'd gotten loose on the premises. That could be the key.

Or not.

■ ■ ■ ■

Later, we returned to HotRescues with all the animals, including those who were likely now to be adopted. I helped to get them into their enclosures once more, then started the administrative work to sign them each back in again.

We'd had a fairly successful day, with quite a few potential rehomings — although I would definitely follow up as quickly as possible with visits to make sure the adopters were as kind and caring as they'd professed on their applications and in person. I'd also make sure they had the suitable facilities they'd described for their new pets.

I realized several things as I returned to my office and collapsed.

A few people I'd hoped to see there, including James Remseyer, Efram's attorney, hadn't shown up. That didn't gain him any brownie points with me. He was still a suspect.

The other thing that I found particularly interesting — and disturbing? Well, I'd heard stories of how Dante's lady friend, Kendra Ballantyne, the lawyer, had solved quite a few murder cases. She'd done it in odd ways, setting things up, often, to have animals she was pet-sitting involved in the resolution.

I'd done something similar today. I'd hoped for an equally good result, determining once and for all who'd murdered Efram.

But despite such a good day in so many other ways, especially for some of our former HotRescues animals, I still felt no closer to determining the killer.

CHAPTER 29

I was about as happy that evening in my office at HotRescues as one of our pet residents who's just been relinquished here permanently by his former owner.

First, I noticed I'd missed a call on my BlackBerry from Detective Garciana. Usually, I was perturbed if I didn't hear my phone ring while easily accessible, in my pocket. Not this time. I'd even missed its vibration with all the excitement of the adoption event going on around me.

That was the only good thing about the call.

At our pet fair, I'd spoken with nearly everyone I'd wanted to talk to that day. Even so, I was no more ahead in figuring out what had happened to Efram than I had been before.

At least the detective hadn't shown up at the park. I definitely wouldn't have wanted to talk to him then. Or now. Or ever. But I doubted I had a choice.

He'd left me a message to call him. He had more questions. And, oh yes, it was fine for us to set up a meeting where my lawyer could be present.

Those questions of his would go on forever. Or until he arrested me for Efram's murder. Whichever happened first.

I had a feeling inside — one that squeezed my lungs into a tight, constricted ball — that it would be the latter. Soon.

At least it was too late to call the detective back now. Tomorrow? Maybe I would forget. Or lose my phone.

I stayed at HotRescues long after my staff had departed. I used the excuse to them, and to myself, that I still had a lot of administrative work to do.

That was true.

It was also true that I didn't have to do it all myself. Or that night. But I wanted the distraction.

When the last to leave, Nina, got on her way, I waited for a few minutes, then walked through the shelter area, greeting all our residents who were still around.

Was I nervous after everything that had been happening around here? I'd have been a fool not to be.

But would I let it stop me? Never!

I even smiled and waved at the security cameras, in case they were working and being monitored by someone under orders to watch my every move — and to pray I did something really awful that they could record and show to the cops and to Dante.

I stopped to open gates and hug as many dogs as I could — and especially to commiserate with those animals who'd been at the fair and had to return here.

Perry was among them. We were ostensibly boarding him now for Si, and if we happened to find him a good home that would be fine, too. I tempted fate — and Si's amazingly excellent training — by first putting my arm through the fencing and petting the formerly vicious dog. I half expected him to bite a finger or two off. Instead, he came over and let me pet him. I went inside his enclosure.

"You're wonderful," I verbally caressed him, too. "It's so much better for you to be so calm and sweet. I wish we'd been able to learn where you came from. Well, if we can't figure it out, we'll find you a new, loving home that's just right for you. I'll make sure of it."

I hoped I could deliver.

With a final hug for that night, I reluctantly slipped out, locking Perry's gate behind me — making sure I'd done it securely. I always checked, or tried to, with all our residents. I especially didn't want to take a chance on Perry's getting out in case he reverted to his prior aggressiveness.

The HotRescues grounds were fairly bright, thanks to our lighting. The dogs barked a lot, as usual. Now and then, I got a whiff of an enclosure that needed cleaning, and I stopped to take care of the offending piles inside — using that as an excuse to hug another lonely dog.

I went into the center building and provided a similar pep talk to the smaller dogs and the cats who came back here. "I know you don't show it as much on the surface," I told a ginger and a Siamese cat who'd both been at the fair, and who deigned to look at me now, "but I'm sure you were hoping you'd find a new human servant to take you home with them today. It'll happen."

My current round was over. I'd visited everyone who lived here.

I stood outside the central building, close to the spot where Efram had died. It wasn't far from where Perry had all but attacked me. From there, I went back to Honey's enclosure. "I'm really surprised you're still here," I told her sadly. "I'll bet you are, too.

We'll figure something out."

What I figured just then was that I needed to visit the storage building. I yanked the door open, flicked on the lights, and went in. I stomped through both floors and left again.

Outside, I again walked from one end of the shelter grounds to the other.

And then I realized what I was doing: tempting not only the security company, but, even more importantly, the killer, the person who'd been inciting all the mischief around here. My moving around the entire facility was a challenge. A dare. *Here I am . . . again. Come and get me.*

Show your face, you damned coward.

But except for the animals who watched me, sometimes barking, occasionally whining, and nearly always alert, I was alone. And disheartened.

I needed answers. Right away.

Before I was confronted once more by Detective Garciana.

Before I lost my mind from frustration.

But what could I do about it now? I supposed I'd have to sleep on it. There wasn't a lot I could accomplish that night.

Shuffling in discouragement like a hurt child who'd been sent to her room, I returned to my office.

The only thing I could think of to slather a temporary balm over my mood was to check out the reports on our adoption fair — or add one if no one else had so far.

I went to the Southern California Rescuers Web site I sometimes visited where pet rescue administrators keep in touch. Since I'd seen no one I recognized from other shelters at the park that day, and no one had introduced themselves to me as being in the same capacity, I assumed none of the members had been at our event. There were no "attagirls" on the site, so that still seemed a reasonable assumption.

I went to the blog area and posted a lengthy, upbeat description of how things had gone. I'd read similar posts by others who also let the world know about the good and bad things that occurred, and I tended to keep what they said in mind to try to avoid making any similar mistakes.

I noticed that one of the members from Palm Springs had posted a cautionary tale about something that had happened in her area. Not at her shelter, at least. But a local resident known for his fostering of pets in need, and helping to teach people how to take care of animals of all kinds, had been hospitalized because of a traumatic situation.

He had been beaten, and his own, long-time dog had been petnapped.

Sad, I thought.

The guy had known enough to get his friend microchipped, but so far no one had turned him in or otherwise located him.

The situation captured my attention, at least for this moment. I wondered if there was anything that I, or HotRescues, could do to help. I sent a personal e-mail to the shelter administrator who'd posted the blog, then shut down my computer.

It was finally time to go home. I did, however, take one more walk through HotRescues before I left, again tempting fate, and the killer, all but calling out, demanding a confrontation. It didn't happen.

Just before locking up for the night, I called the dispatcher at EverySecurity — hopefully for nearly the last time — and let him know I was leaving for the night. Time for them to earn their big bucks while they could. Especially if they wanted to try to redeem themselves.

Still nothing. Nothing at home, either.

Nothing to give me a shred of optimism that I could keep myself from being arrested in Efram's death.

■ ■ ■ ■

I did manage to sleep that night, to my surprise. At least I did after rehashing the high and low points of the day in my mind as I lay in bed.

I woke up early and soon headed for HotRescues, grabbing a cup of coffee on the way.

Nina wasn't there yet, but volunteer Ricki was, sitting in the welcome room behind our big cat lookalike counter, reading a book on animal health. Not surprising. Her veterinary tech school would start soon.

"Good morning, Lauren." She gave me a huge, welcoming smile. "When's our next adoption fair? This one was so cool!"

I laughed. "Soon, I hope. Who's here?"

So far, she said, only Pete was around, starting to give our residents their breakfasts. "We also got a couple of phone messages. Some people who were at the park yesterday and walked away are now regretting it. A few will be here later today to consider adopting the animals they met."

"Excellent!" I went into my office, put down my coffee, and pushed the button to start my computer's morning routine. One item was to add a file for scheduling home visits to our newly adopted former residents. Then I did my first walk-through of the day.

Pete Engersol was right there, feeding little Honey in the first enclosure. "Good morning, Lauren. Honey just asked when we're doing our next adoption thing. She's getting eager for a new home." Pete had been the only HotRescues employee to stay here yesterday, making sure that those babies we hadn't brought along for possible adoption remained okay despite their loneliness.

"I know she is, Pete." I joined them inside the gate and gave Honey a big hug. "And you deserve it, sweetheart." I told Pete about the people who'd seemed interested in her but never came back. "I'm not about to call them. If they're not eager, they don't deserve Honey. I'm wondering, though, if the people who called this morning might be a different couple than those who spent a lot of time with our Honey at the park yesterday."

Pete and I went out to the path together, and he took me aside. "You shouldn't say that in front of her. You'll disappoint her if nothing happens."

He wasn't joking. And I got it. Who knew how much animals really understood?

"You're right," I whispered. "You know,

I'm going to make a special effort to get Honey the right forever home even more quickly than just waiting for someone to find her."

"Good girl!" Pete said.

I watched as he hustled along the path, past the place where I'd found Efram's body, and into the rear shed, where Honey had been used as vulnerable bait to get me inside . . .

Pete loved animals. He'd hated what Efram stood for. He had the wherewithal to get inside HotRescues at any time, to do anything he wanted here. Like bring in a vicious dog and let him loose.

Since I hadn't outed the killer yesterday at the event, maybe that person hadn't been present.

Maybe he had been *here* — no matter how much I hated the idea that it could be this wonderful, kind, animal-loving man.

My mind was churning when I got back to the welcome room. Pete? I definitely hated to think so. I even let my muddied thoughts consider whether Ricki could have done it all.

Dumb. Ineffectual. But I realized I was just trying to protect myself. I knew I'd hear from the detective again sometime that day.

Maybe go talk with him.

Maybe be taken into custody. It had been weeks since Efram's death. The police undoubtedly wanted to arrest someone so they'd look better.

That someone could be me.

I hadn't achieved what I'd intended: the ability to hand over another suspect, complete with evidence to turn their official scrutiny away from me.

Surely it was the Shaheens. It should be them. Incarcerating them forever for killing the horrendous man whose animal cruelty they had fostered was absolute poetic justice.

But I'd found nothing to prove it. And they'd said nothing yesterday to change that. Neither had any of Efram's other acquaintances who were there.

The lawyer, then. I'd do something — I wasn't sure what — to confront him gently again, get his confession . . . ? Unlikely.

Sighing, I checked my e-mail. Not much of interest, except that I'd gotten a response from the Palm Springs shelter owner about that poor animal lover who'd had his beloved dog stolen.

I gasped aloud and nearly knocked over my chair as I stood abruptly. The description of the missing dog was so familiar . . .

It sounded exactly like Perry.

Not only that, but some of the other information she conveyed astounded me.

I pulled my chair back where it belonged and sat down, my breath fast and my mind as confused as if I'd drunk a whole bottle of vodka. Fast. Without anything at all to sweeten or dilute it.

I closed my eyes, thinking everything through. Something was pinching at my consciousness. Turning bedlam and angst into utter clarity. Could it be?

It certainly seemed logical. And illogical. All at the same time.

But I now believed I knew who'd generated all the chaotic events at HotRescues — including Efram's murder.

CHAPTER 30

I considered long and hard about what to do. I believed I now knew the killer's identity, but even if I told Detective Garciana every bit of my complicated reasoning, I had no proof. Nothing that even a TV detective could get a major "aha" out of to ramp up to the climax of the show.

I was no detective. But I remained a suspect. What could I do to change that — especially now, when I was in such jeopardy and knew who had put me there?

An idea came to me gradually. Probably foolhardy, yes, but it also involved making sure I had backup there when the truth came out.

I had every intention of making sure the truth *did* come out — no matter what the risk to myself.

And to my backup? Well, I'd explain it all in advance, so no one would be in danger without being fully aware of it. We'd all be cautious.

I made some phone calls and waited in my office.

If I was right, it would all be over soon. If I was wrong . . . well, it might still be over soon, along with, possibly, my life.

But just mine, I hoped. At least I wouldn't be endangering any of the animals here at HotRescues. Otherwise, I wouldn't be doing this.

I took one more walk through the shelter area while I waited, hugging dogs and cats and making sure they knew I cared, no matter what happened.

When I got to Perry's enclosure, I looked at him closely. He looked back, without growling. I went inside, knelt and hugged him. "I think you know a lot more than you're saying, boy," I told him. "Am I doing the right thing?"

The first to arrive was Si. He was waiting for me in the welcome area when I returned after my shelter visit.

I ran toward him, let him hug me. It might appear that I was wimping out, or, worse, leading him on, but at that moment I wasn't about to turn away from a semblance of comfort.

Holding me tightly, he whispered into my

hair, "I'm so glad you called me, Lauren. And that this will all be over soon. Tonight. But are you sure you're doing the right thing? Shouldn't you have called the cops first?"

I pulled back, still holding his hand, and led him to the visitors' table. He'd donned a long-sleeved blue shirt tucked into jeans, as well as a grave expression that made his normally youthful forty-something face look its age.

As we sat, I explained to him a bare-bones version of the rationale that had tap-danced through my mind and ended with a shaky bow. No applause. Not yet.

"If my suspicions were physical evidence," I told him, "that's exactly what I'd have done. But right now I just want to talk, to see if I can get a confession, especially in front of a credible witness like you."

"That's great," he said. "I'll do all I can to get him to talk."

I heard a noise at the outside door and peered out the adjoining window. Ed Bransom was there, wearing a security company uniform and an officious frown that he aimed at me. "I'm on duty myself tonight," he told me as I let him in. His light brown hair was poufed up in front, as if he'd combed it just for this impending fateful occasion. Whether or not HotRescues continued to use EverySecurity in the future could well depend on what happened this night, and he undoubtedly knew it.

"Fine," I told him. "Let's go talk." I excused us from Si's presence and took Ed out into the shelter area. I felt like the director of a movie, discussing the upcoming scene and the cast members' roles in it and ready to shout, "Places, everyone."

Only, this scene would be especially fateful for one of the actors . . . or so I hoped.

I told Ed to stay here, just outside the reception area, and to listen to what went on inside. He was in charge of making sure that everyone — human or not — remained safe.

"Is your backup outside?" I asked. He nodded. "And you're prepared for any emergency?"

"Sure thing."

I gave him a couple more instructions, then went back inside. I returned just in time to let Matt in. He studied my face for a moment with eyes even warmer than their usual toast color, then approached Si with his hand out for a shake.

It resembled something like, "Gentlemen, shake hands and come out fighting."

Ed Bransom had certainly taken his place

in all this, too, even without a handshake.

I was ready.

I told Matt and Si that our security guy was making his rounds, so we could talk in privacy. I motioned for them both to sit at the table. I remained standing, my back against the leopard-print counter, as if the cat it resembled would lend me courage.

A good thing, since I'd already told enough lies to fill a shelter that night in the name of getting to the truth, and there would be a lot more to come.

"Thanks for coming," I told them both. "I want to tell you what I just learned yesterday and what I think it means. Some of it's speculation, but I think I now know what's been going on around here. I trust you both and wanted your opinion before I go to the authorities with it."

I watched the expressions on both faces — and got the impression they would each be great high-stakes poker players. Not a hint of what they were thinking altered either's demeanor.

"Here's the scoop I learned from a fellow pet shelter administrator: a guy in the Palm Springs area was beaten up a couple of weeks ago and his dog was kidnapped. The dog isn't famous, but people in the area knew him and some of his personality quirks. Others in pet-related jobs could have heard about him, too. Right, Matt?"

"What are you talking about, Lauren?" Matt sounded as irritated as if I'd accused him of something.

Which I had.

"Okay, let's assume you don't know what I'm referring to." I hoped my smile seemed as neutral as I intended. "You've met the pit bull mix who attacked me here, right? We're calling him Perry now and Si has taken him in, although we're boarding him temporarily. Si's hoping to find him a new, wonderful forever home. The thing is, he has an old, wonderful forever home. I should have had him checked for a microchip first thing, but I worried that he'd attack again. Once he took Perry away from here, Si brought him to our vet clinic to determine the condition of his health, which was, fortunately, good. They found his chip — but the information tied to its serial number belonged to a person who'd died years ago in another state. But I'm sure he's the missing dog."

"He's the dog who was stolen in Palm Springs?" Si asked. "Wow! How do you know that?"

"Because that dog — whose name is actually Bubba, by the way — is an educational film star of sorts. He's a poster child — er, dog — for having a split personality under some circumstances. When he was a pup, he got sick and was given the drug Prednisone. Instead of getting the usual sedative effect, he had a rare, opposite reaction that made him highly aggressive — so much so that he's almost unique. His owner keeps Bubba off the stuff most of the time. But the extent of his reaction is so unusual that Bubba is used in films sometimes to demonstrate how vicious dogs can be if mistreated or trained to fight or whatever. The drug isn't administered often, and always under a vet's auspices. And most of the time, as long as he's not under the medication, Bubba is nice and mellow." I looked straight into Matt's face. "Those training films have been made available to Animal Services groups all over Southern California."

"And you're accusing me of finding out about this Bubba, stealing him, and bringing him here?" Matt was standing now. "Why would I do that?"

I stood, too. So did Si. He and I faced Matt over the table. "I'll tell you my thought process. And I warn you, it's so complicated that it makes my brain turn flip-flops. But as you knew, there were three situations that occurred here at HotRescues, and they've all got to be related. You agree, right?"

I looked from one to the other. Both nodded. The look on Matt's face was speculative. Si's expression was even more curious.

"The person who killed Efram was angry about the puppy mill situation and that Efram had been released from jail," I began. "That person followed Efram and saw him come here that night. Or, possibly, he hid his anger, pretended to be chummy and on Efram's side, and accompanied Efram here, where Efram could have shown him how to get by the security system. In any event, once they came in our gate, I believe they got into a nasty altercation. My assumption is that Efram grabbed one of the knives we use to open bags of food and started to attack, but that person used it on him instead. Or maybe the killer grabbed the knife in the first place. Either way, end of story — of Efram, anyway."

"Interesting." Matt's expression had turned as cold as the face of a glacier. *That* was interesting. "Go on."

"Sure. So, I was accused, since I was physically present, and I certainly wasn't quiet about disliking Efram. The person who killed him might even have wanted to frame me in the first place to keep him from becoming a suspect. I believe he was also angry with me for something, like accusing him of doing a shoddy job with his own responsibilities."

I hoped that Ed Bransom was listening . . .

"Or maybe he had another motive for wanting me to take the rap. But the cops didn't arrest me, so he took the next step, making it appear even more like I tried to lay the blame on someone else — the reason for the setup with Honey in our storage shed. I claimed it wasn't me but the killer who did it. Poor little me. I was even stabbed. The cops didn't buy it. They still liked me for Efram's murder but needed more evidence. Plus, something was done each time to foul up the security cameras, at least temporarily, so there was no proof that another person was even around here during either situation." Some of that was guesswork on my part. I'd asked Every-Security and gotten excuses. I'd asked Detective Garciana and gotten evasions. In any event, no one was depending on the security cameras for answers.

"This is pretty damned twisted," Matt growled.

"So's the killer. But even the Honey situation didn't get me arrested. One final scenario was devised: stealing Bubba, giving him Prednisone, letting him attack me. Once again, everyone was supposed to believe I had set it up myself to throw suspicions elsewhere. I know dogs and their personalities. I could have found a vicious dog somewhere — like after the dogfighting scheme that occurred right around the same time — and brought him here to attack me, or at least appear to. Although that was my first thought about you, Matt, since you had access to those rescued dogs. In any event, our security company couldn't even tell whether the person who brought the nasty dog here was male or female — wearing my hoodie, or one like mine. But no one around here, except whoever brought the dog to HotRescues, knew the vicious pit bull mix was actually fairly mild-mannered Bubba. That was the killer's mistake: assuming no one would ever learn about that. But you knew about Bubba in the first place, didn't you, Matt?"

"I could have," he admitted.

"So, end of my story. I'd like yours now. Will you confess and make it easier on all of us?"

Silence. Matt said nothing.

Ed Bransom didn't appear, although I half expected him to rush through the door and take Matt into custody, thus exonerating his security company from its former negligence.

Although, of course, everything I'd accused Matt of could just as easily have fit Bransom.

"Hey, this is supposed to be the time that the villain stands up and confesses," I asserted brashly — to hide the insecurity fluttering inside me. What if this didn't work? "Don't you watch cop shows?"

Matt shrugged.

I turned to Si. "What do you think? Does that scenario make any sense to you?"

"Sure," he said. "Come on, Kingston. Tell us why you did it." He came toward me, apparently ready to put his arm around me. Instead, I backed away to face these two men.

And then I turned toward Si.

"One thing really troubles me about that conclusion," I said. "Maybe you'll be able to shed some light on it, Si. You told us how much effort you put into retraining the dog you called Perry. It didn't surprise you that he became such a model animal in less than ten days?"

"I was amazed, too," Si said quickly. "He just seemed so smart, so willing to change."

"I know you considered that he might already have known some of the lessons you taught. With your background in dog training for shelters, did you ever try to find out if anyone had lost a smart, already trained dog like him? Did you check him yourself for a microchip before taking him to the vet?" I paused. "Or maybe you knew about Bubba. And maybe you changed the information tied to his microchip from the get-go."

Si's turn to become silent. He just looked at me. For a moment, the sweet, caring expression I was used to seeing him aim at me turned as vicious as the pit bull mix who had attacked me. Then it disappeared.

"Why don't we get the cops here now, Lauren?" Si said. "You can tell them your suspicions about this Animal Services freak."

"If I bring them here now, Si," I said softly, "I'll tell them this all was a setup to see how you would react, not Matt."

"Me?" His voice grew as shrill as a Chihuahua's yap.

"Everything I said in accusation of Matt would fit you even better," I said. "I suspect that you killed Efram in the first place for his showing up here at HotRescues and threatening us all. You did it to protect me, in some ways. But then you were afraid of the consequences. You knew at last that I wasn't going to reciprocate any romantic feelings you might have for me — so you decided I was the right one to take the blame for Efram's killing. You had easy access to HotRescues, more than any of the outside suspects I looked into. More than Matt. Maybe even more than our buddies at EverySecurity."

Si's glance moved toward the shelter door where we'd last seen Ed Bransom. Bransom wasn't there. Si grabbed the nearest chair and looked like he wanted to hurl it at me.

Matt moved around, but I put my hand out, waving him back. I knew that animal control officers could carry guns for euthanizing injured animals. Probably commanding officers, too. Did Matt have his with him?

Si released the chair. I assumed his thoughts had been going over what I'd said.

The smile he leveled at me was almost angelic. "You have such a wonderful imagination, Lauren. I'm sure that's how you dreamed up such a complicated series of events to try to exonerate yourself in the first place. But no one is going to believe you."

"Oh, I'm not so sure about that." A familiar voice sounded conversational as Detective Stefan Garciana entered the room

406

from the shelter area, followed by Ed Bransom. I'd told Bransom to watch for the cops and let them in the back way.

Allowing Bransom to feel the anxiety of possible suspicion resting on him and his company was part of my scheme, of course. But I knew by then who'd been responsible for it all.

Now Si was going to realize it, too.

"You're the police detective who's been after Lauren, aren't you?" Si's tone was a friendly welcome. "I'm so glad you're here. Did you hear all the things she said? She accused that Animal Services guy, there — Kingston. But I'll bet all of this is just blowing smoke so you'll get off her case. She's such a smart lady, but I think she finally outsmarted herself."

"Or you," Garciana said. Tonight, he had put a suit jacket on over slacks and a white knit shirt. "I was listening out there to part of what she said. Interesting stuff. She'd told me a little about it before. And I'm quite impressed about how she used my own case-solving exercise, scoping out all possible suspects, no matter how unlikely. I think it worked well this time — even more for her than for me, although I shouldn't admit it. But there are some things she

407

didn't mention, because she didn't know them."

All eyes were on the detective. His face was ramped up into what appeared to be a triumphant smile.

"When Ms. Vancouver told me her outlandish story, I had to check it out, of course. And guess what. The authorities in the Palm Springs area recently discovered fingerprints that they believe came from whoever stole Bubba, the dog, and assaulted his owner. This matter isn't the highest on their agenda, so they haven't run it through AFIS yet — the national fingerprint system — but I think I'm going to make it easy for them. I suspect they'll match yours, Mr. Rogan. And although we didn't make it public, there were a few partial prints on the knife used to kill Efram Kiley that hadn't been wiped away. Mr. Kiley's, of course, and we weren't surprised to find that others matched employees here at HotRescues, including yours and Ms. Vancouver's. That kept her on our suspect list. But she actually fed the animals sometimes. Why would a part-timer who only trains animals here leave prints on a knife used to open bags of food?"

Leaping sideways, Si again grabbed the chair and hurled it generally in my direction. Matt yanked me out of the way and pushed me to the floor.

I nevertheless saw Si reach the door to the parking lot and pull it open . . . only to be confronted by the uniformed officers that Detective Garciana must have called in as backup that night.

Si was busted!

CHAPTER 31

The next afternoon, when things were finally settling down again at HotRescues, I took some time to hang out in the welcome room near our front door, with Carlie and Nina.

Carlie had arrived only a few minutes before and apparently talked her way past those cops who still hung around the parking lot. She had sped here, demanding the whole story, in detail, after I'd called her. Which I'd had to do, since the media had started to point their ugly, oversized noses in this direction again and were screaming all over the local news, and even networks and cable stations, about Si Rogan's arrest. Carlie would never have forgiven me if I'd not given her a heads-up, even a slightly late one.

And, yes, I'd called both Tracy and Kevin even before Carlie. My kids would have been outraged if they'd heard about this, too, on YouTube or their favorite online news source. I asked them to tell Grandma, Grandpa, and Uncle Alex, too, since I was still too busy to contact them all. We'd talk later.

I'd stayed the night, catching quick dozes on the couch in Mona's office. The place was still busy with cops who were looking for additional evidence in Si's office. I didn't think they'd need to disrupt anyplace else at HotRescues, but just in case I had put together another list of employees who needed to get in to help care for our residents. That included Nina and Pete Engersol, who had both come early, Angie Shayde, and some of our most reliable volunteers. Dr. Mona had called and promised to come and give counseling to all of us and our residents later this afternoon.

At the moment, Carlie faced me, hands on her blue-jeaned hips. She cocked her head so her blond hair unevenly fringed out along one shoulder. I knew that look. She used it often on her animal health TV show when unhappy with some owner's approach to a pet's care. Now, she was about to chew me out. "So you set things up here last night, pretending you were sure that gorgeous Captain Matt Kingston of Animal Services first killed Efram, and then kept doing things around here to make you look bad to the police?"

"That's right," I answered mildly, taking a seat at the table. If she was going to ream me, I might as well be as comfortable as possible while she did it.

"Did you really think it could be Matt?" Nina, standing beside Carlie, sounded amazed. She'd just come inside from feeding and otherwise caring for our residents. "But he's such a nice guy."

"That's the point," Carlie said. "Matt was in on it, too, wasn't he?"

"Yes." I answered Carlie but looked at Nina, who seemed confused. "I was already pretty sure, because of some things I'd learned about the dog who attacked me, that the one who'd done it all was Si. Plus, he'd had access at any time to HotRescues and would have had no trouble pulling off one, or all, of the incidents. He bought a hoodie that looked like mine — and wore it when he thought the security guys might see him hanging around outside. He eventually stole mine, too — probably when he didn't have his new one around."

"He seems so obvious now," Carlie said, sitting down opposite me. "Didn't you know before that it was him?"

I narrowed my eyes into a hot glare that I

412

hoped would weld her lips together. "You don't know Si very well," I told her. "He just seems like the nicest guy, always courteous, willing to help, training animals with love, staying in the background."

"I get it," Nina said. "Just a sec." She hurried through the door to the kitchen and returned a minute later balancing three mugs filled with coffee in her hands. "He's in love with you, Lauren. You know that." I shrugged ruefully. "That's his motive, of course. And why he never even tried to teach me to train animals, like he once promised you — since I'm not you. It all makes perfect sense — well, in an awful kind of way. He hated that Efram fooled you. Fooled us all. Then threatened us. So, to protect us — you in particular — he killed Efram. Right?"

"Right," I said. I tasted the coffee. Good stuff — with just a hint of hazelnut. I took another sip. "But . . . well, I'm just speculating, but I think he expected me to cry on his shoulder about the threats, then be thrilled Efram was gone. I'd considered strangling the guy myself, but I just felt awful when he was killed at HotRescues . . . especially when the police were sure it was me. Si was really sympathetic about that, too. Offered me that shoulder again. But all

I did was to try to figure out an alternative suspect for the cops. By then, Si was frustrated."

"And maybe a little scared that you'd figure it out or the cops would?" Carlie leaned her elbows on the table and sipped her coffee.

"Exactly. He even called in an anonymous tip to the cops that I'd threatened Efram. Of course that was no surprise to anyone. I'd even told the detective about it. When the 'tip' didn't result in anything exciting, Si conceived of this additional plot to make me feel bad — and look guilty. He put together the whole scenario with Honey in the storage shed. Apparently he jammed something into the security camera's mechanism to keep it from panning around and photographing him when he moved Honey, then removed it later. At least that's the official speculation. Detective Garciana just confirmed it to me, and it's what they'll assume during their interrogation of Si." I sighed and looked at both of them. "I suspect now that Si was glad I was actually stabbed — a little bit more vengeance."

"That detective seemed so sure you'd done it yourself to try to make the cops look for another suspect," Nina said, sitting back at the table with us.

414

"That was Si's intent." I put my coffee mug down. "He even phoned Matt from here that night, making it look like I'd called him to direct suspicion from myself . . . again."

"And you still didn't take Si's offered shoulder, I gather," Carlie added.

I shook my head. "I liked the guy. Had no indication he was loony. Or, should I say in the interest of being politically correct, mentally unbalanced. By then, I was even more scared but determined — both to fix things for myself and not rely on anyone else. Not even Si, who tried hard to get me to lean on him — all the while also trying to get me to take the blame. So he dreamed up the last of his scary events."

"Bringing in a nasty pit bull." Nina shuddered.

"Not so nasty," I corrected hastily. "I've notified Bubba's owner. The guy sounded so nice and relieved. He's coming today from Palm Springs and staying in LA till his dog is released back to him. Poor Bubba is evidence at the moment. Since Si only worked here part-time, it was easy for him to go unnoticed to Palm Springs, beat up Bubba's owner, and steal the dog. A dog he knew could have a short temper with the use of the right drug."

"Poor guy," Carlie said. "Guys. Both the dog and his owner."

I nodded and smiled. "My sentiments exactly." I took another sip of coffee and continued. "At least the security company is cooperating. Apparently Si was talking to them, acting completely innocent as he expressed concern about my mental stability and how I might be hurting HotRescues with all the things I was doing around here."

"Men suck," Nina pronounced, taking a longer swig of her java as if she'd spiked it. Of course she had every reason to think so. But me? Well, I'd been lucky to have Kerry in my life. And even after all this nastiness I maintained a sense of optimism that not all men sucked, even if a lot of them did.

For some reason, Matt Kingston's quick kiss last night, before he was taken into another room for a cop interrogation, butted its way into my thoughts, and I kicked it right back out again. Did I like him? Sure. Would I go out for a drink with him, or dinner? Why not? But that didn't mean I'd succumb to a mad, passionate love affair. Let alone a caring relationship.

"So how did you determine it was Si?" Carlie demanded. "I know, when you pushed through that adoption event and invited everyone you suspected to come, you weren't ruling anyone out." She had the grace to look slightly embarrassed when Nina looked at her, then me.

"Did you really think I could have done it all?" Nina's hoarse voice all but shouted out her pain.

"Like Carlie said, Nina." I kept my tone gentle. "I was afraid to rule anyone out until I could be sure. I didn't think it was you, but . . ."

"But," she repeated sadly.

"But I'm really glad it wasn't." I stood and hugged Nina's shoulder as she continued to sit there.

"So you had to do something so dramatic?" Carlie pushed. "I mean, really, why pretend that you were sure it was Matt Kingston and get that Si guy on your side to bring him down?"

"It's more fun than just making accusations," I said with a half smile. "But, really? It was because I needed to do something more than point fingers. I'd been doing that all along, and the detective on my case just ignored everything I suggested. This way . . . well, one good thing about our damned security company is that we just set up a new, higher-tech camera with a microphone right in here. It's all there for the cops to see."

My BlackBerry rang. I took it out of my pocket and glanced at the display. Dante.

"I've got to take this," I told the others, and went into my office to be alone, in case the guy who funded my job decided to yank it away from me because of all that had happened. "Hi, Dante," I said when I was sitting down behind my desk.

"So is all that stuff over now, at last?" he demanded with no greeting.

I took a deep breath to prepare myself for whatever nasty discussion might be impending and said, "I certainly hope so." I leaned forward, holding the phone to my ear with one hand and planting my forehead on the other as I rested my elbow on the desk. Maybe I could keep my head from aching this way.

"The media's all over the place with this, but there are insinuations that you staged some kind of scene last night to get the killer to confess. Right?"

That sounded so much like the path taken by his significant other, Kendra Ballantyne. I'd even tried her way with my pet adoption event and it hadn't worked.

And yet, when trying to fix things for myself, I guess I did, subconsciously or otherwise, try to control things by creating a unique dog and pony show of my own to get the situation resolved.

This time, it had succeeded.

"Simple answer?" I said to Dante. "Yes, that's right."

"Good girl! You want a raise?"

I laughed. "I always want a raise. You paying?"

"We'll see. You've gotten some good publicity here for HotRescues, after all."

"That's why I did it," I joked, leaning back and smiling. But then I grew serious. "We still need to talk about our security around here. I involved Ed Bransom last night. I still had a niggling doubt about his innocence, despite being all but certain that Si Rogan was our bad guy. Bransom did come through, letting the cops in and all, but EverySecurity really screwed up all those times before."

"Yeah, they did. They won't again. I've had a long, nasty talk with my buddy, the CEO. Bransom is on probation for now. He apparently had an excuse for the way he acted — some supposedly confidential discussions with Si, who 'let' Bransom drag out of him how confused you seemed to be. Bransom claims that was why he felt so sure you were setting everything up. With that behind us, I'm fairly confident that they're still the best outfit to protect HotPets, especially since I've got . . . Well, you'll find out soon. That was another reason I was going to call you. Expect some company any minute. And let's you and I get together soon to talk about what's best for HotRescues, all right?"

"Sure," I said, puzzled yet smiling as I hung up.

What company was he talking about?

I heard some additional voices as I returned to the welcome room. A couple I'd met before were there. Were these the people who'd expressed an interest in adopting Honey?

They were!

The Lees had been waffling before about if this was the right time for them to bring a dog into their lives. Then Mr. Lee had gotten a stomach virus and they'd had to contend with getting him better. Then — well, they had lots of reasons why they hadn't made an immediate decision. But right now, they both seemed thrilled that Honey was still here and available. They'd answered our questions before and brought along proof that their apartment building allowed pets, so I believed I'd be able to approve this adoption.

Smiling at Carlie, I excused myself and Nina to go with the Lees back to the shelter area, where Honey remained in the first kennel. She leaped at the gate and seemed utterly in heaven when Mrs. Lee took her into her arms, closed her eyes, and hugged the small white dog.

"Come with me so we can go over the paperwork," Nina told them. "Assuming everything checks out, you'll be able to take her home today." She looked at me, and I nodded my approval. This adoption had been pending for a while.

"Thank you!" Mrs. Lee murmured into Honey's neck, and her husband embraced them both.

Nina told me she'd handle the details. She ushered them all — adopters and pup — upstairs to the more private area there for filling out forms.

Carlie was still in the welcome area when I returned.

So was Brooke Pernall, with her dog Cheyenne. Oh, no. Was this upbeat day about to be ruined because the poor, sick woman was here to leave her beautiful golden retriever after all?

But Brooke looked a lot better than the last time I'd seen her. Her hair was styled, complete with highlights. She wore a businesslike suit jacket over dressy slacks. And she was smiling. Except for some tiredness behind her eyes, there was no sign of illness now.

"Hi, Lauren," she said. "Congratulations on solving that guy's murder and the other junk that's gone on around here. Won't happen again. You can be sure of that."

"I can?"

Carlie, who'd been standing, sat back down at the table, regarding us with interest. She reached over and started petting Cheyenne, who stood near her.

"Didn't Dante tell you?"

I recalled that he'd said I should expect company soon. Brooke? "No, but —"

"He's one great guy, isn't he? Rich, and he knows how to use money to get the most good out of it. Here's the story."

But before telling me, she glanced down quizzically toward Carlie.

"She's cool," I said, and I waved Brooke to join us at the table.

"Here's what happened," Brooke said. "I'm now an official employee of HotPets — security director. I may have mentioned to you that I have a background as a private investigator. After checking me out, Dante hired me to supervise security for all of his organizations, and that will include HotRescues. I now have an income and medical insurance — and he also sent me to the cardiologist with the best reputation in LA. I'm on meds now that started helping immediately. I'm not cured, but the doc I'm seeing is hopeful that I'll at least keep my heart issue under control, and if things change, he has other medications he can prescribe or possibly a type of surgery that's successful a lot."

"Wow," I said. "That's great!"

"It sure is. Plus, Dante had the clout to get someone at my bank to pay attention, so now my mortgage is manageable. Cheyenne and I can stay in our home."

"This is really something," Carlie said. I could almost see her thought process. How could she work this into one of her TV shows?

"I think we need to keep this private," I cautioned her.

"I recognize you." Brooke smiled at Carlie. "You're the star of *Pet Fitness.* That's a really cool show. But, yes, none of this is to become public — not with Dante involved." She turned back toward me. "I'll be making sure that EverySecurity does its job right, or they'll be gone. Plus, I've got a couple of former coworkers who can moonlight and stay here at HotRescues overnight sometimes to make sure the animals are okay and to keep EverySecurity on its toes. I may even stay here myself now and then as time goes on — we'll see. In any event, the security for HotRescues — and for HotPets, and even the wildlife sanctuary Dante funds, HotWildlife — is going to get a whole lot better."

"That's great!" I exclaimed.

She stood. "I just wanted to drop in and tell you this, Lauren," she said. "And to thank you. If it weren't for you . . ." Her eyes welled up, and I again saw the fragile, desperate woman she'd been when she had come here the last time.

I stood, too, and gave her a hug. "I'm really glad it all worked out," I said.

Giving Cheyenne a quick tug on his leash, she hurried toward the door. "See you again soon," she said. "We'll work out a good security plan then."

I stared after her with a grin on my face so wide that I felt as if it was becoming etched there permanently.

"What a day you're having," Carlie said.

"I'll say." It had been amazing. Perfect. I'd been exonerated from committing murder and the rest, Honey had found a home, and HotRescues' security issues were resolved . . . not to mention Brooke's health problems. Could it get any better?

Maybe I should go home and not tempt

my luck.

"Too bad I can't use that stuff about Brooke and her dog on my show," Carlie said. "I'd have had fun figuring out how to work it in. Oh, well. I need to get back to my clinic now, but I'll call you later. Maybe we can get together for dinner."

"Sounds good." I heard a noise behind me, as if the door to the parking lot was opening. Had Brooke forgotten something?

Before I turned to look, Carlie said, "Well, hi, hero."

I knew who it was, of course. Rolling my eyes at Carlie's attempt at humor, I turned again. Sure enough, it was Matt.

He wasn't alone. He held a leash, and on it was a beautiful, beautiful dog, mostly black and white, with some merle gray. She — I believed, at first glance, it was a she — appeared to be mostly Border collie, perhaps with some Australian shepherd thrown in. My favorites.

"Well, hi, sweetheart," I said, slowly kneeling.

"I didn't know you cared that much," Matt countered. I looked up to see a twinkle in his brown eyes, and I laughed.

"Sure, I care. But I care more about your friend."

"Oh, my heart." Matt bunched his fist

over his chest, as if I'd struck him there. I laughed.

He took a few steps toward me as I rose again. Our lips met in a quick, friendly — yet strangely tantalizing — kiss.

"Gotta run," Carlie said. "I'll definitely talk to you later, Lauren." She left.

I was alone in the reception area with the guy who'd been so great and accommodating and even protective last night, when I'd needed his help.

And with this wonderful dog.

"Who is she?" I asked.

"She was called Zoey by her owner, who was, from all reports of her neighbors, one really nice senior citizen who died a few days ago from a heart attack. She didn't have any family around. The locals weren't sure what to do with Zoey and brought her to the East Valley Shelter earlier today. She's been processed in, but . . . Well, I thought of you right away. And I don't mean HotRescues. You ready to adopt a dog yourself, Vancouver? If not, I'm not leaving her."

"I didn't . . . I mean, I don't know. I haven't thought about it seriously, and . . ."

I looked down. Zoey was staring up at me, looking utterly serious. And lonely.

I had a feeling that the good stuff of this

day was about to be topped with the greatest part of all.

I looked back up at Matt.

"You want to go to lunch with Zoey and me now to talk about it before you make this huge decision?" he asked.

"Yes," I said. I bent again to hug the pup. She was warm. Substantial. Snuggly. And she seemed to lean into me. "How about it, Zoey? Do you want to have lunch and talk about it?"

As if she understood our words — and I had an utter belief that she did — she barked.

I had a feeling I knew what my answer would be.

ABOUT THE AUTHOR

Linda O. Johnston is a lawyer and a writer of mysteries, paranormal romance, and romantic suspense. She lives in the hills overlooking the San Fernando Valley with her husband, Fred, and two Cavalier King Charles spaniels, Lexie and Mystie.

You can visit Linda at website: www.LindaOJohnston.com.

We hope you have enjoyed this Large Print book. Other Thorndike, Wheeler, Kennebec, and Chivers Press Large Print books are available at your library or directly from the publishers.

For information about current and upcoming titles, please call or write, without obligation, to:

Publisher
Thorndike Press
10 Water St., Suite 310
Waterville, ME 04901
Tel. (800) 223-1244

or visit our Web site at:

http://gale.cengage.com/thorndike

OR

Chivers Large Print
published by AudioGO Ltd
St James House, The Square
Lower Bristol Road
Bath BA2 3SB
England
Tel. +44(0) 800 136919
email: info@audiogo.co.uk
www.audiogo.co.uk

All our Large Print titles are designed for easy reading, and all our books are made to last.